The Constellation of Us

Ashli Mildenberger

□

For all those who feel the stars,
no matter the darkness.

CONTENTS

PART I

Chapter 1

Todd
Then

I was standing in front of an ice cream shack on the shore of Lake Harriet. I didn't even see the long line of kids with their parents because I was distracted by the strong scent of waffle cones. My mouth watered in anticipation and my stomach growled for the hundredth time this hour. I knew that the fact that I was hungry didn't mean I would get food.

Except there had been that one time I was swimming with my family at night and someone had mysteriously left chocolate-covered gummy bears underneath what used to be a T-shirt, but was really more like a frayed piece of cloth. It was the best surprise any six-year-old could ask for, especially a starving six-year-old. The mysterious incident only happened once, but that didn't deter me from coming back to the lake as often as I could in hopes that someone would repeat this kind act of fate. I'd do anything for candy—for food—right now. I had been famished for days, with only Pop-Tarts and water to sustain me.

I left the ice cream shack and walked to the drinking fountain around the corner; at least the water would satiate me for a little while longer.

There was a tree, my favorite tree at this lake, and it just so happened to be far enough from the scent of waffles. Perfect. It was hot out and I didn't want to get a sunburn. But as soon as I sat under my tree, I decided to get up. I walked to the next tree over and sat down. I wanted to switch things up, pretend that I had some choice in my life, some control over what happened in my day-to-day.

I didn't know where my parents were. It had been a week, the longest I had gone alone. One time they told me they were going to get gas and didn't come home for five days. I wondered if they knew they didn't need gas. We didn't even have a car. We still don't.

A week ago, they told me they were going to the casino because God told them they'd get lucky that night. I wondered if they had gotten lucky. I had a feeling they hadn't, because if I were really lucky, I'd be able to stand in line and get a waffle cone with two scoops of ice cream. Although I'd consider even one scoop of ice cream a good day.

"Nice and steady now." A man's voice carried across the waters of the lake. He was standing behind his daughter, coasting a sailboat into the boat's slip. The girl looked forward in full concentration. Her two little hands gripped the steering wheel for dear life. She was taking this responsibility very seriously, even though it was obvious that her father reigned over the boat.

"Do you want to steer the boat into the dock?" He turned around to look at another little girl who was sitting on the bench with her arms crossed and a nasty glare in her eyes.

"No," she said harshly. "This is boring." Then she turned her head away from him.

I decided right then and there that I didn't like her. Seemed ungrateful to me. I'd give anything to have my father ask me to go sailing. I watched the father's face fall at his daughter's shunning. I decided I liked him, based on the simple fact that he wanted to connect with her. He tried.

The father turned back to his other daughter and wrapped his arms around her in order to guide the boat into the dock. I watched the boat's wake simmer down to a soft rolling as they slowed and anchored.

"Steady does it," the father said as he jumped out onto the dock. "Throw me the lines." The girl sitting on the bench ignored her father, stepped out onto the dock, and started toward me. I looked down at the ground and fiercely began picking grass, trying to pretend I hadn't just been spying on her.

I counted to ten before I brought my eyes back up to the scenery in front of me. When I looked back toward the boat, the girl who'd been steering was twisting a rope around the dock's cleat, trying to tie a knot. She eventually sighed and handed her father the rope. I saw him laugh and mutter something to her. I felt myself being pulled to them, wanting to hear their conversation. The girl was not bothered by the fact that she failed to complete the knot, judging by the huge grin stretching across her face.

I stared at her smile, mesmerized. I had never seen anyone smile for so long before.

"Hey!" the father yelled, and the girl who clearly didn't want to be sailing any more stopped near me. She smelled like bubblegum and a clean shower. I could practically touch her if I reached out.

She whipped around to face her father at the dock and screamed back, harsh and ugly, "What?"

"Wait for us there!" he yelled. My head moved back and forth between the two. Why did he want her to wait? Why did he want to keep her in sight?

"I'll wait at the car," she muttered and turned her back on her father. I watched her hands curl into fists and then inched my eyes up to the quick rise and fall of her shoulders. She was breathing heavy. I let my eyes keep going up until I could see her furrowed forehead. Then she swiveled her head to the left—to me. I had been spotted.

I cast my eyes to the ground and started picking grass again, but not before I caught her wrinkle her nose in disgust. I knew I probably didn't smell great. It was my bath day, after all, which was why I was at Lake Harriet in the first place. When day turned to night and the pedestrians left, I would jump into the lake and wash the stench of my life off. But I had a feeling that if I explained, she wouldn't understand, so I didn't bother. I looked back up, expecting to meet her prying eyes, but she had already kept walking past me toward the parking lot.

The father and the other girl eventually left the boat in the dock and drew closer to the tree I was leaning against. At first, I was confused—the girls looked identical—but then I remembered learning about twins. I was still shocked, though. I'd never seen twins in real life before.

They were the same height, same build. The girl who stormed away from her father wore her hair longer than this girl walking toward me right now. But it wasn't the second girl's dark hair that I was paying attention to—it was her toothy grin, still radiating off of her and into the invisible bubble I normally put around myself for protection.

When she and her father were less than twenty feet in front of me, I braced myself. I waited for them to turn down their noses and scurry on past me like everyone else did. I held my breath and looked down at my torn shoes, wishing I could disappear.

Soon, the tips of two pink Crocs came in my line of vision. The girl was standing in front of me. I focused on the butterfly piece she attached to her Croc for twenty full seconds. I counted. I hoped she'd leave me alone, but when she didn't move on, I had no choice but to lift my head.

"Hi," she said in a kind, gentle voice. It was exactly the kind of voice I would imagine coming from behind that smile.

8

Other kids didn't normally talk to me, so I wasn't used to casual conversation. "Hi," I said awkwardly.

"Are you okay?" She asked it without judgement, like this was a normal question she asked everyone. I didn't know how to answer, so I stayed silent. If she was bothered by the smell, she didn't say anything, and she didn't hesitate to plop down in front of me, her knees inches from my heap of grass.

Her father, who had been on the phone walking to the parking lot, stopped and turned to the girl. "Let's go!" he yelled.

"I'm coming!" she told him without taking her gaze off of me. We stared at each other, her with curiosity, me with skepticism.

She bent down and brought her nose close to the mound of grass, inspecting each blade carefully. I didn't know what she was looking for, but I didn't care. I had never had a friend and for some reason having someone sit close to me felt a little like friendship.

When she found a piece of grass she approved of, she set to twisting and turning the blade. She bit her lip, and in only seconds, she was done. She smiled again, wide and proud, and held the small ring made out of grass out in front of her, motioning for me to take it. I was confused, but did what she wanted because I was afraid of disappointing her.

"It's a circle," she said, as though this was not already apparent.

"I see that," I said.

"I like circles, because they remind me that no matter what happens, things will come full circle. Although they can also mean that whatever goes around comes around." She shrugged. "You can take your pick of your favorite meaning."

I rolled the ring between my fingers and then slid it onto my pinky finger. It fit perfectly. When it was fully in place, the girl's smile broadened. It felt like this girl walked around with happiness exuding out of her, suffocating everyone, including me. I could feel her joy press and crack my rocklike heart, making the contents spill out like lava. And suddenly, a softness took over.

I wanted to tell her thank you for the ring made of grass, even though her lack of judgement, her smile…those were the real gifts.

The girl's father hung up his phone and raised his voice again, wanting her to come to him. She stood up and wiped off the grass that was stuck to her knees. "Let's go," she said, as if this had been the plan all along.

I frowned. I couldn't follow her. I had a bath to take and...and what? The realization that I had nowhere to go and no one who cared where I went twisted my stomach in knots. My heart was back to rocks.

"What's wrong?" she asked.

I craned my neck to look at her standing above me. "Where are we going?" I hedged.

She stretched out her hand. I stared at it, weighing my options. She didn't waver.

Finally, when I'd thought through all the choices and came up empty, I took her hand. She hoisted me to standing directly in front of her. I was a little taller, which gave me a burst of confidence, but I forced my chest to deflate and my heartbeat to slow back to its humble pace. I didn't want to make a bad impression on this kind stranger.

She held my hand and started walking to the parking lot, to her father and her twin sister.

She must have noticed my hesitation, because she tightened her grip with gentle reassurance. "Follow me."

Chapter 2

Ruth
Now

My mom and dad are standing around the kitchen island, palms pressing into the countertop. I am staring at their knuckles as they turn ghostly white. I look at mine, also white. I push away from the granite counter, relieving the pressure. I take a deep breath.

There are trays of lasagna stacked in the kitchen. My stomach churns. I'll never be able to look at lasagna the same way again. Bright tulips are dispersed between the pity dishes that people have brought to this occasion. My sister's funeral. One big lasagna-filled bright-flowered occasion. More people are starting to arrive, judging by the chatter in our foyer. We can't hide forever.

"Look," my dad starts, breaking the silent stare-down we were having. "Today is not an easy day for any of us. The last thing we all want is to be around people, but"—his voice breaks—"but we are going to tough it out." He points to the foyer. "Those people out there have travelled far to Minneapolis to pay their respects. We will let them."

"And then we will kick them out," my mom asserts. She stands tall and firm despite the solemn mood. It's her greatest defense against pain.

I nod and put in my two cents. "And then we can throw away this shitty lasagna. Riley didn't even like lasagna."

"Not the point," my dad scolds. My insides recoil, just a little. I'm continually shocked at how even at twenty-three years old, I'm still affected by his words.

I stare down at my black dress and heels and interlace my fingers in front of me. I twirl the simple band on my index finger— the one that looks identical to the ring my twin wore on her index finger. I swear under my breath at my own stupidity for not retrieving hers at the funeral. That ring belongs up here with me, not six feet underground.

Our family heart-to-heart is interrupted when Aunt June barges through the swinging kitchen doors. She looks from me to my mother before landing on my dad.

Please don't ask us how we are doing, I think.

Aunt June's eyes are pools of sorrow. She inclines her head. "How are we doing in here?"

I cringe and slowly back away from the counter toward the French doors to the patio. My mom's eyes shoot daggers at me. She's clearly angry that I am sneaking away and leaving her to the wolves. I mouth I'm sorry and quietly tug on the doorknob. As soon as the cool, spring air hits my face, I hear my dad repeat our family's latest mantra: We are hanging in there.

The backyard is quiet. I gulp in the scents of freshly cut grass and lilac from the bushes lining our driveway around the corner. Although it's April, the air feels as crisp as it did in winter. A small breeze sweeps my hair into my face, and I grip the porch railing.

I hear an uneven cacophony of breaths, tiny gusts of fog billowing out in front of me. I watch the little clouds dissipate and then reappear with each short inhale and exhale, a reminder that I am living.

I slam my eyes shut, trying to ground myself in the darkness behind my eyelids.

This day is too much.

The people.

The potpourri.

The stark contrast between the white interior of the house and the black garb of everyone in it. The reminder that my world is drenched in darkness, tainted, no longer crisp, clean, and clear.

The sorry looks—and, even worse, the sorry statements—are just too much for my heart to carry.

My eyes shift to some movement near the treehouse in my parents' yard. Smoke. I panic. I don't take my eyes off the spot where the smoke had just come and gone as I cross the yard. The rickety ladder is just as I remember it from my youth—precarious, especially in high heels. I count the rungs from muscle memory—ten—and then I'm at the top, peering inside. A man is sitting in the corner of the treehouse, legs outstretched in front of him, relaxed. His eyes are closed, a small, saccharine smile on his face. He is high as a kite.

As I approach, he opens his eyes. Blue—dark blue—eyes, staring back at me. "Jesus!" he yelps. "What are you doing here?"

"Me?" I am confused, still clamping onto the last rung of the ladder. "What are you doing up here?"

He quickly stubs out what appears to be a joint, his face turning crimson. Good. He should be embarrassed. "I brought the flowers today." He waves his hands in the air dismissively, a nonchalant kind of explanation. "My mom owns a flower shop."

So he's the one who brought the damn tulips.

"That still doesn't explain why you are smoking weed in the backyard," I note.

He crosses his legs and leans forward. "Well, you see, I don't particularly like delivering flowers for my mom, considering I am twenty-four years old and fresh out of college."

I do the math, quickly. He either started college late or was on the six-year plan.

I crawl into the treehouse and scoot into the farthest corner, which, considering the size of the treehouse, isn't actually that far from this stranger at all.

"I still don't understand why this means you can smoke weed in a random person's tree house."

"I smoke to ease the shame I have in being a delivery boy at twenty-four years old. Not sure if I can get any clearer than that."

"Right," I say. I lean my head back against the wall and rest my eyes. Maybe I will stay up here until the reception is over. That way, I can avoid Aunt June and all the lasagna lovers. I can avoid the stories from my Riley's high school cross-country team and her favorite med school professor highlighting her laurels and triumphs. She was a high achiever—a perfectionist, really. That type of people always get recognition. I'm not jealous; I'm just not ready to hear other people share their memories of her. Because that brings her back to life. And when their story is over, the cold truth will hit. She isn't alive. She is gone.

I hear a shuffle and blink one eye open. The stranger is looking at me with curiosity. He runs a hand through his ebony hair and then scratches his short beard.

"Why are you up here and not down their at the reception?" he asks, his voice less mocking than before.

I cross my arms, debating how much energy I have to tell him my true reasons. "This is my treehouse." I shrug. "She was my twin."

"Who—" His eyes go big as saucers and his mouth rounds in realization. "Oh, no."

I nod. "Yeah. Oh, no." The words are dry coming out of my mouth.

"Shit," he whispers. I wait for the pity to wash over his face or pour out in his words, but he says nothing. It's only silence, and in this very second it's a gift.

"Thank you," I whisper back.

He squints. "For what?"

"For not saying you're sorry. For not telling me she is in a better place."

"Oh, that common drivel? Nah. I would never." He grins, revealing a row of shiny, white teeth and a small, pronounced dimple on his right cheek. He is handsome without even trying. He's probably never had a zit in his life.

"What was it like? To be a twin?" he asks cautiously.

"Can we not talk about that right now?" My heart shrinks into itself. I'm not ready to say anything about Riley, especially not to a stranger.

"Sure. Yeah, I mean, that was a little fast too soon, I agree." He uncrosses his legs and stretches them out in front of him again. He shivers slightly, and I'm reminded that it is cold. I look at my bare arms. Rows of goosebumps. I hadn't felt a thing.

"What's your name?" he asks.

"Ruth," I respond. "You?"

"Trip."

"I've never heard that name before."

"You've never met anyone like me before," Trip said.

A small giggle escapes me, reverberating through the hardened parts of my body, and I desperately try to hold on to the light feeling it gives me. Trip watches me carefully. I want more of that feeling—any feeling—so I let myself laugh again, a chuckle. It feels foreign. Fake. I don't care.

The small chuckle crescendos into a loud explosion—a release. There have been so many emotions and unspoken tribulations building in me these past few weeks—layers upon layers of unbelievable grief. There is a storm in me, and all I can do in this moment is laugh.

So I laugh.

Trip joins in, although his facial expression borders on concerned.

14

"Does that line work on every girl?" I ask after my fit subsides.

He shrugs. "Usually."

I hum an agreement, and silence follows, the comfortable peace that comes after laughter.

"It's cold," he remarks. "We should get you inside."

"That's the exact place I am trying to avoid," I remind him.

"Right. Well…I have a few more deliveries to make before the day is done. So I'd best be off," he announces, coming to all fours and crawling toward to the treehouse's entrance. No sympathy. No "are you okay"s. Nothing.

I push my arm out, stopping him from climbing down the ladder. "You can't drive when you're high. That's not safe."

"It wouldn't be the first time." He inclines his head at me, his tone patronizing.

"Well, that's something to be proud of," I mock. "You know what? I'll go with you. I will drive." I don't know why I say it. Offering to drive this stranger—this stoned stranger—during my twin sister's funeral reception seems absurd.

Trip bites his tongue. "Isn't it unwise to leave your house right now?"

"You're talking to me about wise decisions?"

He scoffs. "Right." He pauses, considering. "Okay. You can drive me around on my errands. I warn you though, you should be prepared for an abnormal experience. There will be old ladies and awkward singing."

I don't even feel the need to ask, because everything about today, the past two weeks really, has deviated from normal. Thus, the singular ridiculousness of driving around a drugged-out stranger sits just fine with me.

"I'd take awkward singing over pity stares," I say, keeping a deadpan expression.

He gestures to the ladder. "Ladies first."

~

I sneak back into my house to get a coat before meeting Trip in the driveway. I know his vehicle instantly: a white delivery van with poorly painted flowers and the name "Monica Makes Potpourri" on the door.

Trip is in the passenger seat, adjusting the radio, when I climb into the van.

"Please tell me your mom's business is named after that one Friends episode," I ask.

Trip finds a station he likes and sits back, buckling his seatbelt. He motions for me to buckle up. I glare at the irony of his desire to be safe, but I obey. Once the belt clicks, Trip says, "Please don't tell me you've seen every episode of Friends ten times."

I back out of the driveway, past the lilac trees and around the numerous parked cars. I don't look at Trip as I reply. "I'm not that girl. I've only watched every episode nine times."

He barks out a clipped laugh. "The answer to your question is yes. My mom named the shop after a Friends episode. She happens to love Ross. I don't see the appeal, but…not my show, not my shop."

"You're just the delivery boy." That was a low blow. I see his face drop out of my peripheral view. "I'm sorry. Not just the delivery boy."

He looks out the window. I might have offended him. Talking is not my strong suit today.

I switch gears. "So, where are we going anyways?"

"Beehive Nursing Home. You know it?"

"The general direction," I admit, and take a left onto Summit Drive. I survey Trip out of the corner of my eye. He seems relatively coherent, which boggles me, and tells me where to take the next turn.

Ten minutes later, Trip gives me his final direction. "Take a right here, up that hill." The hill is steep, so steep that I can't see over the dashboard of the van. I press the gas, trusting that we will bottom out soon. The van eases and the view of the horizon goes back to something other than the car's dashboard.

The first thing I see is the green lawn, massive and immaculate, surrounding a roundabout brick driveway. The building is white, clean, sterile. Despite the beauty of the landscape, I wouldn't want to live here.

"You sit tight," Trip orders and jumps down from the van. I hear the back door open and close, and then see Trip carrying a large boxed tray of small vases, each filled with short-stemmed tulips. I bang my head on the seat behind me. Damn tulips.

16

My mom and dad are probably wondering where I am by now: my mom more frustrated to have to greet and engage with people alone, my father actually concerned. He'll wonder if I'm okay. That's the therapist in him. Always wanting to find a deeper cause for my actions.

I think of Todd, my sister's boyfriend, and wonder if he made it back from God knows where he'd been deployed. The military moved him around more than I could keep track of, but not anymore…now his obligation with the Air Force is up. He finished his contract just shy of my sister's death. The irony of their situation is enough to tear me in two. I want to talk to him, to support him, but the idea pains me. He reminds me of her, and I'm not ready to go there. I'm still on the train of avoiding any topics related to family, love, and life.

I see Trip walking back to the van with an empty box. His demeanor is light and goofy, in contrast with the dark tornado I feel inside me. I try to open myself up to the positivity radiating off him, just to soak in a warm feeling, but there's a stone wall sheltering my heart.

"Where to next?" I say, switching the gear into drive.

"659 Flowerlee Drive." He reads the address off of scribbles on his palm and takes his phone out to Google the directions. I obey his commands to turn left, then right, then left again. Soon, we pull in front of a brownstone apartment building. Each stair leading to the entrance is decked out with a pot overflowing with vines and bright flowers.

"You're going to want to come inside with me for this one," Trip explains, reaching in the back for something.

"What is this?" I ask when he hands me a cowbell.

He doesn't answer, just opens the door and heads up the stairs. I quickly turn the car off and follow, cowbell in hand.

Once inside, Trip says, "Remember when I told you to be prepared for awkward singing? Well, I hope you're prepared. I am about to do the best rendition of 'Happy Birthday' you've ever heard, and you are going to be my backup musician."

"With the cowbell?"

He cocked his head, feigning surprise. "What better instrument is there than the cowbell?"

"You do singing telegrams?"

Trip winks at me and presses apartment F's intercom. A young woman answers. Trip informs her that he has a flower delivery and she buzzes us up.

"I'd say this is more than just a flower delivery," I mutter under my breath.

"That's half the fun. You see, they think they are only getting flowers, but the true gift is in the song."

His arrogance borders on obnoxious.

He knocks on apartment F and sure enough, a young woman answers the door. She doesn't have to turn around for me to know her butt cheeks are hanging out of her skimpy shorts, and I can't take my eyes off the nipple that is struggling to remain covered by her tiny tank top. I watch as Trip gives her the once over and takes a deep breath. What happens next is a loud, chaotic, terrible rendition of "Happy Birthday." The timbre of his voice makes my skin crawl. I keep my distance behind him and beat the cowbell slow and steady, which makes us only look more amateurish. Trip motions for me to pick up my pace, as if that would help improve the song. But I hit the bell quicker. The woman stands in the doorway, paralyzed.

When the song is over, Trip bows as the woman slowly takes the flowers and backs away into her apartment. Trip turns and lets out a breath.

"Now that was ungodly," he admits.

"You think?"

Back in the car, I peer at my watch. I should go home. As if reading my thoughts, Trip says, "I'm done for today. We really should get you home. I promise, I'm okay to drive." His voice is sincere, his eyes returning to a normal liveliness. I believe that he's okay, but am I ready to go back?

He shifts in his seat to look at me. "I know it's hard back there. There are people who just say that to say that, and people who say it because they have been through death. They have grieved. They truly know what it feels like to be at a funeral."

I watch his eyes soften. So he knows grief too. I want to ask who he has lost and how he got through it, but I haven't been willing to talk about Riley today, so I can't make him talk about who he lost.

He reaches across us and squeezes my shoulder. My eyes shoot to his hand. "It's going to be hard to go back..." he starts, "But you will wake up tomorrow and know you have survived it."

I want to tell him that when Riley and I were little, we used to crawl to each other in our crib and fall asleep like that, our little bodies melted together. I want to tell him that Riley was the brave one, not me. That she could have survived this, but not me. I want him to know that the birthmark in between my eyes that resembles a heart matches the birthmark on Riley's leg. I want to speak of the times I felt as if my world was falling apart, only to find out that I was feeling Riley's feelings. I want the world to know that being the only twin living meant I am a heart with no heartbeat.

Riley had been that heartbeat—the living, exuberant, enduring rhythm. And what is a heart without a heartbeat?

Instead, I say nothing. I let the tornado inside me twist me into knots and the stone wall around my heart grow taller and taller.

Chapter 3

Todd
Then

Adults told us to never get in cars with strangers, but this dad and his two daughters didn't seem like the type to murder or kidnap someone. I didn't think I'd mind being kidnapped by them, though. Because if I did get kidnapped, at least I'd have one friend, and I could live in the mansion they called home.

My jaw dropped as we trundled along the narrow road lined with pine trees. We pulled around their driveway and parked in front of the house.

"This is where you live?" I whispered to the nice twin. She tilted her head as if she didn't know she lived in the nicest neighborhood in town. She had no idea how lucky she was—not in an snotty way, but in a humble one.

"Yes, this is home. Come on, I'll show you around while dad does the grown-up stuff." I eyed her dad as he got out of the car and opened my door for me.

"I need to talk to him before we come inside. Girls, go in and tell your mother we are back. Make a snack for all of us, yeah?"

A snack? My mouth watered at the thought.

Once the twins closed the front door, the father turned to me and rubbed a hand over his mouth. He motioned for me to sit next to him on the porch steps.

"I guess I should have properly introduced myself at the lake. My name is Mr. Schneider." He stuck his hand out for me to shake.

I slowly took his hand with my own and did my best to give him a firm, adult grip.

"Todd, how old are you?" Mr. Schneider inquires.

"Eight," I guessed.

"You don't sound very confident in that," he said mildly.

"Well, sir, I only remember celebrating my birthday once. I couldn't tell you how many years ago." He looked away, like he was disappointed. "I don't mean any trouble, Mr. Schneider," I assured him.

"Todd, correct me if I am wrong here. You were at the lake today to bathe because you don't have running water at home. You haven't seen your parents for a long time, and you've been feeding yourself with whatever you can find. Is that true?" He recounted the truths I revealed to him in the parking lot after the nice twin insisted I go home with them.

"Yes, sir," I said meekly.

"You are a resilient kid, aren't you? A resourceful one at that. You should be proud of yourself." I swiveled my gaze to meet his. I didn't know what resilient meant, but I did know resourceful. But no one had ever framed my life like that before.

"I guess I just do what I have to," I said.

"That you do," Mr. Schneider responded. "Todd, I wish I could have you stay here, but that goes against every boundary I've set between my family and my clients. I'm not saying you're a client, but you know what I mean."

I didn't know, but I nodded in agreement anyway.

"Do you know what a therapist is, Todd?"

"No."

"You know how doctors help you when you're physically sick? Well, therapists help you when you feel mentally or emotionally not well. They listen and provide you with ways to feel better. You can talk to them about anything and everything and they can't tell a soul. Pretty cool, right?"

"Kind of like how we are talking?"

"Just like this." Mr. Schneider smiled, which made creases around his green eyes. "You see, Todd, I am a therapist. It's the best job in the world because I get to talk to people like you and help them. But there are downfalls. Do you know what those downfalls are?"

Of course I didn't. I didn't even know what a therapist was until a minute ago.

I shook my head.

"There are specific occasions when I have to tell someone else about what I talk about with my clients. I don't like it." Mr. Schneider shakes his head in frustration. "I hate breaking confidentiality, but I do it for the safety and best interest of my clients."

I watched his facial features, trying to grasp what he was trying to tell me.

"Son, it's in your best interest for me to call Child Protective Services. I can't say what exactly will happen to you, but I can tell you some of the possibilities so we are prepared for whatever may happen."

We kept sitting on the front steps of his mansion as he told me what might happen to my future, what might happen to my family. I stared at the grass ring on my finger as if it would give me strength. I remembered the girl's smile, and I held onto that too.

"Todd," Mr. Schneider called me back to attention. "Let's go inside now. We can call in a little bit. Do you want that shower now? A snack?"

"Yes, sir," I said.

As he walked up the stairs, he looked over his shoulder at me. "Oh, yeah, and you can stop calling me sir."

Once inside, he directed me to the kitchen while he went to make a phone call. I was guessing it was Child Protective Services.

Mrs. Schneider was sitting at the kitchen island watching her daughters make a peanut butter and jelly sandwich. She wore a white silk shirt that matched her earrings. I think they were pearls. There wasn't a single hair on her head out of place. She matched the outside appearance of this house: neat and clean.

"You must be Todd. Welcome, honey." Her voice was smooth as velvet. "Ruth and Riley are making you a sandwich."

I looked at the twins as they cut the sandwich in half. Ruth and Riley. I wanted to know which name belonged to the nice one who made me a ring of grass.

"I hope you're not picky," the mean twin said.

"I'm not," I insisted.

"Good. Here." The mean twin handed me a sandwich. I stared at it, unsure whether I should eat it right then and there or wait until they started.

"Don't be rude," Mrs. Schneider scolded the mean twin. The girl marched out of the kitchen, unfazed.

The other twin walked closer to me. "I cut your sandwich in a triangle. I hope you don't mind. I like triangles better than rectangles."

I didn't know there was more than one way to cut a sandwich. I usually gobbled it down whole, but not today. Today, I would watch my manners.

22

Mrs. Schneider laughed, a quick and lovely laugh. She looked like the nice twin when she smiled in every way except her eyes. The girl's eyes looked like her father's, green and kind.

"I don't think he cares about what his sandwich looks like, love," Mrs. Schneider said.

I didn't want to eat my triangle-shaped sandwich so fast, but I couldn't help it. We hadn't had peanut butter in our house for months. The creamy texture tasted heavenly. I was licking my fingers when I heard the nice twin giggle. I thought she was teasing me, but then she too started licking her fingers, and she giggled harder, which made me smile.

Mrs. Schneider joined in on the laughter and then turned to me. "Todd, why don't I show you where you can shower before Mr. Schneider and I take you for a ride?"

The nice twin was pouting. Like maybe she didn't want me to leave.

"Thanks for my triangle sandwich. It was really good," I told her.

"You're welcome," she said. "I hope we see each other again."

"Me too," I whispered before following Mrs. Schneider. I rubbed the grass ring on my pinky finger, hoping it would never fall off.

Chapter 4

Ruth
Now

I glance over my shoulder as Trip drives away. He rolls down the window and waves. I walk into the house and the front door of my parents' home creaks, a familiar noise.

There are three people left in the house. Three stragglers talking about Riley. They're sitting on the couch while my parents perch on the ledge of our fireplace. My dad is nodding at something the girl in the middle says, and my mom is rubbing her temples.

When my mom looks up, I can see that her eyes are hollow. Red. She's been crying. I walk slowly up to the couch, behind the stragglers.

"Well." I sigh loudly, announcing my entrance. "We'd best start cleaning up." When the three strangers don't move, I raise my eyebrows at them, hoping they will get the hint.

"Right. Right. We will leave you to it," a girl not much older than me says.

"Great." I smile.

I follow them to the foyer and force myself to close the door gently instead of slamming it the way I want to.

"Where have you been?" My mom asks when I plop myself on the couch.

"Visiting nursing homes," I say. I don't have to look at my parents to know they are concerned. I sigh again, this one genuine. "I went for a drive, that's all."

My mom's lips flatline into an expression of understanding. We all need an escape form today. She stands and begins to gather the plastic plates dispersed in the living room. I watch her move around, my body heavy. I can't help her even if I try. My dad comes to sit on the floor in front of the couch, leaning his head against it.

"Ruth," he begins, "Your mom and I want you to know that you are welcome to stay here as long as you want. I know you have your own apartment in the city, but this is a big house and…you still have your room."

I know he wants me to stay more for mom than for me. She needs me, especially now that I am the only one. Her only child. I bite my lip.

24

"If I am being honest, I want to stay. For a little while at least."

"Your clients won't mind?" Dad asks. I got my degree in social work, just like my dad, but I somehow found my way into being a massage therapist. There's something about the instant gratification of the job, the instant relief clients felt after a massage, that doesn't come with being a social worker. Social work is taxing. Gut-wrenching. Even soul-destroying at times. But giving massages is like giving people the gift of peace.

"I can still drive into the city to work, Dad."

"I know. I know. I hope not for a while, though. Give yourself time to..." He lingers, lost in thought.

"To figure life out?" Without her, I mean.

"Something like that." He grabs my hand and smiles. A sad smile.

"I'll stay, but on one condition," I banter—or I try to banter. I use all the vestiges of my energy to make light of this day.

"Let me guess. You get to pick what we watch at night."

"No, but that is a good idea. I will stay only if we never have lasagna again." The effort of making the joke nearly knocks the wind out of me.

My dad pats my hand—a limp pat, as if he knows I am trying but failing to be okay. Because he isn't okay either. "Okay. Deal."

I leave Dad to go upstairs, to my childhood room. It's a slow process. Each step I have to convince myself to take. But soon I will be in my bed, a place that won't judge my feelings of defeat and exhaustion, but will, in fact, welcome them.

I walk past Riley's room and pause. The door is closed. The white paint is chipping. I focus on the paint for a minute. Two full minutes pass before my fingers find the courage to grip the door handle.

I open the door and try to push my fear away. But it's a feeble attempt, because as soon as I see her room it's as if I am being crushed all over again at the reality that she is gone. Like I am stranded on an island. Like the one person who could come and save me can't, because she is dead. Gone. Chained in a coffin due to events beyond her control.

Everywhere in this room I see her. Her victories are splayed on Steve Prefontaine's smile in the posters of him around her room. I smell her, sweat and roses. I hear her in the pile of CDs by her bed, all basic music that plays on mainstream radio. Multiple trophies sit on her shelf—all of them first place. She has a globe on her nightstand, which I always thought was peculiar. She didn't seem like the travel kind. The adventure kind, yes, toward the end of her life. But not back in high school.

I walk to her desk where her journal is lying open. She must have left it here when she was staying with our parents over Spring Break. The journal is an average get-the-job-done journal. No decorations. No stickers.

The page is open to March and a long line is sketched through all the weeks she was traveling in Guatemala. I flip backward. February was packed. I flip forward. Big mistake. April is blank.

Something in me breaks at the sight of it. The last part of me that was holding on—holding on to what, I don't know—but that part breaks.

A month ago she was here.

I flip the page back to February. When she was very much alive. Gravity pulls my forehead to the pages, to rest on the words she wrote with her own hands. I keep my eyes open. I see black words. Blurry. But there. Living and existing. I almost feel her.

The pages become wet the longer I sit there. I haven't shed a tear this whole day, but now—now I can't stop.

Chapter 5

Todd
Then

"Are you new here?" asked a kid with a round head, beady black eyes, and pale skin. He said down across from me at my corner table in the lunchroom at Centennial Middle School.

"Who's asking?" I demanded, skeptical.

The kid glanced around him and then back to me. "Me. I am asking." He held his hand out. "I'm Xavier."

I picked up my chocolate milk, never taking my eyes off him. I gulped down the whole carton and then picked at the mush the cafeteria ladies called lunch.

Xavier dropped his hand and shrugged. "Cool. Nice to meet you too."

I glared at him. "Why are you sitting here?"

He glanced around the empty table again, confused. "Oh, I'm sorry. Was this seat taken?"

I ignored him and ate my food.

"Look, see those guys over there?" He motioned to a group of jocks sitting in the center of the cafeteria. "They dared me to come over here and intimidate you because they want you to know who rules this school."

I smirked. "Fuck off."

"Right," Xavier said, "That's what I told them too. I also said, 'If you want to scare him, why send me?'"

"Makes sense," I agreed.

"Funny," he said dryly. "They want to see if you will beat me up. Look, you didn't hear it from me, but there are rumors going around that you punch kids to a pulp for looking at you wrong."

"Is that so?" I shoved the last bite of my lunch into my mouth. A memory of my fist hitting the face of a meek boy in my last middle school flashed in my mind. This was my third middle school—and my last chance, according to my social worker.

"Are you gonna do it?" Xavier asked. I peered over his shoulder to the jocks whispering behind cupped hands and then back to Xavier.

"Do what?"

"Beat me up?"

"For what?"

"Was there a reason you beat the other kids up?"

Good question. I shrugged. "Yes and no."

"Huh." Xavier sighed. "Well, it would be great if you didn't beat me up. Maybe I could tell the boys that you were intimidating as hell and that you threatened to kill me before I walked away?" he suggested.

"You know what you could tell the boys?" I said. "Tell them that you aren't their fucking guinea pig and that if they are so curious about me to come talk to me themselves."

Xavier's eyes widened and he gulped. "You know, I think you're onto something here." He tapped a pensive finger against his mouth. "My mom has been trying to get me to make new friends."

"I wonder why," I muttered.

"There's a teeny weeny problem here, though. If they weren't my friends, then I'd have no friends. Zilch. Nada."

"Welcome to the club." I stood up.

"Oh, shoot. Sorry. I didn't mean it like that," Xavier said behind me. I walked away from the corner table straight past the jocks. They cowered back from my glare.

"Watch yourselves," I ordered.

~

If there was anything good about starting a new school, it was the chance to start fresh. I could be whoever I wanted to be. I could be nice. I could have friends. I could sing in the choir. I could play football.

But while it was easy to have that mindset, it was another thing entirely to actually live it. I walked circles in the halls of this unfamiliar middle school until I found the counselor's office. I knew the drill. They'd introduce themselves. Remind me of my past escapades. Warn me that this school is different, that I really had the chance to start over. Then they'd say they'd be here for me whenever I needed to talk about whatever I wanted.

The name tag on the counselor's door read Mrs. Turner. I knocked on the door twice. It swung open, and a middle-aged woman smiled at me. She looked kind, like Mr. Rogers's wife or something.

"Todd?" she asked.

"Yep."

"Right on time. How nice. I'm Mrs. Turner, but you can call me Pat."

She gestured me inside and let me choose where I sat. It was a small room decorated with soft blankets and pillows. She had a jar of jellybeans on her desk and mellow music playing in the background. There was a futon and a worn leather chair. I chose the chair. That way there would be no opportunity for her to sit next to me.

She sat on the futon, a safe distance away, and crossed her legs. She smiled. "How is your first day going?"

"Peachy."

"I saw you sitting with Xavier at lunch." It sounded like a statement, but was meant as a question.

"It was a dare."

"I see. He is a good kid. Bad crowd, but good kid."

"I couldn't tell." My face remained flat, annoyed. "Why am I here?"

"Right to the point and sarcastic. I like it. I can be direct too, you know."

I squared my shoulders, waiting in a silent challenge.

"You smell, for one," she said. "When was the last time you showered?"

When she said she was going to be direct, I didn't think she'd be that direct. I observed the rips in my Vikings sweatshirt. It was my favorite sweatshirt, as well as my only sweatshirt.

"It's my only sweatshirt. My foster family won't let me shower every day."

Mrs. Turner's—sorry, Pat's—features sagged a little, dropping in pity. Same face, different counselor, I thought.

"Well, I will see what I can do about that."

I nodded. I'll believe it when I see it. I fiddled with my hands and looked around her room.

"How many foster homes have you been to?"

"Three," I answered. "This year."

"And how long have you been in the system?" she asked, referring to the foster care world.

"Since I was eight." I grabbed a slinky from her desk and began playing with it.

"It's not easy moving from home to home."

"I wouldn't call them homes," I smirked.

"What would you call them?"

"Hell."

"Fair enough," she responded. "I understand that you speak with your fists rather than your mouth. Where did you learn that kind of anger?"

I met her gaze, trying to decipher if she was getting ready to punish me or genuinely asking me.

"I don't know," I said.

"And if you did know, what would you say?"

I glared at her. "I said I don't know."

"Okay. You don't trust me yet. I get it. Do you get breakfast? Dinner?"

"Sometimes."

"If I put food in your backpack each day, would you take it home with you?"

I deliberated. It had been a long time since I had accepted any form of kindness, because accepting kindness made you indebted to someone. I didn't want to be indebted. I had nothing to give. Nothing to trade.

"I'm not a charity case."

She smiled sweetly. "Everyone has to eat."

Pat had me there. My stomach grumbled on cue, even though I'd just come from the cafeteria. Her smile widened.

"I'll take the food," I said, defeated.

"Good." She opened the jar of jellybeans and handed them to me. "Here. Have some jellybeans to tide you over."

"I've never had jellybeans." The words came quickly, followed by a wave of embarrassment.

"Better have two handfuls, then." She winked. "To make up for lost time."

I popped a red one in my mouth, and watermelon flavor gushed over my taste buds. Pat picked through the jar until she found what I assumed was her favorite. I watched her smile as she chewed on it. The combination of her directness and her compassion made my shoulders drop, relaxing slightly.

"Todd, listen. I'm no dummy. I know kids in eighth grade drink. It boggles my mind, but it's reality. I know that you have been let go by other middle schools not only because of your fighting, but also because of your substance use."

"Let go? That's a nice way to put it."

Pat watched me as her hand went back into the jellybean jar. She didn't care which flavor she got this time.

"I shouldn't have to tell you, but I'm going to anyway. You can't drink at school."

"But I can outside of school?" I teased, completely aware of my poor attitude.

"I'd rather you not, but I'm not your mother."

"No," I said. "You're not. I don't have one."

"And if you did?"

I laughed out loud. "She'd be drinking next to me."

Her mouth turned into a straight line of disapproval. "Is it the pain you're escaping when you drink?"

My face got hot. My fists clenched and unclenched.

"You're getting mad," she reflected. I rolled my eyes. "What are you going to do about it?"

"Punch someone."

"And what good does that do? Do you really feel better after?"

"Sometimes." The truth was that I never felt better, but people were afraid of me and that counted for something. It gave me a power I had never felt before. My peers either followed me or ran from me.

"Hmm. And does the pain of losing your parents ever go away after you punch someone?" Her words hit close to the naked truth: my parents had chosen drugs over me. They had missed every visitation they were allowed, and they had failed they drug and alcohol tests, which meant that they weren't suited to care for me, which meant I had to stay in the foster care system until someone would adopt me. If anyone ever did.

I hated my parents for doing this to me. For making me the kid who smelled and never got enough food.

I stood up and shoved the jellybeans off Pat's desk. The noise reverberated in the room as if thousands of tiny bombs were dropping. I watched green and yellow jellybeans bounce off the linoleum floor, once and then twice. They were like the efforts I made to prove to my parents I was lovable. Once and twice and a hundred times and then done. I kept my eye on one red jellybean as it skidded to a halt at the edge of the room. It was like my anger, skidding out of control until it came into contact with something hard—something concrete. I gasped for air, not realizing I had stopped breathing.

Pat jolted in surprise, but quickly regained her composure. She stood up, nose to nose with me, unflinching. My heart beat loud. I wanted to punch something. Pat didn't follow me as I stormed out of the office and kicked open the front doors of the school.

Chapter 6

Ruth
Now

Two days have passed since the funeral and still my parents and I walk around like zombies.

"What are we to do with all these flowers?" My mom stands in our living room. Her shoulders have dropped, but she still at her five foot eleven, she still looks tall. There are dark circles under her eyes. Probably from the nights we have congregated in the kitchen, all three of us. Eating our separate cereals. The conversation moving like a pendulum, swinging from reminiscing about Riley to avoiding the topic altogether.

I stare at the tulips my mom is currently holding at arm's length. An idea sparks. "Let's bring them to a nursing home."

"A what?"

I think of where Trip dropped off flowers—The Beehive. "A nursing home. You know? The place older people go."

She puts her hands on her hips, suddenly relaxed. "Huh. Why didn't I think of that."

I start collecting the vases and bringing them to the back door. "I know just the place."

~

The Beehive is bustling today. It has to be some kind of special event. There's no other way to explain the flowers, balloons, and people piling in.

My mom parks in the last empty spot in the lot.

"Huh. I never knew this was here. How did you find this place?" she asks.

"I left the funeral with a boy to deliver flowers." I decide to tell the truth.

"I see." She doesn't hear me, doesn't even blink an eye. Her normal response since the funeral—distant. "Well? Shall we?"

The receptionist smiles politely at us as we enter into the lobby, then leave, then reenter, then leave, but the third time we come in with flowers she waddles around her desk to confront us.

"Excuse me. What are you doing?" she croaks.

"Delivering flowers for your event today," I lie.

"You're here with who?" The older woman scrunches her face. I look to my mom for help, but she has already walked through the sliding doors for the last two vases. She turns around and sticks out her tongue at me. Payback for leaving her in the kitchen with Aunt June at the funeral, I guess.

"With no one," I chirp. "We just wanted to be Good Samaritans and deliver these beautiful tulips for your residents."

She doesn't budge. Still confused. Good God, lady.

"Lorna!" a voice booms. I turn to where the voice came from. A man has left a game of chess he was playing in the cafeteria adjacent to the lobby and now walks toward me.

Trip. His voice is the voice that booms.

He is taller than I remembered. His nutmeg-brown hair is clean-cut, shorter on the sides than on top. His face is literally symmetrical with those dark, blue-gray eyes and his lips are…not quite luscious, but close to it. I want to scoff and look away, but his cutting cheekbones hold my attention. He is immaculate all the way down to the clothes he wears. Still, I sense something awry with him, something far from clean and immaculate. Maybe it was what he had told me in the van the day of the funeral. He had known death. I clear my throat and look anywhere besides Trip's assessing gaze.

"Lora, they're with me. Didn't you catch that when they came with flowers?" He wraps his arm around her, and she releases all her air. A giddy, smitten type of release.

"Oh, by golly. You should have told me you were with Trip," Lorna says, as if it's my fault she couldn't put two and two together. She giggles and waves a dismissive hand in the air.

"Quite the ladies' man you are," I taunt Trip after Lorna has made it back behind her desk.

"I didn't even have to use a line with Lorna."

"Skillful."

He rolls his eyes and puts his hands in his pocket. "Seriously, though. What are you doing here?"

"Delivering flowers. They are from our house. We were kind of…getting sick of looking at them."

"I don't blame you," Trip's face turns solemn. Knowing, even. "I hated carnations after my dad's funeral."

Is this the truth, the darkness, that I see in him that sets his perfectionist appearance off-kilter? I gulp, uncomfortable.

34

"It's hard knowing what to say in these moments, isn't it?" He saves me the embarrassment.

"Yes." I nod, unsure if I like that he can read me and articulate exactly how I feel.

"It's okay. You don't have to say anything about it. We are just talking about flowers, after all." He grins, like we share this inside joke. "Listen, my mom is putting on an event tomorrow at her shop. Teaching people how to make potpourri. It sounds lame, but can actually be kind of fun."

Before I can respond, Mom brushes past me with two vases of yellow tulips. She puts them on the only counter space left and wipes her hands clean. When she turns to me, her face widens: her eyes, her mouth, everything open in surprise.

"I'm sorry. I didn't mean to interrupt," she says. Although she wasn't interrupting anything. "Hi, I'm Rebecca." She sticks her hand out.

"Trip." He grins his winning grin. "Nice to meet you."

Mom turns back to me, questions written all over her face.

"I met him at the funeral," I explain.

Trip's eyes dart to me, concerned. He's afraid that I'm going to bust him for smoking in our treehouse. I revel in his panicky expression, far from the arrogant grin he just gave my mother. "He delivered the flowers," I finish.

My mom sucks in her breath. "Oh, dear. And here with are with those exact same flowers." She covers her mouth. "I'm sorry."

"No worries, Rebecca. Ruth and I were actually just discussing how much we hate tulips. And carnations at that."

"Oh..." my mom starts, but then her mouth clamps shut. Trip smiles again, enjoying the tinge of discomfort. I half expected him to break out in a singing telegram.

"I was just telling Ruth here that my mother is putting on an event tomorrow. A gathering of sorts for people to make potpourri." He crosses his arms. "It sounds quite"—he winces—"daft, I guess. But would love to see you both there."

My mom raises her eyebrow at me. I can't tell if it's a signal for I like him, or Should we go? I see a small bit of the version of my mom before Riley's death come out—carefree.

I shrug. It's an answer for both questions.

"That would be lovely, Trip. Perhaps a nice diversion from what we have been doing the past couple days." My mom tries to keep her voice steady.

He claps. "Lovely." I wish he wouldn't smile like he just won a contest.

"Sure, sounds fun. See you tomorrow," I chip in.

"Great. At noon. You know where," he directs the statement to me.

My mom nudges my side when we walk away and whispers, "How do you know where?"

I could tell her about the meaning behind Monica Makes Potpourri, but she isn't a Friends fan. She won't understand. So instead, I shrug. Again. My normal response these days. She doesn't push it.

Chapter 7

Ruth
Now

Sitting outside of Monica Makes Potpourri feels a bit like sitting outside a Hallmark store. From the sidewalk, I can already see random trinkets and Live Laugh Love décor. I've never lived in a Live Laugh Love world, and the sight of those terms of endearment on cups and wood frames makes me die a little inside.

Life is a bit more than those three words, right?

"What did we get ourselves into?" I stare through the window.

"Oh, stop being a poor sport," my mom says. "We're out of the house. That's what's important."

"Right," I respond, and truly agree. I was either falling deeper into a depressive state or having cabin fever inside that house. I needed to leave.

"Ready?" She looks at me.

"Ready." The bell dings as I open the door.

The scent is powerful. I smell lilacs and lemon first, but then cinnamon. And if the smell wasn't overwhelming enough, then the sight in front of me definitely is. Bouquets of flowers are dispersed around an array of novelty gifts. Different types of stationery, candles, coffee mugs, wood boards with quirky phrases like, "You have the same number of hours in your day as Beyoncé," or "Kinda classy. Kinda Hood" are scattered throughout the small shop. I don't know where to look first.

"Everyone, can I have your attention?" A woman's voice, stern but kind, calls from behind the counter. "We are about to begin. Please make your way to our workspace."

The group of older ladies milling around the shop quickly shuffle through a door to the right of the counter. I find myself looking for Trip. He is nowhere to be found. Perhaps he just wanted to inform us of this class, not actually invite us.

Or maybe he thought this would be good for us.

Or perhaps a funny joke.

I'm annoyed that I want to see him.

Mom and I fall in line behind the other women who have shown up today to take the class, two of these women have men accompanying them. Both are grumbling under their breath.

We enter a small but open room with school-style desks positioned in a circle. There are family photos hanging on the wall, some black and white and others in color. I catch a glimpse of one photo in particular of a younger boy being held by two adults, presumably his parents. His father holds the boy's legs and his mother, a younger version of Monica, is lifting the boy's head. All of them are laughing.

The older ladies and the two men claim their seats, most likely their normal spots. Mom and I find the last two desks. My desk squeaks on the tile floor as I sit. Mom looks around the room. Her eyes are wide; she's slightly excited. I let my gaze linger on her, because I know she hasn't felt excitement about anything for a long time.

A middle-aged woman comes into the room and stands in the center of our circle of desks. She is beautiful in a natural way, wild curls and olive-toned skin. Intricate and colorful tattoos on her biceps peep out of her loosely fitted shirt. Her neck is adorned with an assortment of brightly colored mala beads. She seems brimming with life. I watch her in awe. What must that be like, to be overflowing with energy like that?

"Welcome to our monthly potpourri-making workshop. I am Monica. Considering it still feels like spring out there, we will be making another batch of potpourri associated with the season. Just like every month, we will outline the best materials to put in potpourri, the process of making it, and how best to keep all those yummy smells when you take it home. The most important thing is to have fun and don't be too hard on yourself. Now, who wants some wine?"

Mom looks to me, raises her eyebrow, and then she raises her hand. "Yes, please."

Monica smiles and brings over a bottle of wine and a plastic cup.

"She'll have one too." My mom nods at me. Monica's gray eyes find me. Her gaze is uncannily piercing—just like Trip's.

"What did I miss?" The voice is a smooth combination of thrill and confidence and I know instantly that it is Trip. He uses one hand to shut the door behind him and the other hand to juggle what appears to be jars of remnants of flowers. He must have come from a storage room. His black apron is tied around his athletic waist in a nice little bow. Under his short-sleeve shirt, I notice the olive skin tone he must have inherited from his mother. Why had I not seen that before? His pants and shoes are a pristine shade of black. Immaculate. Again.

I feel like a bunny in the middle of an open field. Frightened. Thrilled. A heartbeat too big for my body.

He gives the older ladies a winning smile and they blush. He goes around the circle and hugs them one by one. When he reaches my mom, he holds her extra tight. I watch her melt into his embrace, and I worry he's held her too long or too tight. I wait for the sings of her crumbling in front of me, shoulders shaking, eyes slamming shut. But she does neither. Trip releases her and stands before me.

"Ruth." He bows his head as if I am royalty. "Welcome." I half expect him to kiss the top of my hand.

Then he claps again and moves to the middle of our circle. "Shall we begin?"

It dawns on me. He is teaching the class. Not Monica. I see Monica wink at him and exit the way we came in. Before the door closes, I see her stand behind the front desk of her shop. I bring my attention back to Trip, but fail. My curiosity distracts me from his words and I barely listen as he guides us through each step of making potpourri. A heavy fog presses down on my mind.

Still, one sentence pops out. Who are you, Trip?

He doesn't fit into a stereotype, which makes me nervous, and slightly curious. Although I have to admit, being curious feels better than being sad.

"Ruth, honey. You've got to put your scents into the objects so it smells." Mom leans over. I shake myself back into reality and set to dropping hints of rosemary onto wood chips.

I watch Trip make his way from one person to the next, examining and answering questions. He is playful and passionate.

When he is done praising Mom's work, he walks around the empty desk to my right and sits in it. Energy emanates off him, a positive force field of sorts. Something about him makes me feel a bit more alive, if only for a second. I almost shrink back from the sensation.

"Hi," he says. It's a goofy, high-pitched sound.

"Um, hi."

"What scents did you choose?"

I look down at my handiwork. I can see the herbs in front of me, but my mouth isn't working. He taps his fingers on his desk, a drum roll.

"Rosemary and lemon. I'm considering sage."

"Good choices. Good choices." His face is serious.

"How often do you teach?" I ask.

"Whenever my mom needs me to. It's a bit of a dorky gig, and like I told you in the treehouse, I'd rather not be here at all. But she's done a lot for me, so it's the least I could do."

"That's kind of you."

He runs his hands through his hair and then leans in close to my ear so the others won't hear. "It's just me and her. My dad died and my sister lives across the country. We are all each other's got."

I don't know why he is offering me this information, but I nod anyway, because I understand. I only have my parents now, too.

"You speak about your dad so easily."

He looks at the table, pondering. "It didn't always be like that. I used to be where you are now. In the thick of it. The trenches."

It's true—that is where I have been and where I am still. Deep in the dirt. In the muck. The thick darkness is like a veil over me. A filter that I can't quite gaze through. Sometimes I see spots of colors. But only sometimes.

"Exactly," I say.

"You find ways to get out of it, though."

My ears perk up. "Like?"

"I can't share all my secrets with you yet." He folds his hands on the desk, still looking at me. I'm not sure what my face reveals, but judging by the way his own face falls, it's not good. His eyes are questioning, curious.

I look away. "In the tree house, you said you didn't want to be delivering flowers. What do you want to do then?"

40

He clears his throat, maybe grateful for the change in subject. "Get my MBA."

"To run your own business?"

"I don't know yet. I've sent applications in. Just waiting to hear at this point."

Impressive.

He stands up but leans down and whispers in my ear. "You see, I'd like to think I'm more than just a loser who smokes pot in random people's homes."

He walks across the room to an elderly lady who is waving her hand in the air, demanding his attention. She glares at me over his shoulder. I glare back. A familiar facial expression these days.

I look back at my poor excuse for potpourri and notice a small folded piece of paper on the corner of my desk. I glance at my mom, but she is focused in on her handiwork. I mutter something about going to the bathroom and once the door is locked behind me, I open the note.

I like you.
Call me?
612-245-8022

I reread it three times. I retrace the letters and say the numbers out loud. The filter of darkness lifts, briefly.

The note is corny, but still I put it in my back pocket. And before I leave the room, I look in the mirror. A small smile rests on my lips. Minuscule, but still there. I slap my cheek, ridding myself of that small ounce of joy.

If Riley can't feel joy, I won't either.

Chapter 8

Riley
Then

There was a hole in my bedroom. Approximately six inches. If there were any hole perfect for spying, it's this one. And that was exactly what I did—spy.

I spied on my therapist father as he sat with his crazy clients. How did I know they are crazy? I didn't. But why else would people need therapy?

I didn't find my spying creepy; I considered it educating myself. I was learning people. I was observing body language. I was studying human interaction. It was purely academic. If anything, my dad would be proud of me for using my resources to expand my repertoire of knowledge. Because this was what I needed to do—be smart—especially with crazy people, if I was going to be a doctor. Not all people who go to the doctor were crazy. That was not what I was saying. But there were those special cases. And when they happened, I would be prepared.

Ruth thought I was crazy for spying like I did. That I was a Peeping Tom. If she would only look at him through my hole, she would have understood. But she refused to engage in what she called "nonsense." She could be so uptight. Always playing by the rules, being a suck-up, being the "nice" twin. It was exhausting constantly having to contradict the title I'd been born with—the mean twin. Okay, maybe I hadn't been born with that title. Maybe I just became it. I didn't think I was mean. But compared to Ruth? I would be considered a raging bitch.

Some people thought being a twin must have been great. Frankly, I had always found it eerie. Well, eerie and annoying. We'd dressed the same until middle school (not my choice). We'd been in the same class until fourth grade (again, not my choice). We'd never been allowed to be independent. And I wasn't sure we ever would be. Could you have a brain without a heart or vice versa? I was the brain. She was the heart. Ruth and I were dependent on each other because she would always be what I couldn't be. And I was what she could not fathom being. Our opposites not only kept us apart, but were also the magnet that brought us together—that kept us whole and complete.

If the mole on one of our cheeks didn't tell us apart, our voices would have. Our personalities would. The way we carried ourselves would certainly distinguish us. It had always been that way and it would always be that way.

I worried about what would happen to her in the coming months. She was fragile. Gentle. A kind soul. I worried that her decision to go out of state for college would tear her apart. Especially since I was staying here in Minnesota. Could she do life without me? Could I, without her?

Ha. No. I knew I could. I'd been dying for this independence since I got a little taste of it in fourth grade.

~

That day, as I was spying, I had a sudden thought. This crazy person in front of my father was different than any other clients he'd ever seen. One: he was male (my dad's specialty was couples therapy). Two: he didn't seem crazy. Three: he was my age (my dad usually saw old, or at least middle-aged, people). My father never saw clients my age, especially not alone. He said the reason for not seeing clients in high school was that it hit a little too close to home. I wondered if he realized that having an office in the heated garage of our house was a little too close to home—literally.

Most clients my dad saw completely lacked dynamic emotion (probably because they were all depressed) or were so antsy I could almost feel their foot tapping. But not this one. He was dynamic.

He was angry. Livid. Sometimes he laughed. There was a certain unspoken connection between him and my dad. They had some sort of quiet understanding that I couldn't read from my place in the ceiling.

I decided to name him Generic. Why? Because he was far from your generic eighteen-year-old. At least, that was how old I thought he was. He wasn't like the boys in my senior class. He seemed distinct. Mature. A tad bit wise and a lot bit angry.

I had to admit, the anger was the most intriguing part.

I wished therapy appointments lasted longer than an hour, because an hour was not long enough for me to observe him to my fullest ability. My dad turned his body toward his computer sitting on the coffee table beside him. That was his signal that the hour was up and he wanted to schedule the next appointment. Dad typed a few things into his computer while I watched Generic's face. The anger he'd come into session with had faded, leaving only lightness and what seemed like relief. Typical. All dad's clients left therapy looking this way.

I was just about to hoist myself up from my bedroom floor when Generic looked up. At the hole. At me.

I watched confusion spread across his face, and then his eyes widened in surprise. I stared back. I was not about to balk, not now that I'd been discovered. If I was going to be caught, I wanted my last spying session to be me locking eyes with Generic. A smile played on his lips; a quick laugh escaped. He leaned forward and dropped his gaze towards my dad, trying to block my view. I didn't see what happened next, but I didn't have to. I already knew my dad was trying to make psychological sense of Generic's unexpected laugh.

Chapter 9

Todd
Then

I was sitting in Pat's office, which was not unusual. I'd come to visit her weekly since I graduated from middle school. The middle school didn't seem to mind that a senior in high school snuck into the building after the last bell to snag a handful of the counselor's jellybeans. I skipped the blueberry ones, though, because I'd learned that those were her favorite.

I lay down on her futon, the same futon she had when I was in eighth grade, as she finished typing an email.

"Well look who the cat drug in," Pat teased me and pivoted her chair to face me.

"Just came for my daily quota of jellybeans." I smiled playfully.

"And here I thought you came because I was a steady person in your life."

"Well, that too."

She turned back to her computer and began typing again. "Any fights today?" she asked briskly.

"Close, but no."

She didn't press. "Good for you, Todd. For walking away, I mean."

"Who said I walked away?"

Pat squinted at me. I couldn't help but laugh; she was so easy to tease.

"He walked away first. I wasn't going to punch him, though."

"Oh, now I feel better," Pat said sarcastically. "The counselors at the high school say you have an 'A' in physical education."

"You're talking to the high school about me?"

"Of course I am. I didn't adopt you to ignore you and everything happening in your life."

It'd been almost three years since the adoption paperwork went through, and still I wasn't used to having Pat be my adoptive mother. I hadn't called her Mom yet, even though her nurturing presence embodied motherhood. I'd learned these last few years that she was everything a mother should be—consistent, present, strict but fair. She didn't shy away from the crude remarks other teachers made about my behavior, nor did she back down when the high school principal called her in for the second time that month in order to discuss why I had come to class drunk.

I had a problem. I knew it. She knew it. I didn't know what to do with the problem or how to get away from it. I was ashamed, ashamed of my behavior and ashamed because Pat expected more from me and I wasn't living up to her expectations. I didn't know how to be the person she wanted me to be.

"Todd, you can do better than only getting a single 'A.' I'm proud of you for that, I really am, but let's not forget about math, or science, or—God forbid—English."

I groaned. "I hate school."

"That's because you've never tried."

"I do too try. I go to school every day, just like you asked me to." And some days I go to school drunk so I can get through the boredom.

"Going to school and actually being present in school are two different things. You're not engaged, and you're not engaged because you're drunk."

She'd never been one to beat around the bush. I put my arm over my eyes in agony. We'd had this same conversation multiple times. She got mad at me. I got mad at myself for making her disappointed. I told her I would change. I didn't. I drank. Cycle repeated.

"Come on," Pat said. She closed down her computer and put on her coat. "Let's go home."

I followed her to her black jeep Cherokee, relieved that I'd avoided any further discussion of the topic of drinking.

She was unnaturally quiet the entire way home. When we parked outside of her house, my home, she locked the doors and turned toward me.

I groaned again. "What now?"

"You're not going to like this, but I'm not going to sit around and watch you ruin your life." Her expression was particularly somber, and she seemed to be teetering on the line between crying and slapping my face. "You are at a fork in the road," she said, holding her hands in front of her. "You can either go this way"—her right hand swerved to the right—"which is you making the same shitty choices. Do you know where that leads?"

I knew better than to interrupt.

"That leads to you in jail," she said, cringing on the word jail. "You'd be right next to your parents." She let that soak in, staring at me with both hope and disappointment. "The other road"—she moved her hand to the left, away from the invisible road that would lead me to jail—"will lead you anywhere you want to go."

"I don't know where I want to go."

"Anywhere is better than where you are going now!" She sighed and sat back in her seat, almost defeated. Almost. The sight of her like that made something in me scramble, uncertain, scared. I didn't like seeing Pat defeated.

"You are at a critical point in your life, Todd. Each choice matters."

I gazed out the rearview mirror and watched a blue sedan drive to us and then past us. I couldn't look at her, because her pleading words were daggers to my heart.

"I know you're not used to people caring about you, but you know what? Tough. I love you." My heart leaped. She'd said it before, but never with that much conviction. My own mom had never spoken those words. "You have two choices today," she began. "You can start seeing a therapist or you're going to rehab. You decide."

I didn't resist. I pondered my options. Rehab sounded extreme, and too long of a time period. How could I leave Xavier? At least therapy could be outpatient, which meant I could still stay at Pat's house and see Xavier at school.

My mind went back to elementary school, to Mr. Schneider. To the girl who seemed to smile forever. The grass ring and the peanut butter and jelly sandwich cut in triangles.

"I'll do therapy. But only if I can see Mr. Schneider."

Pat perked up at this answer, like she was surprised that I agreed without putting up my normal fight.

"He lives in St. Paul, by the river, in a mansion," I added, like that was enough information for her to find his contact information.

"Okay." Her voice shook with relief. "Okay," she repeated. "I'll call this Mr. Schneider tomorrow."

"Can we go in now?" I asked, hand on the door handle. I needed to leave this conversation and hide in the comfort of my room, small yet all mine.

"Yes."

I was almost to the door when I heard Pat yell my name. I turned, slowly, hesitantly, awaiting another demand.

"I love you," she said again. Her eyes were persistent. Her half-smile warm. I didn't let her see the happiness I felt creeping onto my face.

"I love you too," I muttered.

Chapter 10

Riley
Then

It was 2 p.m. on Tuesday, which of course was Generic's normal time to come for therapy. Except this Tuesday was different, because I'd forgotten it was Tuesday. I could have slapped myself for being so careless. Because if I had planned our first encounter better, I wouldn't have made the mistake of looking like a train wreck.

I had just gotten back from a run. A run in the August heat at that. I was sweaty and red. I was disgusting.

Generic was in our driveway. Everything after that was slow motion. He was casually leaning against our garage with one hand was in his pocket and the other was fumbling with a cigarette. He was looking at the sky.

This was the first time I'd seen him face to face. Did he recognize me? Recognize the one eye that'd peered down at him?

He was a perfect balance of grace and indifference with little hints of something else I couldn't quite name—yet. It wasn't quite anger. That I remembered seeing during his first session. No, the hints were something else. Pain, perhaps, like flashes of lightning in the dark of his irises.

So not your generic teenage boy.

As if I'd spoken my thoughts out loud, he looked up.

After watching him for months, he was finally watching me.

We stared at each other.

Smoke from his cigarette floated around his face like a cloud. I took my time with his features. I had never seen him this close. My eyes stayed on his nose, long and prominent, for a while. His sandy blond hair was just a little too long, so that he had to keep swinging his head in a particular way to move it out of his eyes. And those eyes. They were the lightest brown I had ever seen. He was wearing a plain white T-shirt and faded jeans. He must have had no idea what his type of looks did to girls. Because if he did, he'd be smiling at me in that creepy come-over-here-and-give-me-a-kiss way slimy kids my age did.

And then he smiled.

It shattered the silence and the lightning in his eyes dimmed.

"I recognize those eyes." His voice was surprisingly deep. I felt my body moving closer to him, straining to hear that voice again.

"You mean eye?" I teased. He chuckled.

"Yeah. One blue eye. Hard to forget. I see them every Tuesday at 2 p.m." His shoulders relaxed.

I smiled then, not because what he said was funny or because he was softening around the edges, but because his laugh was better than I had imagined it would be.

"You do know I can't hear a word you say though, right? I promise I am not a creep," I assured him.

"I know you're not."

"How can you tell?"

"If you heard me, you probably wouldn't be talking to me right now." His face turned solemn, shadows passing through his eyes.

"Your story doesn't scare me."

"You don't even know my story." He threw his cigarette on the ground, smashed his foot into the cement, and stood up straight, hands in his pockets. I looked at the cigarette, annoyed. I'd have to clean that up when he left or else mom would erupt.

"Maybe not, but I am not afraid of whatever it is," I told him.

"Brave." He took one step towards me.

"You might say that." I shrugged. "So what is your story, then? Since I know nothing about it."

"It's one I am sick of telling," he said softly and gently. He was getting slightly uncomfortable, I knew, because he had done this before in therapy: rolled his shoulders down and cranked his neck in slow motion as if he wanted to crawl out of his own skin or shake off the nerves. It was a subtle shift.

"I can tell. Your eyes say a lot about you," I responded.

"Like what?" he countered.

"Like the fact that someone ruined you." I took a risk. "And you're learning how to not give a fuck."

Now it was his turn to shrug. "Plural," he finally countered, like this was the only answer I need. When I didn't make a move to speak, he continued. "Someone didn't ruin me. Two people did. So it's plural."

I nodded, because I didn't know what else to do. "What now?" I challenged.

"You tell me." His feet moved again so he just an arm's length in front of me. I stepped closer to him. Even though I looked like a disaster, I wasn't going to back down. He wouldn't see me weak.

"Your body language says a lot too," I said. Ambiguous, I know. But those sentences tended to draw people in and I wanted to draw him in to me.

"Like?" His eyes twinkled in expected curiosity.

"Sometimes, you give in and let my dad take that weight off your shoulders, and sometimes he hits a nerve and you shrivel up into yourself." He looked down. "You don't ever come back after that," I finished in a whisper, trying to soften the blow, but failing. If I were Ruth, I'd be softer, kinder. But I wasn't. I didn't know how not to be straightforward.

The silence was excruciating after that. I thought I'd blown it.

Then he said, "Your dad is good." The right side of his lips curved into a half-smile.

"Yeah. He is." I held tight to that half-smile. "Imagine trying to hide anything from him. Nothing is sacred in this house."

"Sounds nice actually…having a dad and all." His face fell flat. I immediately regretted my choice of words. Again. Dammit.

"Is the dad thing what strikes a nerve for you?"

It took him a moment to realize what I was asking, but when he figured it out, he responded shortly, "Yeah, something like that. Hey, what's your name?"

"Riley. You?" This was the moment I had been waiting for. It was the split second of adrenaline I felt at the starting line of every race I had ever run—and won.

"Todd."

"I knew it."

"Knew what?"

"That it wouldn't be John," I said. He tilted his head, curious. Confused. "I just mean you wouldn't have a generic name is all."

"Why is that?" He smiled.

I shrugged. Keeping him guessing. "I'll tell you. Tonight. Meet me here at eight o'clock?" It was brazen, I knew, but I felt a pull to him that I couldn't ignore.

He crossed his arms and looked into the distance, debating. His golden-brown eyes found mine again. "Your dad wouldn't like that."

"He doesn't have to know."

He examined my face. I wondered what he saw.

"Deal," he said.

Sweet victory.

Before I could push another question in the air between us, he told me he had to go inside. It was finally 2 p.m. His normal appointment time.

I ran through the house and into my room. I moved the dresser and laid flat on the ground to look in the hole, just to get that one smile I knew he'd have for me. He sat down across from my dad and looked up. We made eye contact for five long seconds before he cracked a smile. I smiled back, even though he couldn't see my lips.

Chapter 11

Todd
Then

Mr. Schneider was just how I remembered him. The only thing different about his appearance were the dark-rimmed glasses on his face and the flecks of gray beginning to show near his ears. He still had an aura about him that demanded respect, and because he was genuinely interested in my well-being as a child, it was easy for me to give him that respect.

He remembered me instantly. I could see him wanting to embrace me in a hug—his infectious smile and approachable demeanor told me so—but we settled on a firm handshake. It was a mundane gesture, but it made me feel like his equal. I thought back to the time he spoke to me on the steps of his home, like I was not a lost little boy but a person capable of communicating with an adult—an equal.

Their home appeared just as it had all those years ago, grand yet welcoming. I didn't expect his office to be in his home. The thought of being in therapy so close to the twins made me anxious, but also thrilled. What if I saw the twins? Would they recognize me?

I felt a twinge of disappointment when Mr. Schneider took me through the garage door rather than the front door, because this lessened my chances of seeing them. He led me to his office and waited as I picked a seat. I had a flashback to eighth grade, when I had to choose between Pat's futon or the leather chair. I looked around his office. He had two chairs, a couch, and a coffee table. All modern and clean. We both took a seat in the chairs.

"Did Mrs. Schneider pick this furniture out?" I asked impulsively.

He laughed. "You're good. Yes, she has impeccable taste. Although I did get to choose the colors." I looked around at the different shades of gray in the room and the one bright blue pillow on the couch. There were a couple windows in the room, letting sunlight in.

"Todd, it's really good to see you," Mr. Schneider went on. "We have had you on our mind for all these years…wondering where you've been. You'd have to be about seventeen years old now, right?"

They'd had me on their mind? Who? Mrs. Schneider? The twins? I wanted to ask about them all, but I didn't know where to start. I didn't know if it was appropriate.

"Yeah, I'm seventeen. A little older than the last time you found me," I said.

He chuckled. "I'd say so."

I rubbed the palms of my sweaty hands on my thighs and folded my arms across my stomach. I sighed, not sure where to begin. Not sure how this therapy thing worked.

"My adoptive mom, the one who called you, wanted me to see a therapist and your name kind of just popped into my mind. I remember you talking about therapy." I uncrossed my arms and shrugged. Mr. Schneider threw me a stress ball. I uttered a thank you under my breath and squeezed the fidget toy tightly.

"I'm glad you remembered me. So, why don't you tell me why your adoptive mother wants you to be in therapy?"

I bit my tongue. Tendrils of shame crawled up from my gut to my throat. I squeezed and released the stress ball.

"Turns out I am becoming my parents."

"Is that so?" Mr. Schneider inquired. He waited for me to continue.

The silence got uncomfortable. "Yes. I am not doing whatever hardcore drugs they were doing, but I am doing something."

"I see. And what might that be?" He crossed his legs and let his forearms rest on the sides of his chair.

"Mostly drinking."

"Beer or hard alcohol?" Like this made a difference.

"Both," I responded. "But mostly beer."

"And who are you mad at?" The question was unexpected, and I needed him to repeat it. I thought about everyone in my life who made my blood pound. The list was long. Then Mr. Schneider asked me to name the one person who I was mad at most.

"My parents." The words flew from my mouth. "And myself. It's a tie."

"What about your parents make you angry?"

"Isn't it obvious?"

"Perhaps, but I'd like to hear it from you."

"I feel as if I should not even exist. They should have never been parents. It wasn't my choice to be born. It was theirs and they didn't accept the responsibility. Now I am left picking up the pieces of a life I've got no say in."

Mr. Schneider eyed me carefully, forcing the words I'd just spoken to sink in. I chewed on my inner lip, embarrassed by my sudden disclosure. I hadn't known I felt that way until the words came out.

"And is that true, that you have no say in your life?"

"Sometimes it feels that way."

"Yes, it may feel that way. But our feelings are not facts. Is it true that you have no say in your life?"

"No."

"No. It's not true. So, who does have complete say in your life?"

"I do," I muttered.

"Ah. You do. Interesting. And what do you plan to do with that control?"

I pondered that word, 'control.' Wasn't that what I'd been fighting for all along? Wasn't that what I'd hoped to gain by intimidating other people?

"I guess I've never known that I don't have to get control..."

"No. You have control already. It's quite spectacular, really." He smiled and adjusted his glasses. "Fighting and drinking are signs of being out of control, and if it's control that you want, then there are other ways to obtain it."

We spent the rest of the session talking about anger: how it felt, where it came from, the messages it gave and the ways to channel it. We spoke about coping skills and how to use releasing exercises like sports—boxing, more specifically—to manage my anger. I listened attentively, curious about the world behind my anger.

When the clock struck three o'clock, we both stood. I told Mr. Schneider that I would tell Pat about my newfound interest in boxing. I agreed to come back next week at the same time.

Mr. Schneider hugged me at the door. I didn't know if it was proper protocol for a therapist to hug his clients, but I figured we both knew our connection ran deeper than most therapist-client relationships. He let me leave alone, and so I retraced my steps through the garage and out the door to my car.

I'd taken two steps down the driveway when I saw her. My body involuntarily halted. One of the twins had tied a tightrope between two large oaks in the front yard. Her body was swaying side to side as she tried to balance on the rope. I'd seen people do this in public parks, but never with such grace.

I was not sure if this is the mean or the nice twin, but whoever it was had grown. No longer was she the eight-year-old wearing little Crocs. She was wearing neon shorts and a loose, white tank top. She looked athletic. Her hair was in a high ponytail and yet the ponytail reached her mid-back. The kind of girl that every guy at school would want to date.

She stopped in the middle of the tightrope, one foot in front of the other. Hands out to the side, creating balance. And then she looked up. I inhaled quickly, and felt my body go back in time to being eight years old at the lake. Did she recognize me?

Suddenly, she fell off the tight rope. Even her fall was graceful. I heard a curse in the distance. She looked back to meet my eyes, and I didn't know what to do, so I did nothing. I made my feet move toward my car and I got in.

It was only when I was a safe distance from their house that I reached in the center console and picked up a small grass ring.

Chapter 12

Ruth
Now

Mom and Dad are sitting at the kitchen island when I return from getting new clothes from my apartment in the city.

Two trays of peanut butter cookies are cooling on top of the oven, which is never a good sign. Mom is a stress-baker. Snickerdoodles means she's lonely. Chocolate chip means she's anxious. But peanut butter—that means she's feeling plain old sad.

Dad motions for me to come sit.

"We found some news out...about Riley." His voice cracks at her name. It has been four weeks, and still her name makes us stutter.

Anxiety creeps like a snake from my toes up through my stomach and into the knot in my throat. I clasp my shaking hands together. I feel lightheaded and have to force myself to inhale. I shuffle my leaden feet towards my parents and take a seat on the other side of the island.

"What?" I whimper, afraid of he'll say.

My dad's expression is unreadable. "There is going to be a trial to determine the fate of the man who killed your sister. We have been asked whether or not we want to participate in the hearing."

"Your dad and I know our answer, but you, of course, can make your own choice," Mom declares, surprisingly calm.

I imagine attending the trial and seeing the man that killed my sister. What would it be like, to finally come face-to-face with the last person to see her? Would he cower his head in our presence? Would he even feel guilty? Even this made-up image of my sister's killer makes me sick. I can't do it. It happened—he killed her. I don't want to be immersed in what happened or even reminded of that story. It's already been playing on repeat in my head. I used to think that seeing her killer, a tangible entity that I could point a finger at and blame, would make me feel better, but now I am not so sure. My heart will be drenched in sorrow either way—whether I blame him or not, whether I see him or not.

"If you aren't going, then I am not going. It doesn't change anything." Both my parents nod in understanding. "What's going to happen to him?"

My parents look at each other. "We don't know." Dad rubs a hand over his face. "We just have to trust that justice will be served."

I stare at the space at the end of the island, the space where Riley would be sitting if she were here, and I choke back a sob.

Oh, Riley. I miss you.

"I'm going to go for a drive," I say meekly. I need to clear my head.

"We will be here if you want to talk," Dad says to comfort me, and Mom nods in agreement before turning her back to me. She cuts a stick of butter in half and throws it into a bowl, starting a new batch of cookies. I don't wait to see what kind.

Before I start the car, I take out my phone. I sift through my contacts until I see his name.

Trip.

I don't know why I want to be with him in this moment. I hardly know him, but I know he knows death, so he has to know this feeling. This unexplainable concoction of emotion. I haven't seen him in almost a month, but that doesn't matter. He doesn't seem like the kind of man who needs an adjustment period with people.

I wait anxiously after I send the text. I try to focus on the soft wind tousling the trees lining the street. I try to name the shades of blue I can see in the sky. I take a deep breath before I look back at my phone.

Trip: Meet me at the shop. I have a place we can go.

I don't use Google Maps on my way, as the route feels familiar now. Easy. The roads are clear tonight, a blessing that allows me to get into the city quicker than normal.

Trip is standing outside of Monica Makes Potpourri when I arrive. My stomach tightens at the sight of him, and before I have time to reflect on what that means, he gestures for me to roll down my window.

"We'll take my car. I'll put out of my spot and you park here," he tells me. I nod and wait for him to pull out before I parallel park.

He is cautious and quiet as he drives, not so charismatic as the previous times I'd met up with him.

"What?" I practically yell after a while.

His eyes widen. "You called me, remember?"

I bang the back of my head against the seat. "I'm sorry. I just needed…" I struggle to find the words.

"Not to be alone?"

"Something like that."

He pulls away from the shop and toward the highway. "I have just the place to go."

~

I thought I knew Minneapolis highways well, but as the cars pass by Trip's 4Runner heading west, I know I'm headed in a direction that I normally don't go. He takes an exit near the airport and cruises into an abandoned parking lot near the runway. He parks the car so we are directly facing airfield, the path made visible by rows of the red and blue lights, shining like stars in the dark night.

The Delta airplane hangar stands in the distance, and multiple Boeing 747s are lining up on the jetway. We're not that far from the highway, but the trees surrounding the parking lot muffle the noise of traffic.

A plane pivots slowly to face us, getting ready to take off. Trip rolls down the windows as the plane rushes forward. I look at Trip, marveling at the scene in front of us. One of his hands takes my own, and the other opens the sunroof to his 4Runner.

The plane picks up speed.

"Three." Trip starts to count down. The front of the plane is hurtling closer to us.

"Two."

The plane's nose tips up ever so slightly.

One.

"One," Trip breathes.

The plane is at full speed now, giving it enough lift to ascend.

Suddenly, we are looking out the sunroof at the gigantic underbelly of a 747. Trip pinches my hand and just like that—it's over. The plane is on its way.

When my eyes adjust to the black sky, I immediately search for a constellation. It's not long before I spot Draco—the dragon. Trip lets me sit in silence, holding his hand.

A familiar warmth washes over me looking at those glistening dots. They have been my companions through periods of turmoil—big or small—in my life. Sometimes I find myself searching for a specific dot, that one particular star, but mostly I search for how they all connect. I look for how they all come together to make a shape, a character. If only the constellations were people. They'd be my true companions. What is a companion, after all, if not for someone who has seen your darkness and still chooses to shine for you?

Perhaps Riley's essence is in the stars, moving peacefully and ceaselessly through the constellations.

"Come here," Trip says, bringing me back to the present moment. He reaches into the backseat and grabs two blankets, then opens his door to step out. I get out too, and watch him do his best to make the hood of his 4Runner comfortable enough to lie on.

Using the front bumper, I hoist myself up onto the hood, then lean back against the windshield. Two satellites glide briskly past each other overhead. I find Draco again.

"Here comes another one! Get ready." Trip is elated. Two bright lights on the airplane's wings are coming full speed, straight at us. I am glad that we are outside of the car this time, because when the plane flies over, the noise drowns out everything else. My thoughts, my heartbeat, my feelings are muted.

"I get it."

"Right?" Trip agrees. "I love this place, this exact spot on Earth. It's peaceful out here. My dad used to take me here when I was little. We'd stuff a cooler with beer for him and pop for me. And maybe pop doesn't sound like a big thing, but my mom is a health nut, so we never had it in the house. We'd come here on my birthday every year." Trip laughs as if suddenly remembering details that have been tucked into the corners of his memory.

I turn my head slightly to look at Trip's profile. I want to see him trust me enough with these details.

"My real name isn't Trip, by the way." He glances sidelong at me.

"I knew it was too good to be true."

"What do you mean?" His voice spikes.

"It's a great name. Only someone really unique could have that name for real. It's a disappointment that it's not you."

"Funny," he says.

"What is your name then? Chris? Please don't tell me it's John."

"God, no. My real name is Jason."

"I can see the comparison to Trip." Trip snickers at my sarcasm, and I revel in the sound.

"My dad gave me the nickname. I think because he was obsessed with traveling. Either that, or he was on some sort a drug-induced trip when I was born." Something about that statement makes Trip drop his head in shame. The words themselves reprimand him.

"What happened to him?" I venture, afraid of pushing Trip too far.

"He overdosed." Trip's gulp is audible. He right hand pinches the bridge of his nose. "Can you imagine? Your father, the pharmacist, overdosing on pills." He pauses and drops his hand between us. "What a joke," he murmurs.

It's not a funny joke, and he knows it, too. I can physically feel his pain. My first instinct is to say I'm sorry, but those words didn't fit in this moment, just as they didn't the day of Riley's funeral. There are no words to express the pain of losing someone you love.

I reach for his hand, which is limp and cold.

He continues. "I'd like to think my dad named me because of our tradition—to come to this place. I used to pretend that he named me Trip because he hoped that one day we'd be one of those happy families flying in a plane together. When I was older, I realized that was my hope."

I turn my body on the hood of the car so I am lying on my side, facing him. He is on his on his back, looking up.

"We were happy when we came here, so at least I have that memory to hold onto. After he started calling me Trip, everyone else did too."

I get the sense that he wants to dispose of his name, despite the nostalgia that comes with it. But that's the point of nostalgia, to simultaneously pull us closer and further from the past, to draw us into a specific feeling time and time again until it's finished, felt in its fullest form.

Trip doesn't explicitly hate his father, but there is resentment. There is grief unfinished.

Another plane glides above us, a dark mass against the already dimmed sky. We stay silent as four planes take their turn at taxiing and taking off. Trip lets go of my hand and rolls on his side, too, using one arm as a pillow. We lie facing each other. He scans my face and gently reaches to tuck a piece of my hair behind my ear. The simple touch sends vibrations through me from head to toe.

"I have something else to tell you." Trip speaks hesitantly. When I don't respond, he continues. "I didn't handle my father's death well. What you found me doing in the treehouse? Let's just say that is the best of it."

He rolls back onto his back again, putting distance between us. He folds his hands behind his head, elbows out. He can't look at me.

"I ran from my grief. I avoided it. I covered it up. I basically put a Band-Aid on it by using...all sorts of things. Because I couldn't deal." Now he looks at me. It's as if he is challenging me or waiting for me to sit up in protest. His jaw clenches.

"What kind of things?" I say, barely above a whisper.

"Drugs, mostly. Sleeping with women. It helped, briefly. But it was never enough." The truth he is sharing is raw and bold, and although it may be too soon in our friendship to share these details, I am glad he trusts me with them.

"Do you still do them? Drugs, I mean."

Another plane flies overhead, filling in the space where his answer would be.

"Sometimes," he admits.

I shove my disappointment aside. Who am I to judge this man I hardly know? Who am I to judge the different channels of grief?

"Why are you sharing this with me?" I ask.

"Because if you know the worst parts about me in the beginning, then it can only go up from here."

"And that was the worst part about you?"

His shoulder hunches up in a mini shrug, and he sighs. "It's a nasty part of me, but the most disgusting part of me is that sometimes I don't want to give it up—the Band-Aid, I mean."

He speaks frankly about himself, his faults, and the dark desires. It's alarming. It's intriguing.

"Perhaps, in time, you will find a solution more powerful than drugs to get you through," I offer.

"Perhaps," he echoes, unconvincingly.

I take my eyes off of him to look at Draco and then back toward the runway, where another plane is coming our direction, full speed and without hesitation. If Trip can share a vulnerable side of himself with me, then I can at least return the favor.

"There is going to be a trial," I begin, keeping my voice steady. "A trial for the man who ran over my sister, and the lawyer asked me and my parents if we wanted to be involved." A small weight lifts off of me at the admission.

"What are you going to do?" Trip props up on his elbow and looks down at me.

"Not be involved."

"You're not curious about the man? About what will happen to him?"

"I'll read about it in the paper."

"Huh."

"Why huh?" I ask, surprising myself with my defensiveness.

"I didn't get closure with my dad. One day he was here. Then he wasn't."

I consider. "What does that word even mean, closure?"

Trip doesn't miss a beat. "Seeing the man who killed your sister face-to-face and then watching him walk away to rot in a cell is closure."

"Is that so?"

"Damn straight. I'd want him to decay."

If I weren't numb, I'd flinch here, at the harshness of his words. His intentions.

"I don't know how I feel," I admit. "It's not like anyone gets in a car determined to go run another person over." The words don't sound right. "But I shouldn't think that way, should I?" I muse. "I should blame that man."

"Think whatever you have to in order to get through the pain," Trip says.

It's not advice I'd normally follow, but since Riley's death, I feel like a ship lost at sea and am open for direction.

"Why did you call me tonight?" Trip asks.

"I don't know," I utter. Again, the truth.

Trip reaches out for my cheek again, and the sudden movement surprises me. He stills his hand. When I don't pull away, he hugs his fingers around my neck and pulls me close to him. It's not hasty, but it's sure. Our lips touch at the same moment the plane's roar stifles the pounding of my rapid heart.

It's the only moment I can recall where Riley isn't at the forefront of my mind.

Chapter 13

Todd
Then

This was the first summer I had not drank. No afternoon pick-me-ups, shower beers, or road sodas. Ever since I'd started seeing Mr. Schneider, I'd been sober. He insisted it was all my doing, but I felt like he had a part to play in my sobriety. It wasn't the therapy, although that helped. It was the fact that for the first time in my life, I saw an older man who'd made something of himself. An older man whom I admire and respect. He didn't need to drink to feel okay, and so I didn't either.

I'd found that I like this responsibility over myself. This new type of control.

I was driving to Mr. Schneider's house now, except this time not for therapy.

I'd never wanted to lie to Mr. Schneider, and at some point, I would come clean. But not tonight. Tonight, I wanted to take his daughter to the river like we'd been doing the past couple months. I wanted to talk to her, to know her more, and to kiss her full lips. Because soon we wouldn't have the opportunity to. Basic training started soon.

I parked a safe distance away from the house and put some deodorant on. I had just come from boxing and didn't want to scare her away with my stench. The sun had set, and the sky was turning a few shades toward night. The street was quiet except for my footsteps, slow and steady.

When I could see their house, I waited for her. She would come to the street to meet me, just as she had for almost every night for two months. My heart was fluttering in anticipation of seeing her.

The porch light came on, our signal that her parents were preoccupied with their nightly routine and wouldn't notice her gone. A few moments later, I saw her silhouette in the doorway. She jogged to the street and jumped into my arms. I lifted her off the ground and inhaled the flowery scent of her hair.

She was perfect.

"How'd the escape go?" I asked as I lowered her back down to the ground.

"Easy peasy." She grabbed my hand. We walked at a comfortable pace down the street until it dead-ended into a small park. Once we got to the park, we pushed carefully through the brush and down the steep trail that lead to the river. I went down first and caught Riley's hand in order to assist her the rest of the way.

At first, the way we settled into silence had made me uneasy. But now Riley knew all about my parents, my drinking, the anger, and the adoption. Now, I found these periods of silence to be comforting; she accepted me for who I was, despite my past. I didn't have to pretend or withhold from her, just like all those years ago by the lake when she didn't balk at my tattered and rancid clothes.

But she didn't know that I was the boy at the lake, and I didn't have the courage to tell her. What if she remembered that moment and was disgusted? What if she saw me differently after I told her? Besides, I saw no use in bringing up the past. How would that help us today or in the future?

"A penny for your thoughts?" Riley broke the silence. She climbed on top of our picnic table, and I followed suit. Our spot was nestled in some thick Minnesota greenery. A small trail from the picnic table led to the Mississippi river moving lazily nearby.

"I'm thinking about the end of this summer. Dreading it," I said sheepishly.

"Me too. I don't want to say goodbye to you. Maybe…we don't have to?" Her eyes widened with hope, pleading for me to change my mind about the military.

"Rile, you know how much this means to me."

"I know. Just wish that you didn't sign a six-year contract. That seems like eternity. When will I ever see you?"

"I'll fly to you when I have leave. You can fly to me during school breaks. You have the advantage of flying out of Minneapolis. It's a major hub."

I hadn't thought about that before, but I was suddenly thankful that she was staying in the Twin Cities for college, because Minneapolis was a major hub. She could fly to see me.

"Flying to see each other?" she whined. "It's going to be torture."

Yes, it would. How was I going to do all of this without her? She was the one who ultimately got me the help I needed. She was the one I called when I felt the urge to drink. She was the one who picked me up and drove me to boxing when I was angry so I wouldn't do anything self-destructive. It was her idea for me to join the military—to have them pay my way through school.

She was a light, and I never wanted it to stop guiding me.

"It will be tough, but so are we." I tried to my best to sound strong. "We can do it, Rile. We've been through worse." Like not seeing each other since we were eight years old.

"You're so confident in us, and it's hardly been three months." Her voice was soft.

I put my arm around her and brought her closer. She melted into me. "That's because I love you." And I did, down to the deepest parts of me. I had loved her a long time. That smile when she was sailing. Her small hands, pulling me up.

She pushed away from me to look me in the eyes. "What did you say?" she breathed.

I kissed her lips, so soft and always ready for me. "I love you." I traced her smile with my eyes, drinking her in. Her beauty was the classic, heartbreaking kind, and I couldn't believe she was mine.

"I love you too, Todd," she echoed, much to my relief.

"We'll write love letters, just like they did in the old days."

"You'd better write me. Even if the other soldiers make fun of you, you better write me."

"I will write." I placed my hands in between her thighs and tugged her closer to me. "Someone has to make sure you are studying. Becoming a doctor is no cakewalk, Rile."

"Are you saying you don't believe in me?" She was teasing, but I knew her well enough to know my comment stung.

"I believe you are capable of anything. I just think with running cross-country in college and studying in order to get into med school is going to be a lot for anyone. Not just you."

"You may have forgotten, but I am Superwoman." Riley pinched my arm. Her lack of humility was more charming than irritating, because I wanted to know where that confidence came from. I wanted to be like that.

"Yeah, yeah, yeah. You're Superwoman, all right. Still, you're my girlfriend, and I'm allowed to be worried."

"I wish you weren't."

"Tough."

"Just like me," she teased. I squeezed her knee, sending her into a fit of good-natured curses and giggles.

"Come on," I said. "I better get you home or Dr. Schneider is going to be worried."

"Yes, about him. As much as I love sneaking around, it would be nice to go on an actual date with you. You know, in public."

I had thought about that, too. I wanted to take her on a date, to roam around the lakes and do normal couple things during the daytime. I especially wanted her to meet Pat.

"I agree. I will tell him about us in my next session with him."

"Oh, that will go over well," she said. "No, let me talk to him first. I'll tell him how madly in love with you I am and then he will have no choice but to allow me to see you."

My heart practically sprang out of my chest. I picked her up and swung her around, kissing her all over her face, vowing from this moment on to show her, more than tell her, how much I loved her.

Chapter 14

Riley
Then

I'd stopped spying on Todd. Not because I wanted to, but because I'd started to develop feelings. I'd go as far as say I respected him, which to me, was more intense than feeling infatuated.

According to my calculations, we had only one month to figure out whether or not we wanted to try to make something work. In one month, I'd be going ten minutes away to the U. In one month, he would be flying to Texas to begin basic training for the Air Force. His decision to go into the military was equal parts quarrelsome and admirable.

Pros of him going into military:

One: if we didn't work out, great. I wouldn't ever see him again.

Two: we'd have space from each other. We could be independent.

Three: he was actually doing something with his life (so being far from a bum, in other words).

Four: he would get strong. Chiseled. Hot. Everyone would be jealous.

Cons of him going into the military:

One: if we did work out, I wouldn't ever see him

Two: distance sucked when trying to make a foundation in a relationship.

Three: …there was none. Which just proved that it was a good idea for him to go.

Every night spent together had only gotten better and better. Each encounter with him made my heart fall a little closer to the ground. In a good way. And if my heart was falling, I knew the rest of me was tumbling after it. I was in love, and it was terrifying.

What if our relationship held me back in school? Could I manage the prerequisites of medical school on top of traveling to see him? When it came down to it, would I choose love over a career? No.

And that's what truly alarmed me. Because he would. He would choose me. His eyes told me so. He loved me in a way that ran deep, a depth that didn't match our time together. And this, too, made me doubt us, because who had he fell in love with in this short amount of time?

Me.

When he looked at me, I felt like he saw parts of me I had even yet to discover. He looked into me and found a better version of me than I believed myself to be, and I couldn't understand why. All I knew is I'd found myself wanting to become that better version of me, the one he saw. And so when the time came for him to leave for the military, I wouldn't complain. This would be a great race, and if I knew anything about races, it was how to win them.

~

We were going to a concert tonight in the city. Todd, me, and Ruth. I wished I could say I enjoyed spending time with Ruth, but the time between now and when Todd leaves was dwindling. I'd rather not entertain my sister when I could be with him...alone.

But he had insisted, telling me that he spent years being excluded and wouldn't do the same to others if he could help it. In the same sentence he would also refer to Pat and the importance of paying kindness forward. This freely given kindness was not foreign practice in my family, but that didn't mean to say it was a natural for me. The way I saw it, kindness was a reward.

"Ready?" Ruth yelled from the living room.

"Ready," I said as I came down the stairs and through the front door. I saw Todd waiting in his truck for us.

"Hello, ladies," Todd said. He kissed me on the cheek. I scooted my seat forward for Ruth to climb into the backseat.

When I settled into the passenger seat I asked, "What is this band called again?"

"White Elephants!" Ruth squealed.

I saw Todd look in the review mirror at her, smile, then look at me. There was a knot of jealousy in my stomach when he looked at Ruth that way, and it rattled me. "You'll probably hate them, but you're being a good sport," he told me.

"I swear, sometimes I feel like I am dating Ruth for how much you two have in common." It sounded spiteful, but I didn't intend it to.

They didn't say a word. Ruth changed the subject.

The drive to the city took a while due to the steady traffic on a Friday night. Todd asked Ruth about her plans for college—when she would be leaving and what she wanted to major in. I tuned them out, watching people mingle in the restaurants we passed.

We left the car in a parking garage and started walking the three blocks to the venue. If Ruth weren't here, Todd might have leaned down and kiss me. He would have stopped in the middle of the road to get the perfect kiss. Instead, he grabbed my hand and winked at me. I heard Ruth behind us, trying to keep up. There was no line outside the theater when we neared it, which only confirmed my suspicions that this band was lame.

Once inside, I could see that I was mistaken. The theater had three sections: the ground floor near the stage where people could stand, the middle section of about thirty rows, and then the balcony. Every seat was full.

Todd held my hand as he weaved through the crowds of people. The opening band, some bore-you-to-death group, was already playing a typical mellow indie song when we arrived at our seats—which were on the end of a row, thank God. Easy escape.

In my peripheral vision, I could see both Todd and Ruth were smiling.

Dear Lord. Get me out of here.

I forced myself to listen to three songs before I excused myself to go to the bathroom, stifling a yawn on the way.

"Riley!" A girl's voice yelled in the foyer. It was Kitrina, who ran the last leg of the four-person relay in track. She was faster than me. I hated her for that, but she'd never know it.

"Kitrina!" I zigzagged through the people crowding the bar until I reached her. She gave me a limp hug. "You like White Elephants?" I asked.

"God, no." Kitrina waved at me dismissively. "I know the bartender, though." She looked over her shoulder to the bar in the center of the lobby. The guy was older and clean-cut, but also a little…slithery, for lack of a better word. "He gives me free booze and I hang out with him after shows."

"Hang out?" I raised my eyebrow.

"Please, don't act like it's a big deal. You here with your hot boyfriend?" she asked.

I liked knowing Todd attracted the attention of my frenemies.

"Yes, sitting with Ruth. I had to leave for fear I'd die of boredom."

Kitrina nodded. "You know what solves boredom?" She inclined her head toward the bar.

I looked back at the slimy, but semi-cute, bartender.

"What are you drinking?"

She giggled with pleasure and grabbed my hand. "Come on. Let's go."

~

I thought the opening act was over. I wasn't sure. My brain was fuzzy. My limbs loose. I kind of liked it.

Kitrina and I stood close to the curtains that separate the foyer from the auditorium. We were laughing, but I didn't remember about what. I heard clapping. We both started clapping too. I knew I must have looked childish, but I didn't care.

I peeked past the curtains. I spotted Todd instantly. He leaned down to hear something Ruth said, and then he smiled.

I felt a pang in my heart. A quiet stab. I wanted to be the one to make him smile. Not her.

I cleared my throat and excused myself.

When I get to Ruth and Todd, I tugged on his arm. He wrapped it around me, pulling me in close. He didn't even ask where I'd been. He leaned down to give me a kiss, but stopped midway and jolted back. Then his lips came to my ear.

"Have you been drinking?" he asked.

"So?" The word tasted like venom coming out.

I couldn't explain his face in that moment. And the booze in me made me not care.

"Come on," I practically yelled. "Let's go dancing. Being here is killlllling me."

He looked over my head to Ruth. I hated that. He should have been looking at me.

I knew he wanted to stay, but I wanted him to choose me. His shoulders sagged, defeated. I saw his mouth form the word, "Okay."

I pushed Ruth out of the aisle and told her the new plan as we walked into the foyer.

"Bye, Riley," Kitrina called, picking up another drink from the slime ball bartender.

There was dancing two streets down, according to Kitrina. A restaurant/bar that allowed underage kids in.

Todd said nothing as we walked there. Party pooper. Ruth looked nervous. Not much of a dancing type. Both of them were furious with my mini tirade, but still I walked on.

Once inside, loud techno music and disco lights hit us full-force. It was the type of place you could get lost in, let go in. Both sounded appealing tonight. Todd found a booth in the corner of the room. Typical. He would find the quietest, most removed spot in the club. I walked by the booth, straight to the dance floor.

Soon Todd would leave me for the military and Ruth would be states away. I would be alone studying day in and day out. Tonight, I didn't want to worry about any of it. Zilch.

Let go. Let go. I repeated in my head. I snagged a full drink off an empty table near the dance floor and downed its contents. The booze hit me fast and so did the pulsing beat of the music. I let vibrations shave off my worries about the future and my jealousy until I was left with nothing but pure euphoria. I was reduced to nothing but this moment and in this moment I felt the sweat trickle down my back and my heart expand two fold.

Todd walked toward me. He was most likely walking at a normal pace, but it seemed like I watched him for minutes until he firmly grabbed my shoulders. My body swung back and then forth, trying to find balance in his arms.

"Why are you doing this?" he asked. I knew I was hurting him. I was disappointing him. His eyes never lied. I wanted to reach up and shut those eyes, but only after I told him See…you don't really love me. You love a version of me that I will never be.

I wrapped my arms around his neck. "To let go. You know, you should let go too." My words slurred. He reached up to grab my hands.

"Let's go, Riley."

"No," I said. "I am not done dancing." I'm not done letting go of the pain that I know will come in a few weeks when you leave me.

He stared at me a few moments, both of us like statues in the middle of the dance floor. He wouldn't force me to leave. It wasn't in his character.

He walked back to the booth, where I could see Ruth sitting. She looked at me with concern and nodded at the door. I shook my head no.

I couldn't say how long I danced, but I can say some nice man shared his drink with me. Then he decided to get grabby, and even though I was not in a logical state, I knew the liberties he was taking were not okay. It was my cue to leave.

Todd and Ruth weren't at the booth when I got there. They were nowhere to be found. They'd left me. Typical. He would choose her over me.

Emotion stuck in my throat. That damn knot from before.

I searched the entire club, even the men's bathroom, before I walked outside. Or wobbled outside, more accurately. I ignored the pity stares as I passed people waiting in line to get in the club. When I got to the end of the line, I spotted Todd. Ruth was standing next to him, talking to an older couple. Who, based on their baggy clothes and slick hair that could have been either wet or greasy, were probably homeless.

Typical Ruth, helping the poor.

I walked up to Todd and grabbed his arm. He didn't look away from the older couple. Now that I was close, I could see their expressions. Hopeful. Proud. Familiar.

"Who are you?" I asked, trying to enunciate over the slur in my speech.

Todd didn't say a word. He looked away.

The man, who had a large nose and something of an intimidating presence, said, "We are Todd's parents."

I didn't know what to do. Ruth looked heartbroken. So I masked my face into something that might resemble sad, but it felt more like a grimace.

Then my hand flew to my stomach. Oh no, I think. Not now.

I closed my eyes as I retched everything out of my insides onto the pavement between us.

Chapter 15

Ruth
Now

"What do you have in these boxes?" Trip pants. This is his second trip from my bedroom in my parents' home to my car.

"Clothes." I cringe, shoving my yoga mat deeper into the backseat. "I didn't know how long I'd be staying."

Summer is around the corner, which means my parents will be busy. But this also means I don't have to worry about them, and so the guilt has waned to a manageable amount. I can handle the echoes of my apartment knowing that my parents at least have each other.

Trip's slender but toned arms barely fit around the box he is carrying. His face is turning red and his cheeks puff like a chipmunk's with each inhale and exhale.

He drops the box behind my car and it lands with a loud thud. Trip tries to catch his breath. "You have heard of a washer and dryer, right?"

I glare at him playfully.

He is right. I had far too many belongings here considering I live just fifteen minutes away. I watch him struggle to lift the last box into the trunk of my car and then close the hatch. He turns to me, his hands on his hips.

"Never again will I help you." Even as he says it, I see a hint of a smile.

"Please don't. Saves me hearing the complaints."

He scowls but closes the distance between us to wrap me in his arms. His shirt is drenched in sweat. I make a face and pull away, but he holds me tighter. Punishment.

When I am done resisting him, he rests his arms on my shoulders. His eyes find mine and he gives me a true smile. Not like the ones he gives the old ladies at potpourri class, but different. Vulnerable. He kisses my nose. It's a familiar move now, but his kisses took some getting used to. Because if they felt good, which they did, did that mean I was moving on from Riley's death? Wasn't that too fast? It felt wrong to be happy and to live when Riley couldn't.

"Listen, there is this event going on soon at The U, a marketing convention of sorts for those interested in applying for their MBA program come fall. It's not really a huge thing, but can you come? With me?"

He is flustered. And he is minimizing. It's the first time I've ever seen him acutely nervous about anything. His insecurities are normally overshadowed by his loud humor.

"I don't know. I may be too busy unloading all these boxes," I tease.

He narrows his eyes. Tilts his head.

"Fine. Yes, I will go with you." I laugh to dispel his nerves.

"Good." He smiles and kisses me briefly on the lips. "See you at your apartment?"

I nod and watch him drive away before going back into the house. I have one more thing left to do.

I find Mom in the kitchen—her normal spot when she's not in the bath. She is humming and rolling dough. Thank God it's not for cookies.

"Hi, honey."

"Hi, Mom."

"All packed out of here?" she asks, trying not to sound forlorn at my looming departure.

"All packed. Where is Dad?"

"With a client." She avoids eye contact. I know she is trying to avoid this moment entirely.

"Mom, I live in the city. Not even ten miles away. I will see you soon."

"I know. I know." She wipes her hands on her apron and walks around the kitchen island to hug me. "Come over for dinner next week? I think Todd is coming."

My heart skips a beat. Todd. The sound of his name bounces through me. Images of him come quickly. Why I haven't thought more of him until just now?

"Where has he been lately?" A sudden flash of anger courses through me. Where has he been? Why hasn't he been here when I needed him most? Doesn't he need us?

"Away. Like the rest of us." She cups my chin in her hand. The wrinkles under her eyes are more pronounced than ever before. I know she is implying that all of us have been distant in our grief, but it felt like that statement was directed toward me and me alone.

76

Perhaps she is right. Perhaps I've been lost in my mind. Not quite myself.

Chapter 16

Todd
Then

I looked at my watch for the hundredth time. Where is she? For someone who prided herself on her accomplishments and work ethic, she sure didn't care about being on time.

Today was the day Riley was supposed to meet Pat. We were having dinner at my house—Pat's house. This was the day that my adoptive mother was going to meet my girlfriend. It wasn't just any meeting; it was the meeting. The summer was over, and I left for the military in a few days. This was the only chance for Pat to meet Riley.

I paced back and forth in my room, which was medium-sized and square with not much more than the basic necessities. Pat had tried to get me little knickknacks and memorabilia, but the clutter made me uncomfortable. Or perhaps I just wasn't used to having stuff.

I looked at my watch again. It read 5:55. I looked at my cell phone. Nothing from Riley. Damn it. She wasn't going to come. Of all the days to be late, today should not be one of them. I shoved the lump of disappointment down my throat and into my knotted stomach. I went into the kitchen, where Pat was making dinner.

"Todd, where is this infamous girlfriend of yours?" she asked, pouring herself a glass of red wine.

"Um, well. There was a miscommunication. She thought I was going to pick her up, so," I pointed to the door. "I'm just gonna go do that. Be right back." I walked out of the house before Pat could say otherwise.

I fumbled with the keys. Where could Riley be?

I drove to the Schneiders' home and parked in their roundabout driveway. I sprung up their steps and knocked. Ruth answered the door.

"She isn't here," Ruth said.

"Shit." I ran a hand through my hair, and spun in a circle. "Do you know where she is? Should I be worried?"

"I don't know, but no, I wouldn't be worried. She doesn't answer my texts most days either. What's gotten into you?" Ruth asked, stepping outside and closing the door behind her. She crossed her arms. In this moment, she looked so much like the mean twin at the lake when we were all eight years old. I'd feared her then, and I still did. Ruth wasn't necessarily mean, but she was intimidating. She was on a pedestal—not that she knew it—because of her grounded demeanor. She was smart, and intensely quiet. At times I didn't know what she was thinking.

I stopped spinning, a sudden thought coming to me. It was unlikely that the idea would work, and it was twisted but...

"Look, I'm about to ask you something really crazy, but I'm desperate." I paused and consider what I was about to ask. It was insane.

I thought of Pat and her thrilled expression when I'd asked to bring my girlfriend over for dinner. She was expecting someone. She wanted to know who I'd been spending my summer with. I couldn't let her down. On the flip side, I had to cover for Riley. What would Pat think of a girl who just stood me up?

"What is it, Todd?" Ruth asked, with an air of caution.

I released a breath. "I need you."

"To do what?"

"To have dinner with me and my adoptive mom," I said.

Ruth pointed to herself, her eyes bulging, and shook her head. "Me? Why?"

"Because Riley is nowhere to be found and this is the only time Pat will really get to spend time with Riley before I leave for the military next week. And...I can't disappoint her."

Ruth tilted her head back, looking at the porch ceiling. She bit her tongue. I wished I knew what she was thinking. Then I cringed. I hated that I was putting Ruth in this situation. No—I was annoyed that Riley was putting me in this situation.

Ruth looked at me head on. "Fine," she said, resigned. "Do I need to change?"

I looked at her outfit: tight jeans, boots, and a cream-colored sweater that was much too big for her.

"You look perfect." I smiled. She started for my car and I turned to follow her, trying to keep up. "You don't need to get anything else before we go?"

"Nope. Let's do this."

We discussed our strategy the entire way to my house. Ruth would tell Pat about her dream to become a doctor and the reasons she loved running. I would talk about our plan for the next six years, if the topic comes up. Minimal touching. We'd act as if we liked each other, but nothing that would overstep boundaries.

We parked in the garage and walked up the short flight of stairs to the door that led to the breezeway. Ruth grabbed my hand, and I yanked it from her. She laughed. It was a rare sound and gave me pause.

"I'm sorry." I squeezed the bridge of my nose. "This is weird for me."

"Hey, your idea," she replied. I couldn't tell if she was teasing me or blaming me for the absurdity that was about to take place.

I grabbed her hand this time, noticing the subtle differences between her touch and Riley's. Ruth's fingers were smaller, fragile, whereas Riley's almost matched my own. Ruth squeezed my hand for encouragement, and I opened the door.

The kitchen smelled like heaven. There was turkey on the dining table, surrounded by sweet potatoes, broccoli, and bread. It felt like Thanksgiving. Pat had the music turned on low, a classical melody. Her back was turned, so she didn't see us come in. She was singing loudly, a beautiful and inviting sound. I'd never known she could sing. Pat took out something from the oven—a pie, by the looks of it.

I glanced at Ruth, who was smiling wide at the sight in front of us. She didn't seem awkward in the slightest. She almost seemed…happy to be here.

"Hey Pat," I said to announce our entrance. She turned around quickly. Her eyes dropped to our interlaced hands.

Ruth dropped my hand and walked up to Pat. She hugged her. Pat accepted the hug and met my eye over Ruth's shoulder, an approving expression on her face. She winked at me quickly before stepping away from Ruth. I released a pent-up breath. So far, so good.

"Well, well, well. The brilliant Riley." Pat held Ruth an arm's distance away, gripping her shoulders. "Dear, I am so glad to finally meet you. I've heard a lot about you."

80

I couldn't see Ruth's face, but I heard her respond. "Thank you for inviting me. I've been looking forward to meeting you as well."

My heart skipped a painful beat. It should have been Riley here saying that. Had she looked forward to meeting Pat? Did she care?

I watched as Ruth helped Pat finish setting the table and preparing the food. Ruth moved with ease, smiling at what Pat says and asking questions at the appropriate time. I could see Pat falling in love with her by the minute. The fact that Pat was welcoming Ruth and not Riley into her open arms irked me.

Ruth and I sat on one side of the table and Pat on the other. She watched us carefully, eyes shifting from me to Ruth, trying to figure us out. I attempted to adjust my facial features to whatever expression meant I wasn't pretending to be on a date my girlfriend's twin sister.

The usual table talk ensued during dinner. Pat asked about Riley's hopes for college, as we suspected she would. She also noted the impressive amount of medals Riley had racked up during her time in cross-country and track. Unlike Riley, who would have basked in the compliments, Ruth didn't seem to know how to handle this praise. She shifted in her seat and glanced at me. I could see her eyes pleading with me, begging me to take the attention from her.

I changed the subject instantly. Pat caught on to what I am doing, though, which only made her eye Ruth more closely, with more interest. Pat was queen of reading deflections.

There was a lull in the conversation, with nothing but the music in the background and our silverware clinking.

"Todd leaves for basic training soon. How do you feel about this, Riley?" Pat took a sip of her wine and cordially wiped her mouth with her napkin.

Ruth shifted in her seat. I reached for another roll, feigning indifference to the answer that was about to come.

"I have to admit, I didn't like the plan when we first started talking about it, " Ruth started. Her voice was gentle, soothing. "But I believe that there will be a certain level of growth that will happen because of that distance. And I can't say that I fear growing."

I listened to each of her words, because I didn't have that opportunity very often. Riley had a tendency to overpower Ruth when we were all together.

Pat inclined her head and smiled. "A girl who is not afraid of a challenge. I like it."

I cleared my throat. "It won't be easy being apart, but we plan to see each other as often as we can."

"And we both realize the significance of communicating and trusting each other through the distance," Ruth added. She glanced at me to see if this had been an appropriate thing to say. I nodded, because it was the perfect thing to say to Pat. I couldn't help but wonder what Riley would have said.

"Yes, well, trust and communication will be key. It's a lofty endeavor, but I know Todd and I know he doesn't give up easy."

We all took a bite of food and the quiet overtook us again.

"How did you meet?" Pat asked.

Ruth's fork stopped mid-bite. Did she know this story? On instinct, I looked at Ruth's eyes, remembering Riley's blue eyes peering through the hole in the ceiling, the one right above her father's office.

"We met on a field trip," I started, my palms sweaty.

"A field trip?" Pat was surprised. "I don't remember you going on any field trips in high school?"

Ruth piped up, "Yes, well. It was a surprise trip. We had walked…to the colleges near our high schools. It's our introduction to college life, so to speak."

"All the high schools walk to the colleges nearby, and you happen to be at the same college at the same?" Pat was confused.

"Precisely," Ruth said. "My senior class and Todd's were at the same college that particular day…" Ruth eyed me and continued slowly. "I had gone to the bathroom and when I came out, I realized I had lost my group."

I cleared my throat, holding in a laugh. "And I found her outside the bathroom pouting—"

"I was not pouting," Ruth scolded me and shoved my shoulder. I winked at Pat, trying to convince her my words were true.

"Anyway, I found her lost, dazed, and confused," I said. Ruth tilted her head back and laughed. "And I offered to give her a tour of the school myself."

82

Ruth picked up where I left off: "I had no idea he was a high school student when I first met him. I thought the whole time that he went to the college. I only found out he was not a college student when he kept walking me in circles. He was clearly lost." She turned to me, wanting me to finish the story. My mind scrambled, trying to find the perfect ending.

"What can I say? I'm a charmer. I asked for her number. You know, in case she ever got lost again and I needed to help."

"Like I'm some damsel in distress all the time," Ruth joked.

Pat had followed our story with interest, but I could tell she was skeptical. "I highly doubt you're a damsel in distress, my dear," Pat told Ruth. "No damsel in distress would be attempting to go to med school. Plus, Todd likes you for your independence."

Ruth smiled in agreement, like this was a compliment for her herself. Pat rose from her seat to gather the plates and bring them into the kitchen.

Ruth quickly got up to help with the dishes, much to Pat's delight. I didn't feel right sitting there, so I too helped clear the table. Ruth rolled up the sleeves of her sweater and set to washing dishes. Pat was next to her, drying the dishes and putting them away.

The hard conversations were out of the way. I finally felt myself relax and enjoy myself. Even though that seemed wrong without Riley here.

When the dishes were put away, Pat perked up. "How about a good old game of Scrabble?"

I didn't even have time to reject the idea before Ruth said, "I love Scrabble." She followed Pat into the living room and looked over her shoulder at me, shrugging. I shrugged back. A game of Scrabble couldn't hurt.

We played three games, and all three games Ruth won. I was shocked by the repertoire of words in her vocabulary, which only made me realize how many quirks and parts to Ruth I knew nothing about. Pat was also blown away by Ruth's quick creation of words, some of which even Pat did not know existed. It was rare to outwit Pat. Ruth laughed uncomfortably, again unsure what to do with Pat's compliments.

Pat sat up from the floor and informed us that she was going to the den to watch a show. This meant she was leaving us alone—trusting us alone. I knew I was eighteen years old and should be trusted, but still I felt uneasy with the permission she was granting us.

"We did it," Ruth said with a note of relief, her shoulders dropping down her back. She sat cross-legged across from me, the coffee table and Scrabble board between us.

"We did. You did great, Ruth. Truly."

"Thank you."

"No, thank you. I was almost screwed tonight thanks to your twin."

"Sorry about that," Ruth said. She leaned back against the couch.

"Why are you sorry?"

After a moment's reflection, she said, "I guess I don't know. I find myself apologizing for my sister's behavior a lot."

I didn't know what to say to that. Speaking about Riley without her present didn't feel right.

"How do you feel about going into the military?" Ruth changed the topic.

I look into her speckled green eyes and scanned the freckles on her face. I could keep whatever relationship we had superficial, or I could tell her the truth. I found no fault in the truth, so I admitted it. "I'm scared. But I'm also ready to be involved in something bigger than me and this town. I want to make something of myself."

"And you think the military will help you make something of yourself?" There was no ill intention in her question.

"Yes. I think it's a start. Like you said at dinner, we shouldn't be afraid to grow through challenges."

She hummed, remembering the comment. "That did sound good, didn't it?" And then her eyes cast down. "It's true, though. You will make something of yourself, but you already have, in a way." She looked up at me again. When I didn't respond, she confessed, "Riley has told me about your past. I know it wasn't easy, but look at you now. You've become something from what could be called nothing."

She was right. I had changed. I was no longer the lonely little boy or the angry teenager. I felt like a man with a purpose, a sense of direction. I was glad to know the transformation hadn't gone unnoticed.

"Thank you."

She smiled shyly and nodded. I reached for the Scrabble box and began to clean up the small wooden pieces. Ruth joined in. "Where did you learn so many words, by the way?" I asked.

"Reading."

"Right." I laughed. "I should probably do more of that."

"It certainly wouldn't hurt. I will get you a book on how to survive the military. Unless you'd like one on long-distance relationships?" I had to look at her face to know if she was serious or teasing. Her face was still, but there was a lightness in her eyes.

"How about both?"

"Deal." She chuckled, a quick and pleasant sound.

We both stood and I wasn't sure what to do next. If this had been Riley, I'd probably have whisked her to my room and snuck some kisses from her. But it was Ruth. The thought made me check my phone.

There was one message:

I got held up! I couldn't leave. I'm so sorry I missed dinner. Is Pat mad?

I looked back to Ruth, who was fidgeting with the sleeves of her sweater.

"What are we going to tell Riley about this?" I asked, putting the phone on the coffee table, face down.

Ruth sat on the couch and pondered this question. She rested her chin in her palm. "I don't think we should say a thing."

I considered this.

She continued, "You leave next week. Riley goes to college in a couple weeks. Pat won't have a chance to meet Riley, so she can't talk about tonight. No harm, no foul."

I didn't like the idea of lying to Riley, but there was no use in telling her if everyone was parting ways soon. It was like the dinner hadn't happened at all…except it had. Ruth had come to my rescue. She'd met Pat. She'd played Scrabble with Pat. She'd made Pat laugh.

"How can I repay you?" I asked her.

"Please, Todd. Don't insult me. I will be here for you. I'm practically your sister."

My stomach shrank into a knot—not because she'd referred to herself as my sister, but because she'd said she would be here for me. She'd been here when Riley hadn't been.

"A sister who looks like my girlfriend." I tried to lighten the mood.

"It is a bit creepy, isn't it." Her face scrunched up. "At least you can tell us apart. That's more than some past boyfriends."

"That's never been a problem," I said, amazed that others couldn't tell the difference. "Your freckles and that little thing right there"—I pointed to the faded birthmark in between her eyes—"tells you apart. Plus, your personalities are polar opposites."

Her hand flew to her birthmark, and I worried that I'd made her self-conscious, but she didn't reveal any insecurities. "I'm glad you see the difference." She met my eyes. It was an intense moment. I looked away first.

We walked toward the door of the garage, where my car was parked. I yelled to Pat that I was going to drop Ruth off, and then realized my mistake and yelled Riley. Ruth bit her lip to stifle a laugh as soon as her name was out of my mouth. "And to think that could have all been for nothing," she gasps.

I rolled my eyes, irritated with my slip. "Let's go."

In the car, Ruth changed the channel and rested her feet on my dashboard, a gesture that would have otherwise irked me. But today, I let it slide.

Chapter 17

Riley
Then

Todd insisted he wasn't mad at me for vomiting on his parents' shoes that night we missed half the concert he wanted to go to. He wasn't mad for getting drunk in the first place. But he was sad, which was worse.

I didn't realize how my drinking could trigger him. I knew he struggled with alcohol. That he'd almost gone to rehab. I felt like a first-class idiot.

He didn't say a word about seeing his parents. Not one single word. He brushed it under the rug. I pushed. He didn't budge, so I let it be.

Today, I felt like breaking. I felt like I was fracturing in two. The only way I'd feel better was to be with Todd, close enough to touch.

He was leaving for basic training in Texas the next day, and so began the longest journey of our lives. He was afraid he wouldn't succeed in meeting the strenuous demands required of him after basic training and thus be dropped from the running to be a pararescueman. I knew he would make it all the way. He had the mental and physical stamina to do so, and that haunted me as much as it pleased me, because once he was a pararescueman he would be put in danger so that others could live. This made his job both precarious and respected by all forces in the military. We would both be respected. We would be a power couple. Unstoppable.

The night before, I'd driven to Todd's house. The house was small, one-level, and almost unable to contain all the love that Pat exuded.

I climbed into his window.

I spotted him sprawled on his stomach, breathing strong, even breaths. I stood there looking at his features, which were soft compared to the first day we had met.

I crawled into bed next to him. His hand reached for me, as if he knew I would come. He pulled me closer to him, turning on his side so his long form stretched the length of my body, my back against his broad chest. His mouth came to my ear and he murmured, "I love you."

I remained silent, trying to keep my tears in. I failed.

Todd shifted just enough so that his hand brushed the wetness on my cheeks. "Rile..." His voice strained. He turned my body so we were facing each other. He gently caressed my hair. Each time his thumb reached my face, he wiped away another falling tear. He kissed my nose. My right cheek. My left cheek. My forehead, and lingered there. I wrapped my arms around him and pushed myself into his hold.

He lifted my chin with two strong fingers. His mouth found mine, and as if he could sense my unease at this whole situation, he moved his mouth slowly, waiting for me to come around. For a moment, I could make myself forget what tomorrow would bring. For a moment, I could forget.

I opened my mouth to him, willing him to go further. He felt my invitation and his kiss deepened. I moaned at the taste of him. His smell was becoming more and more familiar. I gripped his shoulders, begging him to come closer. One of his hands was cradling my head, and the other was tracing a line down my stomach and downwards. I shivered when his fingers found my wetness. He kissed me fiercely. I melted completely into him.

Neither of us said a word out loud, but our bodies spoke a language all their own. I felt my bones shiver. As much as I wanted to completely let myself go to this moment, I found myself memorizing every detail of him. He was reachable in this moment, and tomorrow...tomorrow he wouldn't be. I closed my eyes and set to committing to memory what he felt like. I spent the longest time tracing the groove from his neck to his waist. Over and over again I traced. I squeezed my eyes tighter to stop the tears.

Over and over again I learned by heart.

~

Todd left the next day. I couldn't bring myself to drive to the airport with him. I was a piece of shit girlfriend for not going, but he knew I couldn't. He knew goodbyes broke me, especially this one.

Last night, after we'd made love, I stayed with him until the sun was shining through his curtains. It was the sun that woke me, even though Todd was next to me, staring at me with those big, golden eyes. There were dark circles under them. When he saw me stir, he forced a smile that looked painful. I put a hand to his strong jaw and attempted my best smile. It felt painful too.

"How am I supposed to leave you after last night?" Todd dropped his head onto the crook of his elbow. He looked so small and fragile lying there.

"That was my point," I said slyly. "I wanted to show you what you're going to miss."

Although it was an attempt to keep the mood light, it failed. He looked at me soberly. "I don't need the sex to know what I am going to miss."

Any other girl would have swooned at that. "Is that what we were doing last night? Just 'having sex'?"

Another attempt to get a smile from each of us. If I was playful, he would be too. If I was strong, he would follow.

He turned his head in mock thought. "Hmm, now that I think about it, yeah, we were just having sex." He pulled me closer to him. "I can't let you leave me without making love first."

"Is that so?" I said coyly, already pulling his oversized T-shirt over my head to expose my naked body underneath.

"I love how you play hard to get," Todd teased. He drew circles across my body with his brawny hands, drinking in each inch of my skin with his eyes. He swallowed loudly. "You are the most beautiful girl I have ever known, and I am so lucky that you are mine." I felt my whole body flush from the inside out.

I let him make love to me...again. Both of us crying at the end, lamenting what was to come in only a few hours. I was in a tailspin of dread. It was only when I could hear Pat moving in the kitchen that I remembered we were not alone.

The climb out his window was slower than usual. When my bare feet hit the grass, I risked looking back at Todd through the open window. He leaned out, tears still streaming from his eyes.

"I can't say goodbye," I told him.

"Me neither."

"No, I mean...I can't come to the airport, Todd."

At first, he looked disappointed, and then he nodded. He understood. He always understood.

"I get it."

"I know you do."

He rested both elbows on the windowsill, hands pressed to his lips like he was praying. He stopped what appeared to be a sob rising in his chest. I clamped my eyes closed.

"I love you," I said.

"I love you too."

I kept my eyes closed, savoring his voice. I needed that to be the last moment with him. Hearing him say "I love you" was enough. It was all I needed to get through this. I couldn't see him broken and in pieces, because then I would crumble too. And I hated feeling weak.

My eyes had still been shut when I turned and walked away.

Chapter 18

Ruth
Now

The night of the convention, Trip picks me up outside of my apartment. He is wearing a tux. I've borrowed a long, navy blue dress that trails behind me and hangs loosely off my shoulders—the perfect dress for the sometimes-unpredictable weather in June. My hair is in a high, slicked-back and classy ponytail as to expose my shoulders and accentuate my collarbone.

"You. Look. Beautiful," Trip says as he opens the door for me. His eyes linger on my breasts, and although it's a tinge annoying, I don't reprimand him.

"Thank you," I say shyly.

In the car, we cruise through the rows of traffic until we get into a lane that's steady. I notice his hands are shaky on the steering wheel. I peel his right hand free and squeeze it.

"Why are you nervous?" I ask.

He laughs quickly, a skittish laugh. "I'm not."

"Please," I dismiss his lie. "You sing telegrams and teach old ladies how to make potpourri. You're hardly the type of guy to get nervous. What's going on?"

He swiftly brings his gaze to me and then back to the road. "It's tonight. All of it. I am not used to wearing this." He gestures to his outfit. "And I'm not sure...I'm not sure I'm good enough." He swallows deeply.

"For what?"

"To impress the school, the teachers, my peers...everyone."

"You are good enough."

"You have to say that. You're my girlfriend."

My hand slackens at the term. We had determined that we were exclusive, but still, the word girlfriend clenches my heart.

"Even so. You are good enough to impress these people, whoever they are."

"Everyone that matters in the MBA program at the U and agencies potentially recruiting graduates will be there tonight."

"Good thing you're not a graduate yet," I say, in hopes of easing his mind.

"Thanks," he says shortly. I realize my mistake.

"That's not what I meant."

He takes his hand from mine and sets his jaw. We drive the rest of the way in silence.

We park the car and enter the ornate hotel where the event is being held. Men are dressed to their finest. The women on their arms are in embellished dresses, longer and more extravagant than mine. I breathe a sigh of relief. Good, less attention on me.

Trip is either too nervous or too upset with me to help me up the long, curving staircase to the grand room. He seems to be in his own mind, set on his own agenda.

The lights are dim in the ballroom—dim enough to hide imperfections, but bright enough to shine on people's insecurities.

Round tables are spread evenly around in the room, maybe a hundred tops. Crystal dishes are laid in perfect order on fine white cloths. It feels like a royal wedding, and I feel out of place. Perhaps I would feel more comfortable on the arm of a confident man, but I feel Trip's insecurity emanating off him like he is a small boy in a room full of men. Scared. Unsure of what to do. I want him to tell to act like the person he is with old ladies: chivalrous, disgustingly handsome, witty.

He plasters a fake smile on his face, meandering about. We share pleasantries with other couples around our age for what feels like hours, but I keep finding my way to the snacks, nibbling my discomfort away one cheese stick at a time. I watch Trip closely. I've never seen this side of him before. His skittish, cold demeanor and dark eyes don't just radiate insecurity, but something deeper. It's as if he truly loathes himself. I can see the self-hatred like bricks on his shoulders, weighing him down. There is a shadow in his eyes when he talks to people, like he is assuming the worst. I've always felt him to be authentic, and I don't know this Trip in front of me.

He mumbles some words to me that I can't make out and walks away from me. I stare at his back as he leaves. His hands rest deep in his pockets and his head hangs low. I watch him like a hawk as he stands in line at the bar. Everything he told me that night at the airport comes back to me. He uses substances as a Band-Aid to feel better. To patch the hard feelings up. I taste blood and realize that I had been biting my lip.

I must be nervous, too. I shove another cracker in my mouth. He will order his drink next. I know that if he reaches for hard alcohol, he is trying to run away from these feelings of insecurity and self-hatred. If he reaches for a beer, it means he feels equipped to handle the situation and whatever he is feeling.

The bartender nods his head at whatever Trip says. I hold a cracker mid-bite, anticipating. The bartender gets a nice glass.

Shit.

A large, solid cube of ice.

Shit.

A shot of whiskey. Two shots.

Shit.

No water.

Trip turns away from the bar. He is facing my direction and my heart drops at the smile hitching on his face.

I twist my body toward the food before he can see me stare for fear that he will see the disappointment on my face. If he knew I was disappointed, he'd be upset. He'd be upset at me.

The night passes slowly for me as I watch Trip transform in front of my eyes. Each drink sends him a little more over the edge of nervousness into a free fall. He stops caring how he presents himself or what he talks about. He walks up to random people, interrupting their conversations. I hang back, embarrassed. They stare him down with disgust. They see him as an amateur.

The defeat on Trip's face grows the more he tries and fails. He is angry, his mouth in a tight line, his eyes glassy, his whole being overrun with insecurity. I want to reach out and console him, but he has a front tonight that I can't penetrate with my words or my feelings.

By the fourth whiskey, I lean into him and say, "Maybe you've had enough?"

"Don't tell me what to do, Ruth."

His emotions are removed, leaving the air between us cold.

"I'm not telling you, I'm simply suggesting that you've had enough." I try to sound assertive, but my voice is soft—weak. I don't like it.

He chugs the drink in his hand and tosses the glass on a nearby table. "Let's go. I'm over this."

I'm all too ready to leave. I follow him out of the darkened room, down the stairs, and out in the night air. He walks ahead of me to the parking garage. I hold my dress high, trying to keep up.

I'm out of breath by the time we reach his car. "Wait," I start, breathing heavily. "Give me the keys."

He twists around to face me. "Why?"

"Because it's not safe." I have a flash to the first day we met in the treehouse. He was going to drive to deliver his flowers while high on weed. I told him the same thing I am now.

"Give me a break." He scrambles into the driver's seat. His voice is different than I have ever heard. Cold and indifferent.

I swing open the passenger side door. "No, I will not give you a break." My heart beats fast. I feel the heat rising in my face. "Get. Out. Of. This. Car."

He starts the engine. I gasp for air, but it doesn't make it down to my lungs. I think of the man who killed Riley. I think of Riley lying flat on the cement. Her life here one second and gone the next.

I slam the door and back away. Trip rolls down the window.

"Get in." His words are bitter.

"No. I'm not driving with you." I want to scream at him to get out. Not to drive. Not to be so selfish.

He rolls up the window and begins backing out. The sob that I was holding in escapes, not all at once but in spurts. I wrap my arms around myself. Trip drives past me. I watch his face in the mirror as he leaves.

He doesn't look back. Not once.

Chapter 19

Riley
Then

Medical school had been my life—eating, drinking, and the very air I breathe. I'd been consumed by it. I feared that I was consumed by medical school because I allowed myself to be. The thirst I had to learn and the drive I had to grow, to be the absolute best, was like a drug in my system. I dove into the work in order to escape the part of my reality that didn't make sense. I was clinging to the matter-of-fact piece of knowledge. It was certain. It was sure.

I wanted that in my life, that indisputable certainty. I needed it, because I didn't know where I stood anymore without Todd.

Each time I got to talk to Todd, which was not very often, we seemed to be fighting. Our phone calls were cut short, and the moments face-to-face were fleeting. The distance was changing me and forming a molten rock of resentment and fear in my heart. We fought because we missed each other, and we missed each other because we were apart. And we were apart because it was his idea. He saw our arguing as growing pains, but I saw these disputes as a black mark against us, as if we were competing against the challenge of distance itself. I never turned away from a challenge, and I feared that was the reason I was still in this relationship.

That wasn't to say I didn't miss him. I do. I missed the way he cocked his head when he looked at me, pondering every word I say. The way he searched my face, trying to catalog each detail. I tried to do the same with him, except I didn't quite focus on what he looked like. I tried to capture the feeling I got when I was with him. I needed to feel something other than resentment. What I wanted to feel was what we'd felt at eighteen.

How I wished we could go back to two young lovers rendezvousing in the driveway. He was broken. I was bold.

I was beginning to wonder if I even knew him at all. Could you truly know someone after spending one summer together? We'd planned our forever with that summer as our foundation. We hadn't known the cracks in our groundwork would eventually fissure apart, the distance splitting us into two. I was here. He was there.

What got me the most is that he didn't see it. He thought we still had a foundation, and I was too scared to point out that it had crumbled. Because if I did, that means we'd failed. Was I ready to fail after sifting through these past years together?

The question. The lack of certainty. The doubt felt eerily like a warning ricocheting off my heart. He wasn't intuitive to how this doubt was crippling me. He couldn't see how I wanted to free the feelings I had caged in my heart. He wouldn't understand how even with this desire to show him how I felt, I couldn't. No words escaped.

He'd been angry with me earlier today. We were sitting in my dorm room. I was on my bunk bed—the lower one—and Todd was across from me sitting in a chair. I wished I could say I lived in a nice apartment with a full kitchen and bedroom, but that would be a lie. I still lived in the dorms for convenience. I rarely spent time in this little square of a room. The library was my home.

I glanced behind him at my desk, which was filled with post-it notes of medical terminology and anatomy. Equations and organic chemistry hogwash were everywhere. Two photos were tucked in the corner, barely visible. One is of Todd and me, the day he graduated from all his trainings and wore the proud title of pararescueman. The other was of my family on Christmas, taken by a random cyclist I had met once upon a time as a barista.

I stared at Todd as he sat in my dorm room—all muscle and strength. He was the physical personification of bravery. His hair was cut short, now; he was practically bald. His strong and pronounced jaw was naked, not even a small five-o'clock shadow even though he'd been on leave for the past few days and he normally chose not to shave. I found myself suddenly craving the longer, golden hair he had when I first met him. Was that man still in there?

So he'd stared me down, not willing to lose this fight. "I'm worried about you, Rile," he said with sincerity, shortening my name to weaken me. He knew how I felt when he called me that. "You look too thin. Your parents say you're barely eating. You practically live in the library if you're not running for the team. Something has to give."

I didn't know what to say, mostly because I knew he was right. I was at my wit's end. I was going to deteriorate soon; it was just a matter of time.

96

I wasn't breaking yet, though.

"This is what it takes!" I bellowed. "If I want to be a doctor, then I need to put in the hard work. You know that."

"At what cost? Your health? Your life?"

I shrugged, and a wave of terror crossed his face. "You got where you are today with pure will and determination," I told him. "I supported you through that. That's the least you could do for me."

"Me?" He gestured at himself, bewildered. "That's the least I could do—support you?" His eyes widened in disbelief and he stood by the one measly window in my dorm room, facing away.

"Everything I have done is for us—for you and for me—so that we can have a future," he said. "I am the one who encouraged you to go to medical school because I believe in you. I know you can do this, but it kills me—it kills me to see you not take care of yourself."

"When I have time. I will," I responded pointedly.

"When will that be? You have to make time, Rile. That's the point. We all have twenty-four hours in a day, but we have to prioritize!" He ran his hands over his buzz cut. I wondered if he missed running those hands through his golden hair.

He sat down on my worn futon.

"Look." Todd held my gaze. "I don't want to fight tonight. All I want you to know is that I love you, and I worry about you not taking care of yourself." He extended a hand, motioning for me to sit on his lap.

I went. I didn't want to fight either. I already knew all the things he told me when we fought like this. I was not stupid. Sometimes just waiting out our fights out was all I can do, because he always said sorry first.

I let him hold me, knowing he had to leave tonight. He would be on a late flight back to New Mexico, and then the next day…who knows? I was not allowed to know. At first it was painful not knowing where he'd be; now I just accepted it.

The dusk had turned to night when he untangled himself from me and threw the words "I love you" into the dark before he closed the door behind him.

He didn't know I was awake. He didn't know I had been awake the whole time he held me in his arms. He couldn't sense the effort it took for me to smooth out the rippling doubt within me. For the first time, I did not feel like home near him. I couldn't bring myself to say "I love you back," the words shoved down by a sinking feeling of loss.

Only when he was long gone did I close my eyes and fall into a restful sleep.

Chapter 20

Ruth
Now

The buzz from my phone wakes me. At first, I am disoriented. My normally simple apartment is currently covered in a blanket of flowers: one hundred red, white, and even black roses. I genuinely forget where I am until I remembered that earlier today Trip sent one hundred roses to my front door.

I'm still upset over how Trip treated me that night in the city at the conference. The hurt and disappointment is fresh. He drove home under the influence. He could have hurt himself. He could have hurt someone else. The mere possibility of it, my past experience with it, was enough for me to call it quits between us.

But these flowers...they are the beginning of an apology I knew would come. And I hate myself for smiling when they arrived, because when I saw them, I knew I wouldn't leave him. Not over this. And that alone makes me sick. Did Riley's death mean nothing?

My phone buzzes again, and I turn it over on my nightstand to see who texted me.

Trip: I'm outside. Can we talk?

I count out full minutes before I respond, giving myself time to reconsider. It would be easy to make this argument the turning point of us. I could easily say no. We could be done...just like that.

My fingers hover over the keyboard, postponing what I know will be a betrayal of my conscience. I write:

Yes. I'll be down in minute.

Trip is sitting on the steps to my apartment complex when I open the front door. He turns to me. It's dark, but I see movement around his lips. A smile.

I plop down next to him, our knees touching. We stare at the summer sky. It's already July. I think of Riley. Four months ago she was here.

It's a full moon tonight. I stare at the glowing ball, saddened that bright moonlight meant no stars. My familiar companions were on a hiatus; my bearings, my exact points of reference, were invisible to me in this moment when I needed guidance most.

"Let's go for a ride," I suggest.

"Okay," he says timidly, eager to do whatever pleased me.

"I'm driving," I announce, trying to gain some sense of control. I also can't be so sure that Trip was sober right now. It isn't a risk I'm willing to take.

I walk to my car, an old Volvo sedan I call Greta. Greta was my first independent purchase. I bought her with the cash in I had saved from working two summer jobs in high school. I keep her spotless and fully stocked with lavender air fresheners. I crank down the window to let the humid summer night in and crawled out of the driveway.

I thank Trip for the flowers, and I mean it. I am grateful for them, for that gesture. I let my hand hang out the window, unfurling my fingers to feel the breeze. Trip is jittery, his knees and hands jumping in their own strange dance. I wait for him to cave, knowing he won't be able to handle the silence.

"Look, Ruth. I am sorry." His eyes are big, sad. He swallows slowly, his gaze downcast. "I was an ass. I drank too much. I shouldn't have, and I never should have gotten in that car. I should have let you drive."

He reaches for my hand, and I let him take it. I should say no. But I don't. I hate myself for letting him make me feel this way— like all my sensible thoughts leave me and I have no control of how my body responds to him.

I stay facing forward, focusing on the center lines of the road. "You hurt me," I begin. "It's not the fact that you drink, it's the driving under the influence that I can't tolerate…not anymore." Not since Riley.

"I know," he says, clearly ashamed.

"Alcohol affects people and sometimes not for the best. Sometimes they don't know their limits and they drink, and then they drive, and then"—I grip the stirring wheel tight with both hands—"then someone gets hurt."

"I know."

"And I don't know if you're still doing other drugs, but I'm not into that either."

He hesitates. And then, like a chant he repeats, "I know."

"This isn't an ultimatum, but if you do it again—if you're using something like you used to, or if you drive drunk, then I can't be with you."

"That sounds an awful lot like an ultimatum." He smirks.

"Fine. Consider it an ultimatum."

His face turns grave, but he eventually agrees to my terms.

I park the car below an outdated water tower that I used to climb. It was the place I came to watch the city lights change colors, but mostly to think.

The need to be higher than ground level consumes me. I want to be above and beyond this—this moment where I am like a yo-yo being tossed between two desires: give in to Trip or walk away. I know that if I can make it to the top of the tower, where the world seems open and the sky expands, the answers may be clearer.

I slam the car door and walk the dirt path to the base of the tower. I climb, carefully placing my feet on each iron step as I go, the moon's glow letting off enough light to guide me. I don't look to see if Trip is following, but I hear his shaking breath a few meters below me. I climb one hundred steps by the time I lift myself onto the landing. I walk to the spot where the wooden landing and the tower meet.

Trip makes it up a moment later and slumps down next to me. He is breathing heavily. We both look out at the sea of trees, and beyond them, the Minneapolis skyscrapers.

Trip reaches across us to brush the hair from my face, urging me to look at him. His hands rest on my cheek. "I would never do anything to hurt you. Never intentionally." His eyebrows furrow in a pained expression. He wants me to believe he was genuine. He truly feels that he's being genuine.

"I hope not. Still, I am hurt." Riley crosses my mind. "But I don't know if it's a pain unearthed or a new kind of pain."

"Maybe both," he suggests.

"Maybe both," I agree.

His voice drops low, serious. "There is a lot to my life that still bewilders me, but I do know one thing for certain. You've changed everything. All I want is to be with you and make this work. If I have to stop drinking, then that's what I will do."

He slides his hand down to my chin. I can barely make out his features, but I know he is asking me if this was okay. He is treading lightly, waiting for me to pull away. I may not fully trust him, but my body remembers his touch. It's become familiar over the past couple months. My whole body sighs in anticipation for what's about to come. Our lips touch and a spark ignites and fizzles in an instant. He kisses me like our whole fight was just a minor miscommunication and I'm not still hurting. He wraps his arm around my middle, tugging me across him so I am straddling his lap.

His hands make a pathway down my back, around my waist, toward my thighs and back again. My hair creates a curtain, shielding us from the outside world. His breathing is strong and even. His eyes are closed, but then he blinks them open and I am lost in time to when I first saw those eyes in the treehouse in my backyard. He was there for me when no one else was.

"There you are," he murmurs, as if he could tell the exact moment I left my anger behind to be in this moment with him. He tucks another loose strand of hair behind my ear.

He pulls my face back down to meet his while his hands move quickly over my body, seizing every inch of me. He kisses my collarbone first. Then he moves his mouth painfully slow up the invisible trail to my neck. My thoughts spiral. And I hate that.

I don't want to think. Not right now. But I can't help it. Thoughts swarm around me and hold my passion at bay.

Trip seizes my gaze. I bite his lower lip and feel the itch of his beard on my chin.

He groans, and I feel him harden. My doubts about us are on fire, screaming to be heard.

Do I want to do this? Sex is never just sex.

His kisses became more passionate as he fumbles with my shorts.

I work to unbutton his jeans. My need to forget what happened between us presses down on my thoughts. Because if I can forget that, then I can forget what happened to Riley.

And I want to forget. Badly.

He moves my underwear to the side. I grab his hips, positioning my body so the tip of him is so close to entering. I hold him there and make eye contact, liking this sense of control. He is confused, but willing. He will let me take the lead.

That's what I needed more than anything.

Control.

Control over my life. My grief. Over us.

Despite his flaws. I want him. I focus on that. The feeling of want. Of desire. And in the focusing of my feelings, I realize I have complete control of my heart. I may not be able to resist Trip with my body, but my heart—I still have clout over that.

Sex doesn't have to mean I give him my heart—not yet.

He breaks free of my hold, impatient, and enters me. I gasp.

Our kisses are a mess, but open and deep. Teeth are clashing. I move on top of him, contracting every muscle in my body, getting closer and closer to the edge. My nails are clawing into his shoulders.

"Are you ready?" His words are stressed and muffled against my shoulder.

I squeeze out the thoughts and the feelings. Releasing it all.

My eyes jam shut when it has ended. I rest my forehead onto his right shoulder, both of us in absolute stillness listening and feeling the rapid inhales and exhales of our breathing.

I am afraid of what will happen in the moments before I move away from him.

"I think I love you, Ruth," Trip admits.

A sinking feeling.

I keep my chin on his shoulder, afraid to see him. I focus on the skies once more, waiting, hoping for a star, a guide of comfort.

"Ruth?" he says. I can feel his breath in my ear.

He is waiting for my response. I hold my heart back, closer to me and further from him. I cradle his face and kiss him, because I don't know what else to do.

If I put the word "think" before I love you, does that minimize the severity of the statement? I could think about love. I could ponder love with Trip, but I certainly wasn't in it or even falling into it with him. At least "I think I love you" gives me more room to define my feelings that "I love you" ever could.

He looks at me expectantly, waiting for me to respond with words rather than a kiss.

"I think I love you too." The words sound hollow—rushed. I don't know why I said them.

He smiles, his eyes lighting up. But I can't smile back. He thinks it's because I am overwhelmed with emotion.

And he is right. But the emotion is emptiness.

I thought that sex was supposed to make you feel more whole—more than what you felt alone—but I feel vacant in this moment.

I move off of him before he can read my lies, both of us adjusting our clothing. He puts his long arm around me and I settle into him. He sighs deeply and juts his chin up toward the stark black sky and neon moon. I want to know if he is the kind of man who can name the constellations.

I choose to tuck the question inside me. No matter what his answer was, it wouldn't resolve the icy, oily dread pooling in my gut.

Chapter 21

Todd
Then

The flight from New Mexico to Minneapolis was short and sweet, despite the blizzard that continued to disrupt the peaceful night. It was Christmas. My favorite holiday, and one I got to spend at home instead of on a mission or in the godforsaken heat of New Mexico.

The frigid weather bit my skin as soon as I walked out of the airport and I couldn't help but smile. I invited the cold into my bones, instantly feeling more at home.

I told the Uber driver to take me straight to the Schneiders' house, where Pat and the entire Schneider family would be waiting. My heart was brimming with excitement to have all my loved ones in one room. It wasn't often that I could leave New Mexico, which meant the times I saw Riley were few and far between. I could already feel her lean body against mine when I squeezed her for that very first hug.

The snow on the road made the drive slow, but eventually the driver pulled up to the house I'd thought was a mansion so long ago. I saw Pat's car parked, and if I looked closely through the living room window, I could see Mr. Schneider in the kitchen with an apron on. I carried my suitcase up to the front door and took a big breath, grateful for this moment.

I didn't even have a chance to knock before the door flew open. I was expecting to see Riley or Pat first, but Ruth was the one standing in front of me. My mouth fell ajar at the sight of her.

It was no surprise that Ruth was pretty, because Riley was beautiful, and Ruth was her twin. Maybe it was because I hadn't seen her for two Christmases, but there was something instantly breathtaking about her. I took in her striking, hazel eyes and long, rich brown hair falling loosely down her cherry red sweater. She seemed changed, but I couldn't quite put my finger on how.

"Todd!" she squealed, which also surprised me. She wasn't one to squeal. "You made it. How was the flight?" She took my suitcase from me and escorted me into the house. The Schneiders' home was as cozy as they come: candles lit, lights dimmed, a large tree sparkling in gold ornaments, the scent of pine, the roaring fire, hints of cinnamon and pumpkin coming from the kitchen.

Home.

"It was fast. I'm glad I could make it in this storm." I looked around the foyer, hoping to see Riley run up to me.

"Riley isn't here yet." Taking in the statement felt like swallowing a shard of glass. I tried to not let the disappointment drench my face. Where could Riley be? She knew when I would be arriving.

I heard familiar footsteps approaching, light and quick. Pat rounded the corner and held her arms open wide even though she was still a few yards away. I met her halfway and held her tightly. God, I loved this woman who I'd come to call Mom. I knew she'd be here, as she was normally invited to every holiday dinner I attended with the Schneiders. They didn't like the idea of Pat spending the holidays alone, and they didn't want to have to make Riley and me split our time between the families. I couldn't have agreed more.

"Sweetheart." She cupped my face. "You made it. Thank heavens." Her hands moved down to grip my shoulders. She gave me the once over, making sure my body was in one piece. When what she saw appeased her worry, she asked, "What would you like to drink?"

Although I wished I could have a real drink, I still feared what would happen if I drank too much. If I let it control me. I was a different person than my middle school self, but still the habit haunted me and taunted me, urging me to go backwards.

"Just water," I told Pat.

I went to the kitchen where I know Mr. and Mrs. Schneider were cooking. They both were wearing festive aprons: his was an outline of a muscular man wearing a Santa hat on his private parts, while hers was laced with glitter and red flowers. It was no surprise that he'd be the humorous one and she'd remain the classy lady she had always been. The sight made me smile.

"Todd! You made it!" Mrs. Schneider cried and gave me a half-hug, her oven mitts coming around me but not touching me. Mr. Schneider took his mitt off and shook my hand, but apparently decided it wasn't enough and gave me a quick, strong hug.

I'd never forget the first time he gave me this exact type of hug. It had been after Riley had told him about us. I was fearful that he would demand us to stop seeing each other, or that he'd tell Riley about my past—all of my past. But he did neither. He'd simply listened to his daughter's wants and trusted her. When he saw me, he shook my hand, gave me this hug, and told me I'd have to find another therapist, not because he wanted to give me up as a client, but because he ethically had to. Much to my surprise, our relationship didn't dissipate, but grew. I was no longer his client, but I had become, in a way, a son-in-law these past five years that Riley and I had dated.

"Help me bring this to the table, will you?" Mr. Schneider said. I took off my coat and rolled up my sleeves, ready to jump into the action.

Ruth was setting crimson cloths on the table, Pat was pouring the ice water, and I was bringing the mashed potatoes out. Mrs. Schneider turned the Christmas music on—"Grown-Up Christmas List"—and so began our traditional Christmas night.

Except…there still was no Riley.

"Where is your sister?" Mrs. Schneider asked Ruth.

"Beats me. I hardly talk to her these days."

That made me pause. It wasn't like Riley not to talk to Ruth every day, even if it was superficial banter.

"Has anyone called her?" I asked the obvious question.

"Many times." Mr. Schneider's voice was low. Exasperated. "She will be here. She said she would be."

Ruth poured herself a glass of red wine and sat at the table. I sat across from her. She looked at me and smiled reassuringly. There you go apologizing for your sister again, I said with my eyes. She shrugged.

Don't do that, I silently conveyed to her.

Don't tell me what to do, she teased with a half-grin.

I rolled my eyes and looked to Pat, who was sitting right next to Ruth. She raised her eyebrows in question. She wanted to know about the silent conversation between Ruth and me, and I didn't have a silent response to give Pat, because I too didn't understand what was happening with Ruth. She was usually a closed book, difficult to read. And that was when I realized how she has changed. She wasn't the shy teenager I used to know.

"Let's not let her hold us up now. She told us to go ahead, so go ahead we shall. You must be starving Todd," Mrs. Schneider noted.

"You know me well," I responded.

"Tell us, how is it going being a pararescueman?" Mr. Schneider asked before grabbing the bowl of salad.

Where did I begin? They knew I'd started my training in Texas, and then moved from Washington State to Oregon and eventually to New Mexico where the small group of pararescueman resided. Being a pararescueman meant that you were in the Air Force's special forces group, and thus the details of my missions were confidential. Still, I found ways to provide information to Pat, Riley, and her parents about my daily life. Because if I didn't, their worry would be overwhelming.

"It's been taxing," I confessed. "I feel like actually being a pararescueman is easier than the training to get there though, so there is that."

Pat beamed with pride. "I still cannot believe how many men started in your program and how many they weeded out. You came far, Todd."

"And the actual training you had to do," Mr. Schneider said. "There are not many people who could get through it. Well, obviously, or anyone could be in the special forces."

"Yes, Todd," Ruth teased. "How did you ever succeed?"

"Pure luck, I tell you." Everyone laughed, and I was glad, because I didn't feel like telling them that Riley had gotten me through training.

She had been the first person on my mind during my first jump from a HH60 Pave Hawk Helicopter. As my toes hung over the ledge, inches from a free fall, I thought of her. She wouldn't even hesitate if she were in my shoes. She'd jump out without a second thought. It was easy to envision her toothy smile and brown hair sweeping recklessly across her face, and those images gave me enough courage to jump that day. I would have done anything for her. Just having her on my mind made me feel invincible.

Mrs. Schneider brought me back to the dinner table. "I still love the motto: So Others May Live. You put your life at risk jumping out of helicopters and such to save people all over the world. It's brave is what it is."

"So brave," Ruth bantered. I glared at her, but then smiled to let her know I too thought I was being praised too much.

"What will you do when your contract is up? You only have a year, is that right?" Mr. Schneider asked.

Ruth chewed, watching me. I could tell she wanted to hear this answer, but something—or someone—caught her attention. Her eyes looked past me and over my head.

"Riley, dear!" Pat said.

I turned quickly and saw Riley standing underneath the door to the dining room. The butterflies in my stomach fluttered until I saw who was standing next to her. A random man.

"Who do we have here?" Mrs. Schneider asked politely.

Riley went around the table and starts briefly hugging everyone. "This is Drew. He is traveling across the United States by bike, but as you can see, got a little caught up." She pointed to the window and the flurries falling. Drew waved awkwardly. He was wearing athletic clothes and looked freezing, and he smelled of sweat and dirt.

When Riley had hugged her parents and Pat, she ended with me. I caught her eyes, which looked preoccupied but happy to see me. She kissed me on the cheek and whispered in my ear, "Hi. Sorry I'm late." I kissed her cheek back, letting her know it was okay. How could I be mad at her? I hadn't seen her for six weeks. The last thing we needed was to be mad at each other, especially on a holiday.

Mr. Schneider pulled up a chair for Drew and ordered him to eat. Riley sat next to me and snatched the bottle of wine from the center of the table. She pointed her at her nose and then pointed to Ruth—their signal for "I love you" or "Hello" or whatever secret code they had.

"So, what did I miss?" Riley asked as she reached for my hand. I watched Ruth watching us and noticed a slight shift in her demeanor. She was retreating into her shell.

"The usual," Ruth said. "We were all giving Todd accolades for his bravery. The real question is…" She tilted her head toward Drew, who as being bombarded with Mr. Schneider's questions. "Who is he?"

"I have no idea," Riley whispered, leaning across the table. "He came into the coffee shop and looked so helpless. I couldn't leave him alone in the snow on Christmas, for Christ's sake."

"That's very thoughtful of you," I told Riley.

"Thank you." She beamed.

Across the table, Ruth rolled her eyes.

The night continued with normal family talk, jests, and questions. When I noticed Drew was on his fifth beer, I got the feeling he would either be staying the night, or we would be giving him a ride somewhere.

Every Christmas we played a game before we opened presents and every year someone different got to pick the game. Pat normally picked a card game, the Schneiders could never get past Monopoly, and Riley was a sucker for charades. This year was Ruth's year.

We all gathered around the roaring fire in the living room. Drew stood behind the couch, awkward and curious about what was happening. He had just come from the bathroom, and his hair was curiously wet. My guess was he'd tried to shower in the sink. Mrs. Schneider couldn't keep her eyes off him. Mr. Schneider pretended not to notice anything peculiar about this stranger in his home.

Riley and I fit into the loveseat. Ruth sat directly in front of the roaring fire, the Schneiders on the couch, and Pat on the floor near Ruth, leaning against the ottoman.

"What will the game be this year?" Mr. Schneider asked Ruth, rubbing his hands in anticipation.

Ruth walked over to the couch and pulled out Scrabble from behind the pillow. There was a single groan, I think from Drew, but one squeal of joy from Pat.

Pat looked at Riley. "Be easy on us, won't you Riley?"

At first I was confused, until I saw Ruth's eyes widen in front of me.

Pat was referring to the night she'd thought she met Riley and we had played Scrabble, when in fact, it was Ruth who had stepped in for Riley.

"I can't make any promises." Riley played along. I glanced at Ruth, who was looking at me, biting her lip. She started to laugh but covered it up with a cough.

"What's going on?" Riley asked softly, so only I could hear.

"Nothing," I whispered.

Ruth handed out the wooden pieces and we started to play.

~

110

It was late by the time we had all cleaned the dishes, opened presents, and said goodnight. Drew, the cycling stranger, fell asleep on the couch just as I thought he would. Mr. and Mrs. Schneider retired up to their bedroom, and shortly after Ruth followed suit.

I drove with Pat to her house, even though I wanted nothing more than to sleep next to Riley. Not feeling her touch for six weeks had been torture. Still, I couldn't let Pat leave alone, not in this weather. So I kissed Riley goodbye, promising to come over in the morning for coffee.

It was only when I'd collapsed in my small bed in my old room that I took my phone out.

Me: You lost on purpose.
Ruth: Pat is too smart. She would have guessed.
Me: Maybe so. Still, never hide how smart you are.
Ruth: Even if that meant we were found out?
Me: ...even so. Thanks for my present.

I looked at the book she'd given me this year: Where Men Win Glory by John Krakauer. It had been our running joke ever since that night she pretended to be Riley. I had asked her how she knew so many words, and she told me she read. Every Christmas and birthday she gave me a new book and each book I found myself thoroughly enjoying. I'd really started to look forward to her gifts.

Ruth: You're welcome.
Me: Night Ruth.

I fell asleep with the image of Ruth's last text: the word "goodnight" in Scrabble emoji letters.

Chapter 22

Riley
Then

I was leaving for Guatemala today with Doctors Without Borders. I wasn't a doctor yet, but that hadn't stopped me from pestering one of my professors who was going on this month-long trip. He had no choice but to let me tag along, even if I was only a pre-med student. I'd learned that if you were persistent enough, you would eventually get your way.

This trip was unique because doctors were traveling with engineers. The engineers would rebuild decaying infrastructures and the doctors would care for the people living within those decaying infrastructures. I wanted nothing to do with the engineers. I didn't even want anything to do with the doctors. I was going to serve the people of Guatemala, and if I was honest, for the adventure.

But plans didn't always work out.

"Excuse me," were his first words to me as we were waiting in line to check our bags. He practically purred them in my direction. "I noticed your attire. Are you on the trip with Doctors Without Borders?"

At first, I was pleased he would even assume such a thing. Maybe I did look like a doctor after all. But then he pointed to the name tag the group leader made us pin to our shirt. It screamed organized group.

I swore and glanced at the ceiling, if only to do something rather than melt in this guy's presence.

"I know you're going on the trip. I just wanted to meet you."

I could feel my cheeks flush in response to his lazy smile. He was dressed in casual attire, and stood around my height, which wasn't saying much considering I was taller for a girl. He had jet black hair that was well groomed and made his baby blue eyes stand out in contrast. His jaw was strong and wide. His skin was an olive tone, as if he might be Eastern European, and I wondered if he'd grown up here or abroad. He held his easy smile and I felt my body leaning closer to him like it wanted to soak in this small amount of affection. It had been a long time since someone—a man, at that— had wanted to meet me.

"Are you going on the trip too?" I asked him.

His head tilted as if he was waiting for me to say more, and he looked...surprised, as if I should know him.

When he realized I didn't recognize him, he chuckled and said, "I am Zeph, but everyone calls me Z."

"Oh?" I asked, peering at his shirt, "And aren't you a little rebel." Now he was the one to look confused. "Where's your name tag?" I finally said. He angled his head a second time, as if he was pleasantly surprised by this question.

"I am with Engineers Without Borders," he said, a note of pride in his voice.

Arrogant indeed.

He shrugged nonchalantly. "I guess we are organized and structured enough. We don't need the name tags."

I smiled at the joke in spite of myself.

"Doctors need a little more help in that arena. We are more into the blood and guts," I joked back, surprising myself. Did I joke? When was the last time I joked around with someone?

He made a face like he was visualizing a horrendous scene and couldn't get it out of his head.

"You're a doctor, then?" he asked.

"Pre-med student. I have a long way to go."

"I'm surprised they let you on this trip."

"Why is that?"

"They don't let many students accompany doctors on these sorts of things. It can get...messy."

The truth was that there was one other pre-med student on the trip, but I bit my tongue. I didn't want to share his attention—not yet, anyway.

"I like messy."

He raised an inquisitive eyebrow. I kept silent.

We stuck together through security and during the walk to the gate. We didn't have far to go, since our first flight was domestic. We'd fly to Atlanta first, then Guatemala City.

Once we arrived at our gate, everyone in the group came to shake Z's hand; they all seemed to know him. I assumed it was because he traveled a lot with these people, but when one nerdy engineer asked Z for an autograph, I got suspicious.

"What's his deal?" I asked the other pre-med student. She was a mousy girl named Jamie who had exceptional book smarts and zero common sense. I normally kept my distance from her, as her passiveness made my blood boil, but I couldn't do that this trip. We'd be rooming together and working side by side. I had to find it within me to be civil to her.

"Jesus. Do you not keep up with anything?" Jamie replied, aghast at my ignorance.

"I'm sorry," I hiss. "I guess between the eighty hours of schoolwork each week I don't have time to scroll through Instagram and stalk people."

Jamie rolled her eyes. "Z is the Lead Engineer who was one of the masterminds behind rebuilding New Orleans after the destruction of Katrina. He was the youngest engineer to help in the reconstruction of the levees that would better protect New Orleans in the case another hurricane struck. His ideas have revolutionized rebuilding strategies for aging infrastructure after natural disasters."

Oh. Oh. So, it turned out that arrogant Z was justified in his arrogance. Damn. No wonder he was surprised by my question earlier. He'd assumed I would know him.

I glanced at Z at the same time his light eyes slid to me. I turned back to Jamie, but not before that damn smile showed on his face.

Jamie sighed. "You are right, though. He is sexy for being an older guy."

"How old is he?"

"In his early forties, I think," Jamie guessed. "According to Instagram."

"Oh, brother. I didn't say he was sexy, by the way."

"Uh huh." She nudged my shoulder. She didn't know me well, but it wouldn't take a neuroscientist to see that Z rattled me…and everyone else around him. Jamie and I watched the flock of people gathering around him.

I tried my best to ignore him, and was able to the entire time the group waited for our plane to board. And I still didn't bat an eye when he stood up after they announced that first class could enter the plane. I didn't look at him until I entered the plane and looked down the long row in front of me.

Still, I felt him staring at me.

Right before I was about to walk past him, he pinched the sleeve of my coat.

"Excuse me, miss," he said, his tone playful. "I think you passed your seat." He glanced at the ticket in my hand. I looked down.

"I think you are mistaken. I'm 33C." I matched his playful tone.

He lips formed a tight line. "Yikes. That's really far back."

"Thanks for the reminder."

"Let's hope you're not in the middle seat. That can be a real doozy." He bit into a biscotti cookie and smiled. He was infuriating and bewitching all in one. He leaned toward the aisle and motions for me to come closer. "Listen. I already asked the flight attendant if anyone was sitting next to me. She said no. You can sit in 33C if you want, but I'd rather you didn't."

I pulled back, considering what I thought he was offering. Still, I asked: "What are you suggesting?"

"I would sit down if I were you," Z said out of the side of his mouth, "The guy behind you looks pissed." I peered over my shoulder. A sweaty, bald man was glaring at me. Behind him, a short line of grumpy passengers were demanding to know what the hold-up was. The first-class flight attendant noticed the line going stagnant and looked for the culprit. She made eye contact with me and firmly told me to take my seat. I looked at her, then at the bald man breathing down my neck, toward the direction of 33C and finally at Z. He patted the seat next to him and took another bite of biscotti.

I sat down.

I'd never flown in first class before. The territory was foreign—hoity toity. As much as I was appalled by the extravagant gesture, the seats did look comfortable.

"I don't need your handouts," I scolded him. It was an admittedly risky comment. I didn't want to offend him, but there was something about his nature that made me think he enjoyed jabs.

"Is that why you're making yourself at home?" He teased me as I plucked a champagne glass from the flight attendant's tray.

"Couldn't get enough of me then?" I asked, averting his accusation. Was I flirting?"Something like that." His charm unfaltering. He took his own drink from the flight attendant—a gin and tonic from the scent of it.

People were still piling onto the plane. A passenger's bag hit my shoulder with surprising force, and I reflexively moved closer to Z. He must have thought I was leaning into him on purpose, because he also leaned in and whispered in my ear. "Wanna watch a movie with me?"

I snapped my head towards him, acutely aware of how close our faces were. He was grinning like a little boy, awaiting my response. Did he ever stop smiling?

"Only if I get to choose," I countered.

"Okay, but if you choose the movie then you have to promise to hold my hand during takeoff."

"What?" I said, incredulous.

"I'm serious." His features softened—a sense of vulnerability shining past his armored of hubris.

"You want me to hold your hand? During takeoff?"

"Takeoff scares me." He said it so matter-of-factly. He was someone people looked up to, and obviously thought highly of himself, yet he had his fears too.

"It's a deal." He set to searching through the movies and making "our" area comfortable while I pretended to be fascinated with the champagne in my hands. I thought briefly of Todd and sent some words, a form of prayer, out into the universe...wherever he might be.

I didn't know why, but the quasi-prayer ended in "I'm sorry."

~

Being in Guatemala, serving these people who live with a dearth of resources, was hard work, and I loved it. I was learning more there than I ever could have in a classroom. I was a sponge, soaking in knowledge. I'd overheard the other doctors speaking admiringly about me more than once, which pleased me immensely. Hard work paid off.

Our camp was small, but sufficient. There were two bunk houses: the engineers were residing in one and the doctors in the other. The bunk houses consisted of multiple bunk beds and no bathroom. There were community bathrooms and showers located in-between the two bunk houses. The kitchen and rec center were opposite the bunkhouses. And just beyond the kitchen were two small, private cabin-like rooms where the lead of engineers and the lead of doctors resided.

It had taken a while to get used to the simplicity of life here. Our clothes were simple. The bunkbeds we sleep on were simple. We had no private spaces. There were no mirrors. I didn't want to know what I looked like, anyway. Half our days were spent traveling windy roads to different villages, and by the time we'd loaded up the truck to head back to camp, we were too spent to take a shower. I knew I smelled rancid.

Even with the primitive living quarters and horrendous medical conditions, I found myself smiling more often than not. Whether I was holding tight to the side of a truck driving through the jungle or waking up with the roosters, I was still smiling.

I'd only ever felt this feeling one time before—when I first met Todd. My mind—and my life—had slowed down. I was living in the present moment. Except this time, the freedom I was feeling had nothing to do with Todd.

In fact, I'd barely thought about him outside of the one email I'd sent him when I first arrived. I knew he was waiting anxiously to hear more, but how could I begin recounting all I had seen? He wasn't here to experience each moment with me, and describing them felt futile. He wouldn't understand. Sharing this experience in words wouldn't do it justice, because he wouldn't be able to feel or see how it had changed me.

I was changed.

I could feel it in my bones.

And I didn't know how to go back to the old me and everything else in my old life.

I had started to not miss Todd, and I knew that meant something. I could see my future without him, and I certainly knew that meant something.

Z didn't help. I'd only seen him a handful of times since we landed in Guatemala City, and each time sent a jolt of energy through me. I wanted more of that liveliness. I wanted more of him.

One early morning, I couldn't sleep. I quietly left the bunk house were all the doctors were still sleeping in order to start a pot of coffee, only to discover that someone else had beat me to it. I found Z drinking coffee and leaning over a dinky plastic kitchen table to get a closer look at a pile of blueprints. I was sure I looked like a disaster, but I didn't mind. Neither did he. He seemed surprised to have been caught so early.

From that morning on, I continued to wake early in hopes of meeting him in the kitchen. He was usually there with that same winning smile. And so began our talks. We talked through the morning until we had to separate and attend to our individual duties and we talked through the night after dinner. Eventually, we found ways to be on each other's teams when we visited various sites away from Guatemala City, some hours from our base. There were rumors about us, but we didn't care.

He was arrogant—there was no doubt about that—but it only came out in short spurts here compared to the full force of it back in America. His entire appearance had transformed when he was working with the Guatemalan people. He listened attentively, rallied them into his plans, taught them new skills, and led them through the beginning stages of building exceptional foundations. I admired him. His knowledge. His experience. Everything about him screamed success. He was mesmerizing to watch and as much as I tried to hold his arrogance against him as a way to protect my heart, I just couldn't.

We would be leaving, all engineers and doctors, in two weeks' time. I was dreading saying goodbye to Z, and I wondered...a small part of me was curious if I would miss him.

Chapter 23

Riley
Then

After one particularly long day in Guatemala City, Z asked if I wanted to go for a walk after we returned to the camp. I knew I'd say yes before the word even escaped my mouth.

When we landed in Minneapolis, I would say goodbye. But until then...I would tell him yes.

Z had his hands in his cargo pant pockets when he stopped by the bunk house where the doctors were housed. His black-gray hair was a bit disheveled and what was once stubble on his face was now a short beard. I exited the room discreetly, hoping to bypass any of Jamie's passive aggressive glares or verbal warnings.

Fireflies were swarming around us as we walked the trail through the jungle from our camp to the little village a mile or so away called Santo Tomás La Unión We deliberately walked slowly in order to not trip over any tree roots that were scattered in the path. I held my breath when I heard a hissing sound, but realized it was not a snake, but a breeze curling through the mahogany tree leaves. I could hear birds chirping near and far, creating a soothing symphony of music in the night.

"I like how you see this..." Z started. "This world. You come alive here, you know. I can see it on your face and in the way you work with these people...not everyone is cut out for this. I would know, too; I have done a lot of these trips."

"And here I was thinking you could say one sentence without puffing your chest."

He laughed, a deep loud sound that resonated through the darkness.

"I didn't want to disappoint," he teased, but out of the corner of my eye I could see his face drop. "Is that all you think of me?" He looked genuinely hurt.

I released the breath I had been holding and looked straight ahead at the winding dirt trail. Darkness was slowly wrapping around us like a tight, secure blanket. No. That was definitely not all I thought of him. Instead of answering that question, I said, "I don't want this to end." Again, I looked out the corner of my eye, awaiting his reaction. A small grin crept onto his face. That made me smile, too, because that meant he didn't want this to end either. Whatever this was.

The mile-long trail ended abruptly. One minute you were in the throngs of the jungle and the next you were on the main road of the small village of Santo Tomás La Unión Both engineers and doctors had packed scheduled that didn't allow for leisurely outings, which meant that I had not had the opportunity to explore what looked to be a quaint little village. I followed Z out onto the street. He waited for me to fall in step with him until we were walking side by side. The village was small, but still there was enough light coming from the tiny convenience stores or tourist stands to light the way.

We took our time looking at the trinkets that the Guatemalan natives had for sale. We watched children kicking a soccer ball against a concrete wall and we stopped more than once to listen to the sounds of the night. Laughter came from dilapidated huts and chants echoed onto the street from a nearby church.

A group of five men wearing dark clothing came out of a dingy building with a neon sign of a beer bottle above the door. They looked more like a gang than a group of men on a cheery night out. I could feel their eyes devouring me. I had yet to feel unsafe in this country, especially working with such a prestigious agency, but seeing these men sizing me up made me stand a little straighter.

Z grabbed my hand. My eyes darted to his face, questioning, but he didn't say a word. I didn't let him go, even when we were long past the hungry eyes of the group of men. Z brushed his thumb back and forth across my hand. An electric shock tremored through me. Up until that point we had been playful. But that…that felt the opposite of playful.

"I thought you'd be protesting right about now." His whisper broke the thick silence around us.

120

"I didn't want you to get scared back there," I told him. "I know this helps." Z looked at me sidelong and a flash of pain crossed his face. I was worried I'd upset him, but he recovered quickly. He stopped suddenly and swung me around so that I faced him. He let go of my hand and moved both his hands on either side of my face. I froze.

"Remember on the plane when we were talking all night? And I told you how I became an engineer? I told you how many kids I wanted someday...and the five most important qualities that I look for in someone?"

"Yes, I remember."

"What did I say?" His thumbs traced small circles on my cheeks. I felt dizzy. "What were my five?"

I muttered the adjectives, trying not to faint. My body was burning, and as if it had a will of its own, slowly leaned into him. I didn't know what was going to happen, but I wanted to know what it felt like to be buried in this chest.

I felt like we were standing in the dark matter between the stars, even if the stars were actually fireflies flashing by. The closer his face came to mine, the more it felt like I was being pulled into the dark matter, far away from this Earth.

"You are honest," Z said before he placed a gentle kiss on my forehead. "Intelligent." His lips brushed my right cheek. "You are so unbelievably funny." He chuckled and kissed my left cheek.

His kisses feathered against my face as he continued, making the floor a little uneven beneath me. I wanted him to kiss me on my lips. I wanted more.

Could he feel my heartbeat pounding through my eardrums? I closed my eyes and leaned into his touch.

"I want to add one, though. It's not a part of my list, but I need you to know it." I opened my eyes and saw him staring deeply, intently into my face. I swallowed and brought my hands to his forearms. For a second, Z stopped, likely because he thought I was rejecting his touch and pushing him away. I held on tight, letting him know this was okay.

121

"You are beautiful." Now I thought my knees really were going to give out. "I thought that as soon as I saw you checking your bag in, but I knew for sure that you were when I saw you working with those kids in our first camp. You had dirt all over your face and in your nails. God, you were a wreck." He laughed and dropped his head back to look up to the sky. "But you were so happy. So happy. That was beautiful."

He could have said this to any girl, and likely he already had to many girls. As bad as I wanted to give him a sarcastic rejoinder, I didn't want to ruin this moment. I didn't want to be just any girl to him. When I searched his face for lies, or inauthenticity, I couldn't find any.

I didn't have time to contemplate my next choice. I didn't have self-control. I didn't even think of Todd when I let Z close the last, short gap between us. His lips covered my own.

We laughed through the kisses, as if we both couldn't believe this was really happening.

He pulled back, still cradling my head, and turned serious: "Who are you and where did you come from?"

I don't know why this pleased me so much, but it did. I answered him with a kiss, because I didn't have another answer. I didn't know who I was.

We snuck kisses with each other all the way back to camp, and when he pulled me towards his private cabin, I let him.

When we get to the door, he informed me that he'd wanted a private room because he knew I'd be in here eventually. I dropped his hand and gave him vulgar gesture. He laughed and added in a serious tone, "No. I am kidding. It's just because I am extremely smart, and they wanted me to have enough space to explore my visions."

He was insufferable. And in that moment, I loved that about him. His confidence took up the whole room so that there was no space left for doubt.

I hated doubt. I hated that that's all that was left of Todd and me. I was sick of being doubtful. Just once—just tonight—I wanted to bask in confidence.

Z laid me down on the bed and took off his shirt. I admired his toned arms and solid chest. He slowly lowered onto the bed until he was on top of me. He kissed me again and I felt a sudden urge to be skin to skin.

122

"Is this okay?" he asked gruffly between kisses.

That question was tantamount to the other question circling my mind. What am I doing?

Yes, I should have stopped. I should have communicated with Todd more. I should have been with Todd...he was my safety, my home, my normal. I should have said no to going on a walk with Z. I should tell Z that yes, we needed to stop. I should have broken it off with Todd if I was even considering doing that with another guy.

Z stared down at me, waiting. He searched my eyes.

I closed my own and sent a prayer to Todd, even though I knew it was more of an atonement. It was an apology for what was to come when I got home, and for all the pain I would cause him one day.

I was not his.

I was nobody's.

I thought of the pain on the faces of people I'd served this trip. I thought of their regrets and love lost. I thought of all the moments and opportunities that passed us by because we were afraid to leave what was safe and what was comfortable. I thought of those who lived with regret for the chances not taken. Those who missed out on the world when they didn't live in the present moment. I thought of how short life was...and how we had to do what we felt was right in the moment, because this moment was all we had.

So I opened my eyes one moment and stared straight at Z the next. I told him "yes" in all the moments after that. I never knew one simple word could change the trajectory of my life forever.

Chapter 24

Ruth
Now

I am just getting back to my apartment after giving five massages. My hands are aching and my back sore. I make it halfway up the stairs to my apartment before I remember the mail. I haven't gotten it for weeks.

I turn around slowly, holding onto the railing as I step down the flight of stairs. I search for box 24, my apartment number, and sigh when I see the stack of mail. I sift through it right then and there, throwing away the ads and coupons I'll never use.

The last piece is a thick, medium-sized manila envelope from my parents. Why didn't they give me this last week when I was there?

I wait to open it until I am in my apartment and in my pajamas. Once I am sitting on the couch, I tear into it.

The contents rest in my hand. A note and a journal. I recognize the journal instantly. It's a genuine treasure in this moment. The note is from my mother.

One of Riley's friends from her trip to Guatemala sent me this. I couldn't bear to read it but though it belonged to you more than anyone.

I love you, sweetheart.

My trembling hands open my twin sister's journal. She's had this since she was a teenager. I know because I used to catch her sneaking out of her bedroom window in order to write.

Her words are in block letters. Precise. Organized. Exactly how she was.

My fingers trace the sentences and don't stop until the last passage. My fingers begin to tremble like china shaking on a shelf...

Chapter 25

Riley
Then

Tomorrow all doctors and engineers will leave for the States. I dread leaving the sanctuary and peace of this land. I already miss the work I am doing. I try not to think about the mirrors I will face myself in again, society's pressure to be a certain way, or the worrisome emails from Todd that are steadily piling up in my inbox.

I haven't had the courage to look at them, let alone respond to them.

Z doesn't know. I don't even know if it's worth telling him and risk ruining our last days together. I've already decided that when I return to the States, I will talk to Todd. I'll have to work to cultivate the courage to speak to him, and I promise myself I will work on that when I land.

I will be brave enough to tell him everything. My heart hurts thinking about all we have been through, all we promised, all we thought was going to be in our future. I cringe thinking of him hearing the news while he is away on a mission. What if he doesn't take it well? What if this piece of news distracts him and he makes a fatal mistake on a mission? I can't be the reason he screws up.

So I will wait. I will wait until the perfect time. Even though everything in my body and bones is telling me I have to end this childhood love.

Todd was there in the beginning of me discovering who I was. He was and will forever be my first love. And yet—I cannot marry a man where all we have is love.

I need someone that revels in my strength but does not depend on it.

Z and I may go separate ways when we return home, but at least I'll have my brief memory of him—the man who showed me what could be.

At least I can say I lived.

~

"Look Riley, I'm not ready to let you go, whether you like it or not," Z had said on the flight from Atlanta to Minneapolis. He had managed to get us first class again. I tried to ignore the look of envy from the poor bastards in economy eating peanuts and lukewarm meals.

"It must be so boring for you, getting everything you want. Where's the challenge in that?" I posed.

"I don't play games when it comes to love."

I halted mid-bite at the word love, but brushed the feeling off.

"Is that why you tried to win me over by buying me a first-class ticket? Manipulated me to hold your hand during takeoff and landing? Flirted endlessly with the other intern before taking me to bed?"

"I knew that bothered you," he said with a shit-eating grin on his face. "It worked, obviously. You practically came crawling to me after that darling." I punched his arm and laughed.

"I don't crawl to anyone."

His face turned serious before he kissed me on the cheek. "I know. You're independent. One of the five things I adore about you."

Todd had never spoken to me like this. A hint of pain burst in my heart, and I tried to push it aside.

"Just five?"

"For now." He pinched my knee. "There is still so much to know, Riley…so much." He settled into his seat, and I fought the urge to spill my guts right then and there.

I didn't know whether or not to tell him about Todd. They both deserved an explanation. But Todd deserved an explanation more. I'd finally read his emails, and each one got progressively more emotional. There were hints of anger in them, but mostly concern for me. In my one response, I had reassured him I was well… maintaining my position of steadiness. I didn't need Todd worrying, especially when I learned he was about to deploy on a rescue mission abroad.

I wouldn't tell Z anything. Not until I had talked to Todd.

"I don't know what is going to happen when we land, but I am glad I met you." I glanced at Z's profile.

He looked straight ahead. "How about breakfast?"

I sheepishly turned my face away to hide my smile.

During takeoff, I looked out the window and chanted my prayer to Todd.

I'm sorry…

I'm sorry…

Chapter 26

Todd
Then

Today was the last day of my contract. I'd been in the military for six years and today—today I would be done.

I'd gotten back from Kuwait last week. It had been my last mission. The last time I would jump out of a plane and rescue a wounded solider. The last time I would live the mission statement: So Others May Live.

That free fall out of the helicopter had been my favorite fall of all, because it marked my last jump and the first day I'd seen the end in sight, the end where Riley would be waiting for me.

This was the completion of our dream. Today.

I packed up my belongings, although there wasn't much I'd acquired over the six years. All my stuff fit into three large duffle bags: two to check on the plane home to Minneapolis and one to carry on. I wore my uniform out of respect. I would leave this base as a solider.

"Whatcha got there?" Sean, my closest friend and a fellow pararescueman, came into my apartment without knocking.

I stared at the diamond ring in my hand.

"I am going to ask Riley to marry me," I said, not quite believing the words coming out of my mouth.

"It's about time," he says dryly.

"Well… it had to be the right time. I wasn't going to be engaged doing distance."

"You do know that she could have moved here and lived with you if you were married though, right?"

"Obviously. She isn't done with med school, though. I'd never ask her to give that up."

"Right. Med school. I forgot your hot girlfriend was also smart," Sean joked.

"Watch it," I warned.

"Lighten up, man." Sean waved a dismissive hand in the air.

I put the ring back in the navy blue velvet box and tucked it deep into my duffle bag. I checked the time. I was going to be late for my plane.

I threw my duffle bag over my shoulder and stood. Sean looked almost sad, and the sight of him that way made me sad too. When would I see him again? We hugged—something we had never done before.

"Two more years for you, eh?" I asked Sean.

"Who knows? I may be a lifer." He shrugged.

"You'd be a great lifer. I'll be in touch." I clapped him on the shoulder and walked out the door to my truck. I heard him follow and shut the door behind him. He walked next door to his own apartment, waving one last time.

I was going to miss these men. My brothers. We'd trained together and we fell together, many times so others may live. They'd been a major part of this chapter in my life, but now…now I was on to the next chapter. To Riley. To our future.

~

On the drive from New Mexico to Minnesota, I thought of my plans for the future. I didn't want to lose my training and didn't want to stop helping others. I had explored many different career options, but the only profession that appealed to me was being a paramedic. I would start there, at least. It was an easy transition from what I had been doing. The adrenaline, pressure, and mission behind the job would be familiar and come easily to me.

The closer I got to Pat's house, the easier it was to let go of the intensity that the military created in me. I felt my heart soften. My lungs open. And the constant strain in my head release. I didn't have to display bravado or be a man's man. I could be me—just me—the me that was lurking underneath the service all those six years. I hadn't lost him. No one realized that was the hardest obstacle I'd faced. Not the grueling training that pushed me to the end of my physical strength, but the mental training to retain what made me human: vulnerability and love, which only made me closer to Riley. It was, perhaps, what had kept us alive, together, as one. That was my greatest achievement.

I thought of living in the same town as Riley and Pat, the two most important women in my life. I could see them on a regular basis. Whenever I wanted. I would have to get my own apartment, preferably in the city, so Riley could live there. The image of her packing up her dorm room and walking into our apartment sent shivers down my spine. This had been a long time coming. Too long.

The states flew by hour after hour, one vast stretch of land after another, until I reached the first lake outside of Minnesota. I drove the familiar highway around the Minneapolis skyscrapers until the highway turned into a quiet road. It was nearing sundown.

Snow covered the ground even though it was March. It was cold. I was surprised to see Pat on the front porch of the house, swaying slowly on the swing. She was wrapped in a wool blanket and wearing slippers, gently pushing off the porch to keep her in motion.

I didn't even grab my bag from the truck, but walked up to her quickly, instantly concerned. She had been crying and her lips were quivering, almost blue.

"Pat! What happened?"

It was then that she broke. I had never seen her cry this way. I sat beside her and drew her close to me, rubbing the shivers away. I let her cry.

"What happened?" I asked again, my concern growing into something terrible. Something had happened. The darkness was loud and clear.

Pat sat up straight and composed herself to the best of her ability. I could tell she was trying to be strong, to say the right words. Her eyes found mine and she began to tear up again.

"What is it?" I asked, impatient.

"It's Riley."

"What about her? I just talked to her not five hours ago. What happened?"

Pat stared at me. My skin went tight, practically suffocating me. "No," I breathed.

Pat let out another sob and looked away from me. "Todd, she was in a terrible accident."

My instinct was to leave, to run, to rescue. The urge to save her was all-consuming. I quickly stood.

"Where? Where was the accident? What happened, Pat?" My voice was rising.

She stood as well, face to face with me. She took ahold of my arms. "She was running. There was a driver. He hit her. He may have been drunk; we aren't sure yet. She was declared dead on the scene. The man has been arrested."

Each word came to me in slow motion like I was in a tunnel, being pulled further and further away from the brutal truth. I could hear Pat, but I couldn't believe it. I heard an echo say, "No. No. No." I thought it was me, but I didn't feel here in this moment.

I was fading fast. Far from reality.

"When did this happen?" I managed to ask, pushing through the static. The white noise. It was so loud in my head. Screaming at me.

Pat shook her head. Her lips didn't move. I needed an answer.

I was fading. The static was closing in, like the fading image on an old TV set, a black line splitting me in two. Soon, it would all be black.

I waited for it to come. Almost ready, welcoming it, because then I wouldn't have to feel anything at all.

But then the rage came.

It forced the static back out of me. I could hear. I could see. I inhaled sharply, gasping for air.

Pat was reaching for me, her fingers wet from wiping her tears. I shrugged her off and ran down the steps. I didn't know where Riley had been hurt, but I was going to find the spot and I was going to see if she needed me.

"Todd! Where are you going?" I heard Pat behind me yell through her terror.

I was drifting, losing my mind, but I couldn't stop. I put the truck in drive and pulled forward.

□

PART II
One Year Later

Chapter 27

Ruth

"Can you promise me you won't be weird?" Trip grabs both of my shoulders and stares at me straight on.

"What do you mean weird?"

"You know...you get a certain way when we go out with my friends. Moody. Distant."

He is right. I do. I do because I can't stand them and the way they yell over each other. Their humor is layered with inside jokes from times way before me. They are eccentric in an I-need-attention kind of way.

I sigh, exasperated. "I will try not to be weird."

"Good. Thank you. It wouldn't hurt to smile every once in a while."

I give him my cheesiest grin.

He smiles back, genuine. "Just like that. Beautiful."

"What?" I ask, curious, unnaturally defensive.

"Look. Don't get mad," he starts. Already I feel guarded. "Could you maybe put on a little makeup? Nothing much," he quickly adds, "but maybe...that eye stuff and whatever makes you have color?"

"Mascara and blush," I say coolly.

"Sure." He shrugs and gives me that smile, that one smile he gives all the older women in his potpourri classes. I rarely get his real smiles anymore.

I hate myself as I walk away from him and sit at my vanity in my closest. My heart burns as I lift the brush to my eyelashes and then glide pink pigment across my cheeks.

I walk back to the front door where Trip waits on his phone. He looks up. "There! Beautiful."

Only when he turns to open the door do I clench my fists in irritation. I look back at my apartment.

My apartment. Still a point of contention between us, as he has dropped numerous hints about him moving in. I laugh the prospect off every time. Not yet. I'm not at the point where I want him in my sanctuary. I gave him a key a month ago, figuring that would silence his requests. It did—for two weeks.

I lock the door behind me and follow Trip down the stairs to the parking garage.

"Oh, and another thing." He turns to me when be both get into the car. "Can you not…be mad if I drink tonight?"

And there it is. The elephant in the room. The big, fat, elephant that never goes away. No matter how many times I tell him it's not the drinking that bothers me, he still doesn't get it. I don't care about him drinking. I care about the way he acts when he drinks, like he can't stop and won't. Not even for me.

"Any other demands?"

"Jesus, Ruth. I can't win with you."

He pulls out of the garage.

"Where are we going?" I ask, changing the subject into safer territory.

"O'Reilly's." His voice is clipped now that I upset him.

"The whole gang will be there?" I ask, referring to Vince, Terrance, Savannah and Ali.

"Yep," he says.

Oh, good. It's going to be another one of these nights, I think. A night of you drinking and me waiting around to drive you home because I'm too worried you'll make a stupid mistake and drive yourself and hit someone.

None of my thoughts leave my mouth, and my feelings stay deep in a place that feels safer than in the air between us. My mind shifts to Riley as naturally and instinctively as a river finds the sea. The words in her journal at the forefront of my mind, all day, every day. I am the brain, and she is the heart.

It's been over a year, and still I cannot get over losing her. How could I? What good is a heart that has no heartbeat, after all?

I lean to the right so my forehead presses into the window.

Oh Riley, what do I do?

134

Chapter 28

Todd

I spray some cologne on myself out of habit, and then the obnoxious honking begins.

Xavier.

By the tenth honk, I'm down the stairs and out the front door of my apartment building. Xavier's parked in a shiny red jeep across the street.

"Look at you!" he booms.

I inspect my red shorts and black V-neck shirt, confused by his statement. My outfit seems appropriate for June.

"Look at me!" I repeat half-jokingly. "What's with the honking? You said you'd be here at eight, and so I would have come down at eight." Time was valuable. I wouldn't waste it being late.

"You look good man. It's been a while." Xavier ignores my chiding.

It has been a few weeks since I reached out to Xavier. Against my better judgement, and despite feeling doused in guilt, I agreed to go to dinner with Xavier, his wife, and whatever friend she brought. Just for tonight. It is not a date. It's four people having dinner together. That's it—that's all.

When we walk into O'Reilly's Bar, it takes a moment for my ears to adjust to the noise. The music is loud, and the lights are dim. I have to squint to see across the room. My senses are heightened by the lack of sight. I don't like not being able to see, an insecurity that didn't bode well a year ago when I was leaping out of planes into utter darkness.

Xavier leads the way back to a corner booth where his wife, Clara, and her friend are sitting. They are engrossed in conversation, leaning forward, faces close and two empty martini glasses in front of them.

"Todd! Welcome!" Clara throws her hands up in excitement when she spots me. "This is Tiffany. Tiffany, this is Todd," she says, introducing me to the blonde sitting next to her before I even had the chance to sit down myself.

Tiffany appears pleased to meet me and gives me an alluring smile. I noticed a small dot of red lipstick on her front teeth. Her perfume—a bit grandma-y and floral—hits me with alarming intensity. Her blonde hair drapes to her waist and her makeup—besides the lipstick—is matted perfectly to her face. Her cleavage also seems perfectly placed, as her boobs are practically falling out of her shirt. I do my best to keep my eyes on hers, which were, not surprisingly, bright blue. Everything about her screamed typical Minnesotan Viking genes.

"What can I get you?" Xavier motions to the bar.

"Lime soda is good. Thanks man," I respond, acutely aware that he is leaving me alone with Tiffany and his wife, who are both one martini deep already. Tipsy women are almost always more brazen, and that makes me want to retreat back to the solitude of my apartment.

"So, Todd. Tell me. How has it been being back?" Clara asks. Her eyes shoot daggers into me. I see the intention behind this question. She wants to know how I am doing since Riley died.

"It's…uneventful." I manage a smile. "Sometimes that is good, though. It's been a nice recovery time."

"Xavier tells me you're working as a paramedic right now. Couldn't get away from the work of saving people, could you?" Clara sounds equal parts teasing and concerned.

"It gives me something to do. Preoccupy my mind." So I don't sit in my apartment and brood all day.

"I bet you get this question all the time," Tiffany chimes in. "But I am curious. How many people did you save being in the special forces?"

I am instantly peeved. She isn't the only one who asks this question after they hear I was in the special forces. Why does it matter how many people I rescued?

"I guess I never really counted," I say honestly. She looks skeptical and repositions her legs so that they are touching mine, a hungry look in her eyes.

"I heard about Riley," Tiffany proceeds slowly. "And…I am sorry for your loss." She doesn't at all seem sorry. Clara shoots Tiffany a look as if to say uncalled for! and then shrugs at me, a look of apology on her face.

Tiffany begins talking to Clara about something else, much to my relief. I don't hear their conversation, because suddenly I am looking at Riley across the bar.

My heart stops.

My stomach hardens into steel, sinking low.

I swallow and blink a few times. Is this an apparition? A sick trick of my mind? No matter how wide I open my eyes, I still see Riley. An overwhelming feeling of loss and longing inflates and extends outside of me, creating a magnetic pull, pulling me toward Riley and everything that use to feel like home.

I can't breathe.

Clara and Tiffany are talking next to me, a faded dull hum, muffled and irrelevant.

Slowly, logic creeps back in. That girl—woman—in front of me is Riley's twin sister.

Ruth.

My heart screams in protest, wanting it to be Riley, but then settles into a feeling of comfort. It is good to see her.

Xavier walks up to the table carrying four drinks. "You okay, Todd? You look like you have seen a ghost."

You could say that.

I try to formulate some sort of sentence, but nothing comes out.

Xavier looks to Tiffany. "It's been a while since he's been around people." Tiffany and Clara laugh out of pity.

"Sorry," I apologize with an equally fake smile and take a sip of my lime soda.

It doesn't take long for my gaze to shift back to Ruth. I can't stop staring. I've seen her parents since Riley's death, but not Ruth. My mind tries to retrace the last time I saw her, but I can't put my finger on a specific date.

She's in a circular booth, bigger than ours. A tall, bald man sits near her, flirting with a girl with violet hair. Another, much larger guy with erratic hair sits across from her. One girl wearing dreary lipstick sat in the booth too, laughing easily. All of them look like they've been friends for a long time, talking over each other without a hint of annoyance. They are outlandish looking, and all are vying for attention—from anyone. Both the girls laugh at something the bigger man says, and Ruth's lips attempt to curl up in a smile, but twitch and falter. She doesn't seem to understand the humor around her.

Another man, just as tall as the one with the shaved head, comes into the booth and situates himself right next to Ruth. He puts his arm around her and just for a slight second, I see her already rigid body flinch. It happens so fast, I almost wonder if I imagined it. But no one else noticed.

Ruth scans the room, her eyes guarded and distant. They look so much like what I see in the mirror: eyes feigning a happiness that is simply not there. She is still the same Ruth I remembered: reserved, guarded at times, and lost in the depths of her mind

The man next to her brings his lips close to her ear and she laughs, but not a full-hearted laugh. I know because her real laugh doesn't come out often, but I remember what it looked like when it did. I can tell she's uncomfortable right now, and the idea of it makes me oddly uneasy.

From this distance, Ruth's outward resemblance to Riley is uncanny.

I can't drag my eyes from her.

She's beautiful.

"What's your next plan?" Clara interrupts my thoughts.

"Sorry?" I ask, caught off guard, painfully yanking my gaze away from Ruth to face Clara.

"What do you plan to do next now that you're out of the military? Or is being a paramedic kind of it at this point?" she rephrases.

I stumble on my words but manage to come up with some sort of plan that makes me appear more organized than I actually am. My attention floats back to the corner booth—back to Ruth—and then darts around the room when I can't find her.

"Excuse me for a minute," I tell the group and slide out of our booth.

Before I walk away, I hear Tiffany ask the table, "Is he fully there?"

Sometimes...

I walk to the back of the restaurant and just manage to spot the back of Ruth's head as she exits through a door by the kitchen.

I don't hesitate. I follow her.

When I get outside, I do a categorical sweep of the alley. It's dark, but there's no movement to cause alarm. Ruth is standing in front of me, facing a brick wall, her head hung low. She taps her left foot repeatedly, seeming deep in thought. She looks so much like Riley from behind.

I wish I could get all caught up in a snare, rising above this scene, watching Ruth for a while before I have to figure out what to say to her. And when I found the perfect words for this moment, I could cut the net and fall back to the earth—right back to this spot in the alley. A few moments pass before she turns around, ready to go back inside.

She stops. Our eyes meet.

Her expression goes from genuine surprise at another human so close to her and then shock when she realizes who the human is. Me. She brings shaking fingers to cover her mouth and we stare at each other.

Images flash by.

Her pleading for me to take the attention from her when she first met Pat.

Her crawling into herself when Riley was around.

Her big eyes.

Forest green.

Her dark trail of freckles.

Her leaning into the music at the White Elephants concert.

Her.

Pretty without knowing it.

In one unexpected motion, she closes the gap between us and flings her arms around my shoulders—easy, swift, without a question. It's the first time we've touched in years. She's on her tippy-toes. A little shorter than Riley, then. How come I've never noticed that before?

It takes me a moment to remember how to return a hug, but when I do, I wrap my arms around her firm body and hold her tightly.

"Todd," she whispers, squeezing me. "You're back." She steps away from me, and I find myself hesitating to let her go from my arms completely.

"I am. I didn't see you at your house after the funeral," I say.

"I…didn't stay long." Her cheeks flush, her eyes shining a calm sort of light. "I didn't see you at the cemetery." Not a challenge. Not a judgment, only curiosity.

"I didn't stay long," I lie. I can't tell her the real reason I didn't go, which was that I was barely hanging on to my sanity. Although something tells me she would understand.

"Where have you been since then?" She tilts her head with kind curiosity.

"Working, living…"

"Trying to forget us?" she says, more a statement than a question. I'm about to refute the statement, but then think better of it. Because that is exactly what I am trying to do. Forget it all. Move on.

Our eyes latch onto each other. She doesn't search my face, because she doesn't have to. She already knows how I'm handling Riley's death, how I feel, because she feels it too. We speak our own language with our eyes, taking turns asking and answering.

I hear her sharp intake of breath and hold my own. So, she feels this too.

She smiles, a chip in the shield I saw earlier. It's a true smile, one I remember from back in the day when she teased me. I find myself smiling back. Her face is burning red as if she is suddenly self-conscious. I watch her look me over head to toe like she's checking that I have all my parts. I inconspicuously do the same to her. The freckles on her face are more pronounced than I remembered. Her hair falls to her shoulders—rich brown and slightly wild. Her jean jacket is a bit too big, but her linen shorts fit just right, revealing short, olive-toned legs.

I silently scold myself for even staring at her. She is Ruth, my girlfriend's twin sister. My dead girlfriend.

"I'm sorry I haven't contacted you to see how you are doing. Now that I see you, I realize that I should have." Her voice brings me back in time, to Riley, to the Schneiders'. Although I thought it would be painful to go back in time, her voice—a mixture of honey and velvet—melts into one sweet melody that instantly puts me at ease. I savor each word.

"It goes both ways," I reply. "I'm the one who should be apologizing."

"Truce?" She asks, giving me a small, yet still real, smile.

"Truce." I reply. "Hey, your birthday is coming up."

Her eyes widen. A shadow crosses her features. "I was kind of hoping to forget about it." She folds her arms across her chest.

"I didn't mean to bring it up to upset you, I just thought...well maybe we could do something together in remembrance of Riley?" She eyes me warily and then looks away. I'd like to think that I asked Ruth to be with me on her birthday because I don't want her to go through it alone, but truly I don't know if I can be alone on that day.

"It's easy to run away from the day by ignoring it, but that won't help. It won't make anything easier," I say, more for me than for her.

She lifts her chin, her grin revealing a small dimple in her right cheek that's all hers and no parts Riley. "Did my dad teach you that?"

"Very funny."

The door behind me flies open. The guy she was sitting next to in the booth comes staggering out.

"Ruth," he demands. "What are you doing out here?" He slurs and then he realizes I'm there, too, and points a finger in my chest. "And who are you?" He prowls around me with shifty eyes.

"Trip, this is Todd," Ruth stands in between the guy—Trip—and me. I can see her cheeks burn. Her body is back to being tense—her guard is up. I can tell she's embarrassed by Trip's behavior. Suddenly, I understand why Ruth flinched in the restaurant. Anger—burning and quick—starts to build. He's drunk.

Trip moves to Ruth's side and puts his arm around her. She recoils.

"Todd," Trip spits. "What are you doing out here talking to my girlfriend?"

I look at Ruth. This is her boyfriend. She shakes her head as if to plead for me to let it go. She must see my anger seething. I turn to Trip and force my words to be smooth. "I was just getting some fresh air." I try to quell the boiling inside me, only for Ruth's sake.

Ruth places her hand on Trip's chest and says through her teeth, "Go inside. I'll be there in a minute."

Trip stumbles back a bit and throws his hands up. "I'm not leaving you here with him." He points to me again.

"Look, why don't you go inside. Drink some water. She will be in in a minute." My tolerance is thinning fast.

He smirks. "Water?"

"You're drunk."

"What's it to you?" His face contorts into something ugly. Does he know how Riley died? Does he not see how this makes Ruth feel?

Ruth is getting even more fidgety. The last thing I want is to make her more distressed. Ruth gently pushes Trip away from me, encouraging him to go inside, and follows him up the stairs when he does. I don't want her to go—not yet. The door is almost closed when she turns around. Her eyes pierce mine.

"I'd like that. To see you on my birthday," she says, like we weren't interrupted at all.

"Okay." I feel my shoulders loosen. Relief trickles through me. "Where can I meet you?"

She looks back inside and then to me. "Should we visit her grave?"

I was going to suggest somewhere else. I haven't visited Riley's grave yet. It'll be difficult…but maybe what I need. I nod. "Yes. I'll meet you there. How about in the morning? Say eight o'clock?"

"Sure."

She starts back inside, but I'm not ready to see her go. I yell her name. She peeks her head back out the door. "Do you need a ride home tonight?"

For a moment, she appears to consider. I find myself leaning forward. I see her gulp and look down to her feet. "I…I will have to give him a ride." She points inside. "It was good to see you, Todd." She gives me one more small smile over her shoulder before she disappears.

142

I let my head fall back so that I'm gazing up towards the night sky. Seeing Ruth should be the most painful reminder of all. But it isn't pain I feel. No—it's a cold guilt and a soft sense of welcome.

Chapter 29

Todd

Pat is at my front door. I know because Pat has a specific knock—soft and slow.

"One minute!" I yell before throwing my sweats on. I crack the door open and there she is, holding a bag of bagels. I hate when people come over unannounced, but when they have bagels? I can make exceptions.

"Good morning, sunshine." Pat walks past me, inviting herself into the apartment. She surveys the small space and then faces me. "Look what you have done with the place! This looks fantastic." She hesitates, then adds, "and clean."

I survey my apartment, trying to see what she does. From the front door, I can see my living room the left: two couches, a coffee table and an average TV. Straight ahead is a meager kitchen table, and on the other side of that, an L-shaped kitchen. My bedroom is through an arched doorway on the right and a guest bathroom is near the front door. It's basic and non-significant. It screams military. Decorating was a slow process and not exactly my forte.

"Thanks. It's coming along. I learned from the best, right?"

"Oh, stop," Pat teases, although I can tell she is pleased.

"How are you?" I walk the short distance from the door to the kitchen and take out two plates from the cupboard. Pat sits at the kitchen table, watching me with her narrow, knowing eyes.

"Fine for an oldie. Why do you look so tired?" She deflects from herself.

I grab a knife from a drawer and spread cream cheese onto my bagel. "It was a late night." I sigh.

"Oh?" She waits for me to proceed.

"I saw Riley—Jesus." I put my hands to my face. "I mean I saw Ruth." Pat's eyebrows rise as I continue to flounder. "I saw Riley's sister, Ruth." I spell it out in a complete sentence.

"I'm glad you didn't see Riley," Pat huffs out a laugh. "I would have been concerned."

I rest my face in the palm of my hands. "When I saw her, I was frozen in time. I thought Riley had risen from the dead."

Pity flickers across Pat's face. "That must have been terrible, and extremely triggering." Her voice rings with pure empathy.

I can't stop thinking about my encounter with Ruth. When the clock read 3 a.m., I was still thinking about her. Did she know how fake she was acting in that booth? Did anyone sense her pretense? Did they not consider how the heaviness of her feelings physically dragged her head down low?

Her facade bothers me, and it irks me that no one around her seemed to care.

Pat touches my shoulder and I jerk my head up. I sigh. "I am sorry, Pat. I was lost for a minute there."

She gives me a drawn-out "hmm-hmm" in her all-seeing way and I laugh. She is good.

"What time is it, anyway?" I ask.

"One-thirty. I've never known you to sleep into this hour. You're usually up when the rooster—"

"Shit! Pat, I have to go," I say frantically, just now remembering the appointment I had booked.

I started seeing a therapist, Heidi, shortly after learning of Riley's death, and still see her on occasion. One of her suggestions is that I get a massage—something about getting comfortable with touch and tuning back in to my body. At first, I was appalled by Heidi's suggestion. I ran away from silence the first six months after Riley's death, because to be still in silence meant I heard every thought associated with grief—loud and clear. The regret, the doubt, and the anxiety each spoke in loud tones of their own. If I had to hear those thoughts and have a stranger touch me? No, thank you. But by the fourth massage, the pain wasn't so loud and when the noise of my broken heart hushed, I was able to soften to the touch. So here I am, off to get my fifth massage.

"Where to?" Pat asks as she gets up and cleans our breakfast mess, calm as deep water.

"A massage," I mumble, slightly embarrassed. I race into my room to put a shirt on and slip into my Chacos.

"Really?" Her eyebrows shoot up. "Good for you," she finishes with approval.

I kiss her on the cheek and leave, yelling, "Lock it on the way out! Love you."

~

I peek at my watch as I enter the spa and smile with satisfaction. Made it with two minutes to spare.

I plop into a seat on the couch and finally allow myself a deep breath. The fountain in the lobby adds a nice echo, and the complimentary drinks and snacks are my favorite. The receptionist—whose name is Laura—keeps glancing up from typing on her computer to stare at me. I squirm in my seat, suddenly uncomfortable. It wasn't the fact that she was staring at me that made my insides tighten into a grimace, it was that she stared at me while licking her lips one minute and winking the next.

Audacious girls have told me I was attractive before. I never really saw what they see. I should be flattered, but instead I feel like that awkward middle schooler too nervous to hold a girl's hand. Dating Riley gave me the best excuse possible to veer away from any interested woman.

Some of the guys I was deployed with would have loved any opportunity to take advantage of girls who threw themselves at them, but not me. The distasteful part, in my eyes, was the speed in which girls moved onto the next airmen after I said "no." I loved being committed to Riley. Saying "no" to other women was the easiest thing in the world for me.

Just as I am about to pick up a magazine to hide behind, Laura says, "Hey Ruth!"

I am stupefied.

No.

Not here.

She can't be here. It has to be another girl named Ruth.

"Thanks for covering Beth's shift. We were really in a crunch there."

My heart stumbles. I want to run away, far from this moment where we will come face to face. But I also want to stay. To remain paralyzed. To come face to face with her again.

At last, I dare to look up toward the voices. That one person with that one velvety voice who's been in my life since forever but whom I am now just noticing.

She is standing at the white marble counter, leaning most of her weight onto one foot, her right one. Her rich, brown hair is in a high ponytail. She is wearing tight black pants and a tight black T-shirt. And I should look away. Look down. Look anywhere, but I don't. I'm frozen in place. Again.

146

I drag my eyes down to my own appearance and take inventory. Shit.

"Your appointment is here," Laura informs Ruth and then points over at me. Ruth turns in slow motion. I feel myself leaning forward, just an inch. I can see her face flush. Her forest-green eyes go wide and try to look away from them, but I can't. I see her gulp. She runs a hand across the side of her head, flattening her curly baby hairs.

I stand up to greet her. It's both an effort and the easiest thing I've ever done. When my feet have led me to her, I see that she's not wearing makeup. Something about her nakedness makes my lips curl up involuntarily. Like she isn't going to hide anything. Like she can't.

Ruth smiles. My heart clenches. I remind it to beat again.

"Hello, Todd." She sounds pleasantly surprised. Thank God.

"Hey," I say. "I didn't know you were doing massages. I swear—I am not following you."

She lets out a quick, open laugh. "I know. It's good to see you again. I am just going to go"—she points to a door off the side of the lobby counter—"get things set up, and then Laura will send you back when I am ready for you, okay?"

Okay. I can do this. I will just have to keep reminding myself to breathe, but I can do this. If she's being professional about massaging her dead sister's boyfriend, then I will be professional too. "Sure," I respond and head back to sit on the couch. I slap my face when my back is turned, trying to wake myself up. To act normal. To remember who she is.

After ten painful, anxiety-provoking minutes, Laura saunters over and tells me to follow her. She leads me to a smaller room for my massage. Ruth walks in moments later. I lean against the massage table for support.

I can tell that she put a little makeup on and redid her hair since I saw her in the lobby and I wish she hadn't. I want to see that stream of freckles flow across her cheeks and nose.

She clears her throat. I realize I am staring at her without saying a word, but the words are stuck somewhere in the mess inside me.

My palms are slightly sweaty.

And then I remember I will soon be naked.

Butt naked.

In front of Ruth.

Then she will be putting lotion on and rubbing her delicate and perfect hands on my body.

I start coughing, trying to interrupt the thoughts from continuing.

This can't be happening.

I almost cancel the whole thing right then and there.

As if Ruth reads my unease, she offers, "You don't have to get naked if you don't want to, it's really up to whatever makes you comfortable. In fact, if this is too weird, we can just cancel?" Her shoulders inch closer to her ears. I don't know what she wants me to say, but something in her eyes tells me not to leave.

"Nah. It's only weird if we make it weird, right?"

Her shoulders melt back down. She is pleased. I think. I could be reading her wrong.

"I'll leave you to it, then," she says before shutting the door softly behind her.

I decide to leave my boxer briefs on and slide onto the table, removing the bolster from underneath the sheets. Too many jumps out of an airplane can create some wear and tear on a person. My back and knees took the worse beatings, and nothing, including a bolster, seemed to help ease the tension.

I squish my face into the headrest, not sure if staring at the floor is better or worse than facing Ruth.

Chapter 30

Ruth

If I knew that Todd would be my first client of the day, I may have cancelled the appointment.

There's something about being in his presence that makes me feel as if I'm betraying both him and Riley. Riley because he was hers first. And Todd because...I know details about him that he doesn't know I know. Riley's entire journal is filled with stories of him. Until the end, that is.

Zeph. Does Todd know about Zeph? He can't possibly. The timeline wouldn't make sense if he did, because she didn't plan on telling him until she returned from Guatemala and Todd returned from his mission.

I am sick with this secret between us.

He deserves to know.

Or does he? What good would it do at this point?

Seeing him in the alley of O'Reilly's was like forgetting and remembering all in one moment. He was old and new at the same time, familiar and yet completely foreign. He looked like the same Todd I knew for years, but also different...mature, striking, comfortable in his skin. His sandy blonde hair wasn't as long as it was the summer after high school, but it was still longer than the mandatory military buzz cut. I hadn't realized how pronounced his jaw was or how his sharp nose fit perfectly between his gold eyes. All night I tried to forget how those eyes held me tightly, fixing me to the bricks underneath my feet in the alley.

I felt my body responding to him last night in that narrow alley, and when you feel like a walking ice cube, numb and cold, for so long, then you notice when your body shifts. It's the same feeling I got when I saw him in the lobby this morning. He was mismatched. His hair was haywire, but he was smiling, and I had to grab the counter for fear that my knees would betray me.

Beth, his usual massage therapist, hasn't spoken a word about Todd to me. She must not remember him, or just chose not to tell me today when I'm covering for her, because she knew I would say no. I don't know whether to thank her for being so coy or to scold her for assuming I could handle massaging Todd.

I pull Beth's file on him and briefly review the notes she had written after his last massage. What I can gather from Beth's chicken scratch writing is minimal. She recorded that his shoulders and back were especially tense, and that he'd had surgeries on his knees and lower back. That doesn't surprise me with the type of work he had done the past.

I also read in the notes that his referral came from his therapist, which has to mean he is still in therapy. A flashback of him outside our house during the days he saw my dad overwhelms me. I feel as if I am invading his privacy by knowing he was in therapy again and wondered if he spoke about Riley in his current sessions. Does he miss her?

Of course, he does, Ruth. How can he not?

There is a comment at the bottom of the case notes. "Possible Acute PTSD from deployments. Therapist says massages are for reintroducing touch and facilitating healthy connection."

From what I know of men returning from the military, they tend to struggle to achieve normalcy when they return home. Many suffer from flashbacks, numbness, avoidance, depression...the list goes on. The symptoms sound a lot like grief, and maybe experiencing trauma is a grief of some kind—a loss of normalcy.

I can't imagine how Todd is adjusting to being back. His plans with Riley have been demolished. The future that they fought six long, relentless years for is no longer—vanished in one quick moment. How is he rearranging himself now? Has he already, a year later? He left the trauma of his career only to return home to a girlfriend who was killed by a drunk driver. He was immersed in two wars, two ultimate losses: his career and his girlfriend.

Despite my best attempts to gather myself before entering the room and seeing Todd, my hands and my heart are trembling. I look in the hallway mirror one last time before I knock on the massage room's door.

"Come in," a low, sexy grunt.

Oh God, what am I getting myself into?

Todd is lying face down, and I notice he has removed the bolster from the table.

"Hi," I breathe softly, announcing my presence.

"Hi," he says, or at least I think he says, into the headrest.

I go over my normal spiel for new clients and then allow silence to take over. Knowing when to talk, where to put pressure, and when to offer silence is an art. I normally let the clients lead the way, but am struggling to know whether or not Todd wants to communicate or let the lull of noise carry us through the hour. How do you navigate a situation with a man who once dated your sister—your twin—who is now gone from both your lives forever? I force myself to remember that I'm a professional, and this is a professional service, because my mind creeps into territory that screams betrayal.

The moment my hands touch his back, he flinches.

"I'm sorry," I blurt out.

"No, it's okay," he assures me, bringing his head up slightly to avoid muffling his voice. "I just...haven't been touched in a while."

A lie. According to Beth's file, he has been here monthly for the past four months. What he means is that he hasn't been touched by me since...since when? Never.

"Oh," I respond, at loss for words. I watch my hands stroke his back, doing my best not to think of all the times Riley had done the same, and I shake my head. I practice breathing mindfully and focus on suffusing his skin with positive energy, easing his tension, and releasing his pent-up pain.

"Are you okay?" Todd asks. I bring my attention back to Todd and realize my hands have stopped moving. I quickly bring them back into motion.

"Yes," I stammer. "I am sorry. This is just strange for me. Being with you reminds me of Riley."

"Tell me about it."

I laugh nervously. Of course, being with me reminds him of Riley. We are—were—identical twins, for God's sake. "It was never hard to be with you before." I can't bring myself to say before Riley died. "But now I can imagine it would be hard for you...to be with me." My words are sincere.

I'm not expecting him to move, but he rolls over onto his back and sits up, revealing a defined chest covered in tattoos. I've never seen him exposed like this. Most of the ink on his chest is unreadable, which makes the tattoos even more somber looking. His abs are just noticeable above where the sheet drapes over his lower body. I have to consciously tell myself to close my gaping mouth and meet his stare. He tilts his head in thought.

"Ruth, I can't imagine how difficult this is for you." His voice strains.

For months after her death, people asked me how I was faring, which I thought was obvious—not well. Those same people never ask how you are a year later, though. As if you're expected to move on.

But for some reason, this shared grief gives me permission to let my true feelings seep through the mask I normally wear. I allow myself to drop my pretenses, if only for this brief moment. I feel out this new face I am wearing—staring straight at him. It's me, my authentic, bare-bones self.

I fight to find the words to say to him. I can't link the pronouns with their proper adjectives. His golden eyes pierce me, and I wonder if he could somehow read my thoughts.

"I miss her," Todd says, unashamed. Honest.

Good. Common ground.

"I do too. Every day I do." Todd doesn't lie back down, so I sit on the stool near him. Quiet fills the room until I break.

"She was everything I couldn't bring myself to be," I say. I don't know where the thought comes from—nowhere, maybe. Or maybe it's a truth that has been deep within me, but unable to get through the all the layers. Layers of days coming and going. Me moving further away from her death. Further away from her life.

"How so?" Todd asks.

"Remember that one Christmas you spent at our home? Riley had been working as a barista for some extra cash during medical school. Leave it to her to have a part-time job during medical school. Anyway, she met someone in the coffee shop and brought him to our Christmas dinner. Do you remember that?"

Todd's eyes glaze over, grasping for that memory. The right side of his mouth curves up into a smile. "Drew. The bicyclist. How could you forget him?"

"Yes! He was biking across America, in the dead of winter of all times, and here Riley is inviting him home for a nice warm dinner. He could have been a murderer for all we knew." My small laugh stops as the word "murderer" leaves my mouth.

"He did suck at Scrabble, didn't he?" Todd jokes, not letting me dwell on what I had just said. I push on, diving into the memory.

"Remember before we played Scrabble, he said he needed to go pee, but came out of the bathroom drenched in water? He could have just asked to use the shower. My parents would have let him. They couldn't decide whether or not they should be furious or pleased to have a daughter so welcoming."

"Your mom was furious, and your dad was pleased," Todd says matter-of-factly. I revel in his insight, because he was spot on.

The quiet consumes us again as we both bask in the memory.

"I like this," I say.

"What?" Todd asks.

"Sharing memories with you."

"It's a bit of a gift, really." Todd looks down at his toes, his legs hanging over the edge of the massage table. "Remembering her makes it seem like she is here with us. Hearing a memory from your perspective makes me feel like I am learning something new about her...a gift," he repeats.

"Let's make a deal," I propose. "Every time we see each other, we will share a memory of Riley—one the other wouldn't know about. It will be our gift to each other."

Todd runs his hand through his hair and down his face, contemplating. For a second, it looks like he's going to refuse, but then he nods curtly. "Deal."

I hop down from the stool and gesture for him to lie on his stomach. I can't let him leave with the tension he walked in the room with. As I begin to move my hands in even, smooth strokes, I feel his body give into me.

I sigh with relief that he didn't ask about Trip, whether on purpose or not. My face—naked, with no masks—would give me away, I am sure of it. Even though I'm not quite sure what I would reveal about Trip, as I hardly know where my heart stands with him these days.

Chapter 31

Todd

I wake with a noxious blend of feelings in my gut. Today is July 20th. I tossed and turned last night, knowing that when midnight came around, Riley's birthday would too. There's some consolation in knowing that I wasn't alone. Ruth didn't sleep either. I know because when I had texted her happy birthday at midnight, she responded instantly. The conversation was short—simple, basic words—but was still a small antidote to the ache in my heart.

It's early in the morning when I get into my truck to drive to the cemetery. A few clouds scuttle across the baby blue sky, and the sun is already casting its light upon the world. My eyes linger on the rising ball of light, intrigued by how the Earth keeps spinning, even when you are shattered.

The skin across my knuckles turns white on the steering wheel and I curse when the thermos of coffee tilts on its side in the passenger seat. Am I nervous? I don't know if Ruth likes coffee, but I need it. Plus, Pat taught me to show up, whether that be with a personality or a cup of coffee. Considering I won't be shining bright today, coffee will have to suffice.

I park the truck at the cemetery gates.

The birds are singing their morning song and frolicking from one tree to the next. There's a small breeze that sends the leaves chattering. There are no other cars in the parking lot, and I take that as a sign that Ruth isn't here yet. I can go and talk to Riley before Ruth gets here, but I fear the grief would pierce me beyond composure. So I sit in the truck and I wait.

My mind drifts from what I should say to Riley to what I should ask Ruth. A stream of potential questions glides through my mind. I don't know how to behave around her, not because I don't know myself, but because I don't know what to expect. We've spent time together, but we don't really know each other. Who is Ruth without Riley?

The clock ticks to five minutes past eight and Ruth has not yet showed. I hate being late, so I make myself get out of the truck. I throw a blanket over my shoulders, the thermos of coffee in my hand, and walk toward the gates of the cemetery. There are two angels perched on top of the cemetery gates, the sun rays bouncing off their outstretched wings.

The cemetery is a massive, square-shaped plot of land near Lake Bodhi. I've heard that there is a rose garden and pond in the center of the cemetery, but I have yet to see it. That would mean I had been brave enough to come here before this moment, but I wasn't.

As I start walking, I notice many smaller paths shooting off the main gravel trail. Those paths weave around groups of tombstones, creating a maze throughout the plot of land. The sound of crunching pebbles fills the air as I keep walking on the main path. I keep my eyes low, gazing from one tombstone to another, looking for the one name that had the power to utterly destroy me.

And then I see her.

Ruth is kneeling in front of a tombstone in the distance. She is still and serene.

I take my time walking up to her, trying to collect myself. I halt when I am a few steps away from her.

My heart is an anchor sinking deeper and deeper into a dark abyss. Riley's name is engraved on a white marble tombstone in front of me.

The last time I saw Riley was before she left for Guatemala on a service trip. An image of her sad smile passes through me like a ghost. There was something wrong, something in disarray inside of her when I saw her last. She was distant. She wasn't the same Riley I had fallen in love with, and only after I had learned of her death did that truly unsettle me. I cannot remember the last time I saw her as my Riley—the fiery girl who dared me to be a better man or the only woman who quite literally embraced me with warm intensity when we departed each other. Somehow, I thought me proposing to her would bring her back to me. I think of the ring I had for her—gone now. Sold. I couldn't bear to look at it anymore.

A bird flies across my line of vision, bringing me back to this moment. To Ruth.

My eyes quickly scan her for any red flags, an old habit from being a paramedic that I can't seem to quash. She's wearing light blue Levi's jeans and a loose white T-shirt. Her small feet are bare and tucked underneath her. Her head hangs low, her chin only inches from her chest. Strands of her dark hair have fallen from her loose ponytail, framing her face. Nothing about her shouts for attention, yet that alone gave me pause. Who are you, kneeling here in such quiet reserve?

"I know you're here," she says softly, not opening her eyes. I stay static, at a distance, not sure if she's addressing me or Riley. "Todd. I know you're here." She turns her gaze toward me, long, navy blue earrings sweeping her cheeks as she does.

"I didn't want to intrude."

"You didn't. I'm glad you are here."

At her words, all the ashes of uncertainty leave my body. "Here, sit on this," I insist, spreading the wool blanket on the damp grass. "Coffee?" I hold up the thermos. She grins, a small light shining forth, and then rummages in a backpack at her side. When she faces me again, she's holding up her own thermos.

It takes me a minute to realize what I am seeing.

Her small hands grip the thermos. I think she is smiling, but her face becomes blurry behind the thermos. Everything but her hand becomes blurry. My eyes fixate on her pinky finger.

It's a ring.

A ring made of grass.

The blade of grass is a vibrant green. Freshly picked. She just made it.

It wraps around her pinky finger. It's delicate, but strong.

Two words that I thought always had described her.

The sight of it squeezes the air out of my lungs. I'm suffocated. A goner. Still, I inhale and keep inhaling until there is nowhere left for the air to go. It reaches the crown of my head and extends to my toes.

I've seen a ring like that before. I still have the remnants of a ring like that.

I'm taken back to being eight years old when I first met Ruth and Riley, and my mind is gone. I am thinking of a time where Riley and I were lying on a blanket in her backyard. She was picking grass, mindlessly. But she never made a ring. She had twirled the grass in her fingers over and over again. And I didn't realize until now how I had been anxiously waiting for her to tie that knot, to instinctively make a ring.

But she didn't.

She couldn't.

Riley couldn't make the ring then, because it wasn't Riley who made the ring first.

The truth hits me like another wave of grief. A loss of what I thought I knew to be true all along.

156

I close my gaping mouth and clear my throat, trying to wake myself up from flashback. I almost tell Ruth everything. The words are on the tip of my tongue.

It was you. All along. You were the little girl with the pink Crocs and the smile that radiated through the world and changed lives. You told me to come with you. And I did. I followed you, yet you weren't the one I fell in love with.

"Um, Todd. You can sit down now," Ruth says, eyeing me with curiosity. I realize I'm still standing in front of her, thermos in hand.

"Right." I try to cover my shock with a light-hearted laugh, although it comes out as an awkward huff. "Riley didn't like coffee, so I didn't know." I curse myself for...I don't know what. Comparing the two?

I sit down next to her, careful to give her enough distance. Being in such close proximity to Ruth when she's wearing that silly little ring made of grass takes me back to an old scene—to this exact moment, sitting next to each other. There is no lake. No tree. My clothes don't reek, but still. It feels the same. In both cases, Riley is at a distance.

I want to be alone to process this new discovery, to figure out how I had made such a catastrophic mistake and how I had fallen for the wrong—the unexpected—twin. But my mind goes blank at the sheer force this realization has on me. It feels too overwhelming to organize.

Ruth waves a hand in front of my eyes. "Earth to Todd."

My head snaps up. "Sorry," I manage. "Just a bit out of it today."

Ruth doesn't seem fazed by behavior. She shrugs and tucks the loose strands of hair behind her ears. "It's okay. Me too."

When I don't initiate any conversation, Ruth fills in the silence. "I envied her energy, that intensity she had without drinking one sip of coffee." Her big, hopeful eyes stare at the tombstone.

"Every day was a list to her, wasn't it? She had a lot to accomplish. I think drinking coffee was too much of an inconvenience to her," I add, fighting to stay in this present moment with Ruth.

"She changed, didn't she?" Ruth's voice is low and serious.

It isn't so much a question as a statement. Still, I answer. "She was different towards the end. Medical school took a toll on her spirit. I was worried about her going to Guatemala. One more thing added to her already abundant list of duties." I rest my elbows on my bent knees and interlace my hands. "We got into a fight before her trip…" I trail off, trying gate up the flood of emotions flowing through me.

Ruth turns her whole body toward me, sitting in the crisscross-applesauce position. Her knees are inches away from my outstretched legs. My closeness doesn't faze her, and she doesn't seem surprised by my disclosure. Her eyes are soft, urging me to talk. I want nothing more than to bite my tongue and lock the door to my heart. At least until I've sorted out what I just learned in seeing that ring on Ruth's finger. But I can't risk making Ruth feel alone in the process. Something deep in me snubs the thought. She doesn't deserve to be alone in this grief. Still, I look away from her eyes as I talk.

"I was worried about her. I didn't used to be, not when we were in high school. The worry started when we were a part and just continued to grow. She became more and more repulsed by it. When she went to Guatemala, I wanted to take the time apart to talk and work through whatever was eating her up inside. We didn't have to talk on the phone, but some form—any form—of communication would have been enough."

"She never wrote."

"Nothing. The whole time she was gone on her trip. The weird thing is that when she came back, she was like the Riley I had met when she was eighteen years old but…different. Better. She looked…" I struggle to find the words.

"Like the best version of herself?" Ruth finishes for me. I meet her eyes. She looks away sheepishly.

I try to remember Riley's face when I saw her after her trip. "You are right. She did look and seem so happy. And it wasn't me who made her that way."

Ruth's brows furrow. "That also wasn't your responsibility. Only she could have made herself happy." She takes a sip of coffee. I follow suit, letting the warmth slither down my throat and heat up my insides. Ruth is right, but that doesn't change how I feel. "Was that your memory?" Ruth asks. Right—we'd made a pact. We'd each share one memory of Riley when we were together—a gift.

"No. That's not the one I want to tell on your birthday." I smile, and Ruth's lips twitch up in a quick smile, too, before turning flat again. She has a way of letting her joy go, as if she doesn't quite feel comfortable in that emotion yet. She didn't used to be like that. I lean back on my elbows and stretch my legs out in front of me. Ruth sets her coffee down and lays her body long next to me. I can't help but notice her delicate form so close to mine.

"It was my twenty-second birthday. I was home on leave and Pat had wanted to have a nice dinner with Rile and me. She planned it all, from the appetizer to the drinks to the roast. She was excited to have me home, and you know how much she loved your sister. She took Rile in as her own child. Although Pat would take in any child as her own."

"True." Ruth giggles.

I clear my throat. "Dinner was supposed to be at six o'clock. I had told Rile multiple times, because I knew she'd be forgetful."

"Like she had been before," Ruth teases, referring back to the time she stood in for Riley the first time Pat was to meet her. My insides split at the memory—warm when thinking of Ruth that night and cold when I remembered how Riley hadn't been there for me.

"She had a million other things going on." I cannot stop myself from defending her. "When seven o'clock rolled around, I got worried. She didn't text. I didn't know where she was. So, I got in my car and I drove. It sounds like an overreaction, but I don't know, I couldn't stop. I just had to make sure she was okay. You'll never guess where I found her."

I could feel Ruth's eyes on me as she rolled her head to the side. I swivel my gaze to look into her eyes, full of wonder and anticipation.

My voice drops like I'm about to give a punchline. "I found her napping on a cardboard box around hundreds of others in downtown Minneapolis. It was a weird chance that I had even ran into her where I did, but there she was. I guess there was a protest at the college. Hundreds of students vowed to sleep on the streets in order to bring awareness to the hundreds of homeless people living without proper healthcare."

Ruth's mouth hangs open in surprise. "She missed your birthday to sleep on the street?"

"For a good cause," I respond, defending Riley again like a reflex.

"Todd…" Ruth opens her mouth and then slams it shut.

"What?" I ask.

"I guess I am not surprised is all. It was a catch-22 with her. Hard to be mad at her for saving the world even if that meant those in her close circle were placed on the back burner."

"Did she have a close circle?" I surprise myself by asking.

Ruth ponders the question and bites her lower lip. "I guess I don't know. Sometimes I wonder if I even knew her at all." I can feel the heaviness of this spoken truth emanate off of Ruth's body and I gladly absorb it. Better to give the load to me then allow it to burden her.

"I'm sorry. I didn't mean for the memory to be tainted. It sounded funny in my head."

"It was still a gift. Thank you, Todd," she says, placing her hand on mine for a second before bringing it back to her side of the blanket. The place she touched vibrates in quiet longing. I am reminded of the night she hugged me in the alley, or the other day when she massaged my back, a warm surprise.

"Are you ready for my memory?" she asks.

"Yes." I rest my head on my hand, not wanting to miss her face as she tells her story. If she's uncomfortable with me staring at her, she doesn't show it.

"Picture this," she begins in a dramatic voice. "Riley and I were just learning how to ride a bike. She got her training wheels off before I did, which wasn't a shocker. She did everything first. One summer, dad thought it was a brilliant idea to drive to Montana to visit our cousins. Riley insisted we bring our bikes, knowing full well that there wouldn't be anything else for us to do at our cousin's farm." Ruth closes her eyes as if trying to go back in time.

"At the farm, there was this cattle guard. As kids, we were absolutely terrified of them. I thought for sure one twist of my tire would have me falling through into the weeds below.

"So, here I am. Parked on my bike, staring at it. Then, out of nowhere, Riley comes flying past me and over the cattle guard." Ruth laughs out loud and I roll onto my back, chortling.

"Dust was flying into the air as she braked on the other side. She looked back at me and screamed…" Ruth cups her mouth.

"'Come on Ruth! What are you waiting for?'"

Ruth paused, all caught up in her memory. "I think…I have been waiting for her to go first in everything my whole life. And she did. She led the way. I followed."

I close my eyes, trying to catch up to the shift in emotions. Our shared grief is oscillating from relief to pain and back.

"That's not how I remembered it," I whisper. "Whenever we all hung out, you had your own agenda. You became your own self, Ruth, even if you couldn't see it." I expect to see tears in her eyes, but there are none. She looks away first and straightens her posture.

She reaches for her phone and I watch as her face falls. Is she waiting for someone to text her? The guy from the bar?

"Are you dating that guy I met in the alley?" I know he called her his girlfriend, but I want to see what she considered him. I'm afraid of her answer.

Ruth's mouth is slightly agape. I can't help but stare at her lips as they make the perfect expression of surprise. She sighs.

"I was afraid you'd ask me about Trip."

"Trip," I mutter.

"Yes. Trip," she says. She shoves her phone into her backpack. "He hasn't called me yet. I guess it's still too early."

"Are you happy with him?"

She looks at me suspiciously and then to Riley's grave, contemplating.

"You don't have to answer that," I rush in.

"No, I want to. I just can't find the words sometimes to say what I really want to say," she says. I wait patiently. "I am trying to be happy on my own, and I am trying to figure out if he will add to that happiness or take from it. I guess I am not sure right now."

"I suppose it's not his job to make you happy." I repeat the same words she gave me earlier. I'll let the subject go. If she wasn't ready to talk about it, I'm not going to push her.

Ruth punches my shoulder playfully and stands. She slips her feet into her shoes and gazes at Riley's tombstone. Her lips move, but I can't hear what she says. She puts her index finger on her nose and then points to the grave. I know she is whispering the word "nose" in her head—her and Riley's code for "I love you."

"Let's go," Ruth says.

"Where are we going?" I stand up too.

"You'll see."

"I don't like surprises," I say as I shake the grass off the blanket.

"Too bad. It's my birthday." She flashes me a grin over her shoulder and swings her backpack onto her back before walking down the path. I look at Riley's tombstone, bring three fingers to my mouth for a kiss, and then touch her cursive name etched in stone. I love you. I will always love you, even if I had mistaken you for someone else.

When I catch up to Ruth, I pull onto the loop of her backpack, setting her off balance. "Hey!" she exclaims, eyes narrowing until she realizes why I grabbed her backpack. I swing her bag onto my shoulder and walk in front of her.

"I could handle my own bag, you know," she huffs.

"Nope. It's your birthday," I tease her, trying to lift the mood. When I get to my truck, I throw my thermos and blanket into the back seat and turn to Ruth.

"Where did you park?"

"I walked."

"What?" I'm shocked. "You walked here from your apartment in downtown Minneapolis?" That's at least twelve miles.

"I'm staying at my parents' place. House sitting. They are driving the coast of Lake Superior today."

I roughly calculated the distance in my head. "Still, you walked three miles here?"

Ruth puts her hands in her back pockets and rocks on her heels. "I like to walk. Gives me time to think, plus there's this whole theory in therapy about bilateral movement. Supposedly it calms you down." I want her to continue, fascinated by what she knows, but she is already getting into the passenger seat of my truck. I try to keep up.

"Where are we going?"

"To get chocolate-covered gummy bears," she says with all seriousness.

I think back to the last time I had chocolate-covered gummy bears, and my heart leaps. It's been years, but you don't just forget when mysterious gummy bears show up in your belongings when you've been starving for days. I almost go back in time to the darker days of my youth, but I force myself to stay in the present with Ruth.

"And where do we find those?" I play along, allowing myself to laugh at her random request. She fidgets with the radio and rolls down the window. I can see her lips curving in a smile. Once she finds a satisfactory channel, she puts her feet on my dashboard, glancing at me from the corner of her eyes, testing whether or not this is okay.

"It's your birthday. Today—today you get whatever you want. But tomorrow, you can't put your feet on my dashboard."

Her grin widens. This feeling, however small it is, shoots through me like lightning. I don't know what to call it, but I think it feels like bliss.

"To Izzy's Chocolate Factory," Ruth demands playfully, pointing through the front window.

I don't know what will happen after chocolate-covered gummy bears, but I know whatever it will be will feel like this. A simple feeling of absolute freedom.

Chapter 32

Ruth

Todd and I eat copious amounts of chocolate-covered gummy bears, play half a round of golf, visit Starbucks for my one free drink of the year, and still I haven't heard from Trip. I feel a hint of worry—perhaps something happened to him? But even as I consider the question, I know in my heart it wasn't true. He's fine. He just forgot to call. I'm thankful that Todd is here with me, but it's getting harder to hide my mortification at the fact that my own boyfriend has not called me on my birthday.

"Still nothing, huh?" Todd asks after I put my phone down for the hundredth time. I shake my head and fold my arms, trying to avoid Todd's all-seeing stare. His eyes are sharp, missing nothing.

"Well, what now?" he asks. "You already beat me in golf and you clearly have more skill in eating chocolate-covered gummy bears. What else do you want to kick my ass in today?"

"You better not be going easy on me," I joke.

"Never." His mocking voice makes me smile. I can't help it. When I first saw Todd this morning, his eyes were glazed over in apprehension. Now his demeanor feels lighter—still cautious, but not intensely so.

We finish our coffee and walk to his truck. We both sit in silence before I push out what I was too scattered to say earlier at the cemetery. "Trip wants to move in together." I sigh. There it is, out of me and into the space between Todd and me. The truth of the matter articulated. Trip wants to live with me. And I...want to run away. I think? I don't know how I feel about Trip—with Trip—and that alone makes me antsy.

Todd doesn't turn the car on. He doesn't ignore me. He doesn't do anything but give me his full attention. His legs angle toward the passenger side, hitting his knees on the center console.

"That's big, Ruth. What are you going to do?" There is concern in his voice. When I face him, his eyes are pools of longing. I don't know what he longs for, and I am not brave enough to ask. My gut turns again.

"I wish you could have met him under different circumstances." I tumble over my words, hating that I feel the need to convince Todd why I'm with Trip, even if I can't articulate those reasons myself.

164

Todd waits for me to finish, but I don't have anything else to say. He turns the truck on and backs out of the Starbucks parking lot. As he looks out the back window, he says, "It's your life, Ruth. I don't get a say in it. I just want you to be with someone who deserves you."

His words make me feel all jumbled up, lost and found in one quick minute. Even though his words cut to the heart of the matter, I still want to ask him what he means. I want him to lay out exactly what I deserve, because somedays it feels like what I think I deserve is not what I need. Somedays I haven't got a single clue.

I have to look at my hands, twisting together on my lap in order to recover from whatever was happening between us.

"I have an idea," Todd announces. "For our next adventure today."

"Okay." I relax back into how we were before the conversation of Trip. "I like the sounds of that."

"Do you trust me?"

Without a doubt. "Yes."

His smile is contagious.

He doesn't drive long. We park in front of a small shop with a tattered roof. When I get out of the truck, I can see the sign. The Nook. A bookstore. Is he going to buy me a book? Are we going to have a reading contest, see who could read ten pages the fastest? I think I would win that contest, but I won't reveal that quite yet.

Once inside the bookstore, Todd walks straight to the back and stops in between two bookshelves. I take a moment to look around. The store is cluttered and tiny, barely enough room for twenty people. The only other person in the bookstore is a teenager popping her gum behind the register. She seems bored, which annoys me instantly. I would have loved this job as a teenager. The lights are dim, gloomy, and the small part of the shelves that aren't holding books has a thick layer of dust on them. If the gum-popper weren't so preoccupied with her phone, perhaps she could dust.

We are standing near books about travel. Is he taking a trip?

"Okay," I whisper. "Now what?"

"Why are you whispering?" Todd whispers back.

"I don't know. It seems like the polite thing to do in a bookstore. Kind of like a library."

"Are you really worried about what a teenager thinks?"

I look back at the employee, who's now picking her gothic nails with a paperclip. I shrug. "Good point. Okay, what are we doing here?"

He rubs his hands together.

"The anticipation is killing me." The words are out before I can stop myself. I feel my heart drop and my body reel with at the word kill. Todd touches my elbow, bringing me back to him. I look down at where his hand meets my body. He self-consciously pulls away. Does he feel this too?

"You don't know whether to live with Trip or not, eh?" he begins.

"Right," I says, flustered at the mere thought of it.

"Well, then we will let the will of the Gods decide!" He throws his hands out wide. The Gods? What Gods?

"Okaaaay," I draw out the word, deciding to play along. What do I have to lose? Maybe the Gods can help me settle the what-ifs in my heart.

He leans against a shelf stacked with books on Italy. "Pick a genre."

"Young adult."

"Oh, interesting. Quick answer, quick answer. Why?" For a moment I am taken aback by his question. My mouth moves, but no words come out. No one cares enough lately to ask me questions, even the simple questions.

He weaves in and out of the rows of shelves until he finds the young adult section. His eyes twinkle with excitement. I loved seeing him this way.

"Because teenagers aren't afraid to feel," I respond. He doesn't ask me to explain further. He only nods, like he already knew what I was going to say.

"Okay, pick a book."

"Any book?" I ask, confused about where he is taking this.

"Any book. There is only one rule."

"There are rules to this game?" Is this a game? I find myself suddenly giddy with excitement.

"Oh, Ruth. It is not merely a game. It is the will of the Gods. It is your destiny. Your path." His voice is serious, but his eyes are shimmering with humor.

"What exactly is the game?"

166

"In a moment, you're going to reach for a book. You're going to open the book to a random page and then you're going to skim the page and stop your finger. Whatever sentence your finger lands on is the answer to your question. It will be your decided path."

Sounds easy enough. I spot a book with a colorful spine and reach for it, but Todd's fingers curl around my wrist, stopping me.

"Oh yeah. One more thing," he says.

"Another rule?"

"You have to keep your eyes closed—the entire time." He crosses his arms.

I smile mischievously. "Okay, then. Here goes nothing."

"May the Gods forever be in your favor," he pronounces. I laugh out loud, not caring if the teenager up front hears. He follows suit, and I revel in the deep, husky sound.

I stretch my arms, preparing myself for the task ahead, which only makes Todd laugh more. I take a deep breath before I begin. Eyes closed, I move my body to the left, extending my arms out and touching the spines of the books. I bend down, choosing a hardcover from the bottom shelf. I split the book in two toward the back, almost at the end of the story, and slide my index finger around and wait for the urge to stop.

"Did you forget the last rule?" Todd's voice says near my right ear. I can sense him standing behind me, peeking over my shoulder. I open my eyes and pivot my head to look at him. He inhales loudly, comically, and says, "No opening your eyes!"

I can't help but feel joy—a silly, crazy joy—when he is playful with me like this. My eyes travel across his features. I like the way he looks when he dishes smack talk. We stare at each other with stark intensity. I stop my finger on the page.

"Found it," I whisper.

He looks down at the page, breaking the spell between us. I follow his gaze.

It is perfectly true, as philosophers say, that life must be understood backwards. But they forget the other proposition, that it must be lived forward.

I understand what it means: that our experiences make more sense when we are outside of them than when we are in them. That we may know the why only after we have lived through the what.

"What does it mean?" I want to hear what he thinks.

Todd takes the book from my hands, holding it open like it was the holy grail of books. At first, I wonder if he doesn't understand, and then I notice the resolve on his features. This has struck a chord for him.

"It means that life is made up of two things: process and content. The experience of life is the process: our greatest teacher. Content is the people, the choices, the present interactions."

I glance around me, at nothing in particular. "Are you sure this is the young adult section?"

He smiles wide and slams the book shut.

"Wait! What book did I choose?"

"That is the last rule. You're not allowed to know. You were given your answer." He orders me to turn around and I hear him put the book back on the lower shelf. "Did you get the answer you were looking for?"

Am I going to move in with Trip?

No.

How can I? How can I live with a man who has never made me feel what Todd is making me feel in this one day? Living with Trip will give him the idea that we're serious, or at least becoming serious. I'm not sure I'm ready to be devoted to him—or to anyone, for that matter. I don't need a quote from the Gods to realize this, though. I need one day with Todd.

"No. I don't think I can." As soon as the words leave my mouth, Todd's grimace transforms into an expression of relief, and I ponder it. Why is he relieved? Why does he care?

Todd doesn't respond to my statement. He only puts his hands in his front pockets and walks out of the bookstore. Thoughts are churning in his head—I can practically see them being tossed around, and every once in a while, thrown to his heart, then thrust back to his mind. What is going on up there?

"Wait," I plant my feet. Todd turns and cocks his head. His smile is back. "You have to do it too."

"Okay," he responds quickly. "Same rules?"

I chew on that. "Yes, but I have to know the question."

He rubs his chin. "That's fair."

I cross my arms, relaxed and excited. "Where to?" He seems like the kind of guy who would pick a historical novel, a book about the aftermath of WWII. So I'm surprised when he leads me to the children's book section.

"Children's books?" I ask.

"Why not? If your young adult book yielded such a philosophical quote, I am curious what a children's book would say. Plus, it's simple. I like simple." Like the idea of simplicity is a luxury. I wonder if he ever knew what simple felt like in his life.

"Your question?"

He trickles his fingers across thin spines and broad book covers. His hand halts on a green book with a tree on it. My heart leaps. The Giving Tree: my favorite. I'm anxious for his question. He watches me watch him. Just as he opens the book, he asks, "What's next?"

What's next? That's what he wants to know? In reference to what? I don't push him to expand, though, granting him the same courtesy he gave me.

He closes his eyes and opens the book wide. He rests his palm on one page. "This one," he says confidently. He hands me the book. "You read it."

I do, reading about a boy who stayed away for a long time and wanted a boat to take him far away, the tree that tells him to cut down her trunk, to sail and be happy.

I quietly shut the book. "What does it mean?"

"That I can speak to trees," he says matter-of-factly. There is a lightheartedness in his features, but still I see more deep thoughts bouncing around inside him. I put the book back where it belongs and gently shove his shoulder.

"That's your destiny? I don't buy it."

He shrugs and loops his arm through the crook of my elbow. I fall into his ease, right next to him, not minding this spontaneous side of Todd one bit.

Chapter 33

Ruth

Todd drives to my parent's house and parks out front. The quotes—our destinies—circled in my head along with what he told me earlier: I just want you to be with someone who deserves you.

I'm not sure being with him was such a good idea. Being together doesn't feel innocent anymore. Being with him threatens the shell I've worked so hard to build around me, to protect me while I figure out how to live without Riley.

I hesitate to open the truck door, whether it's because I don't want to be alone or don't want to be without him, I can't tell.

"Let's make a deal." Todd interrupts my internal tug-of-war. "When you're sick of me, you tell me to go shove myself with gummy bears. But until I hear those words, I am not leaving you."

"Deal." I have to push the word past the enormous lump in my throat. I am thankful he made the decision for me, or else I may have stubbornly situated myself in his car until he dragged me out.

"I hope you don't mind dry humor and prosciutto pizza," I say as I unlock the front door.

He cocks his head and laughs. "My favorite combination, actually."

Silence clings to us when we enter. Although the house is empty, there are hundreds of stories that enshroud us at the door. I swear I can hear distant sounds of Riley's voice, vibrations from the tales told around the fireplace. I look at Todd. Can he feel that too?

He clears his throat. I place a hand on his shoulder and his eyes fly to my hand, just as I suspected they would. Each time I am physically near him, a shadow of disbelief passes his eyes, like he is alarmed to be granted such affection. Where did he learn to believe he was not worth that simple touch?

I remove my hand and clench my fist at my side, suppressing my desire to comfort him. He may not want it, and it may not be my right to give it him.

He slides his hands into his jeans pockets. "I haven't been here much since the funeral. Yet you have. You're living here with her ghost. I don't know if I am envious of you or saddened that you had to go through it alone." There is no premeditation in what he says or how he says it. No hesitation.

"I suppose all that matters now is that I am not alone." It feels like a gamble to mutter those words, even though I don't know what I am gambling away. My heart? My loneliness? I promise myself his answer didn't mean anything—as it shouldn't. We are nothing but acquaintances on our journey through grief. Nothing more.

He turns his back on me and starts for the living room, but not before I hear him say, "You were never alone."

~

A half-eaten pizza lies on the coffee table that both our feet are propped up on. We have watched two hours of Arrested Development. I look at the clock wearily, knowing soon I should say goodbye. I can already feel the crushing weight of silence that will likely swallow me whole when Todd leaves and I have to try to sleep. I push the daunting thought away and plaster a smile of gratitude on my face.

"You need to be home now?" I ask, hating that the question sounded more like Do you want to go? Do you want to leave me?

"Truly, I have no where I'd rather be. It is getting late, though." Todd yawns while looking at his phone. I left mine in the kitchen. Who's going to call me, anyway? Surely not my own boyfriend.

Todd stands up and holds out his hand to me. I take it and stand too, so that we are facing each other. I note the incredibly short distance between us. It takes all my willpower to stare straight into his eyes, unflinching, when I'd rather gaze at his collarbone directly in front of me so at least I have time to gather my thoughts.

"Do you mind if I crash in the guest room?"

An invisible bird flutters in my heart. He's stayed over before, many times. It's not like this will be any different.

I nod and step away from him. "Of course. Let me get you extra pillows." I walk pass the guest room to the downstairs closet. I hear him following me.

I grab a pillow and extra blanket, just in case. When I turn around, he is leaning against the guest room door. His sandy blonde hair is sticking out in all sorts of directions. He looks exhausted, and all because of me.

I began to apologize for making him do this, but knew he will refuse it, so instead I say, "Thank you for today. You could have been doing a million different things and yet you decided to be with a sad, lonely girl."

"That's not what this is, and we both know it." He gives me a kind, reassuring smile.

He would have done anything for Riley, but will he do the same for me? The thought makes my stomach turn. How can I even look at him as anything more than my sister's person? Doubt creeps like a slow mist under my rational thoughts.

"Good night, Ruth," Todd says before entering the guest room and closing the door behind him.

"Good night."

I shiver, as if my body can sense the lack of warmth from Todd's presence. I'm alone.

I climb the curved staircase, past Riley's room and into the darkness of my own bedroom. I crawl into bed. My eyes flutter shut only after I found Riley and my star sign patched together on the ceiling, a cluster of glow-in-the-dark stars in the shape of a crab.

~

I wake with a start. Not because of a noise, but because the silence of the house is rattling.

I try to fall back to sleep but can't, and I know why.

Todd is below me.

I can practically feel his closeness.

There was something in the way he looked at me today, rife with recognition. I felt like he was my mirror—showing me the walls I had built around my heart to manage my grief. He saw my walls and he saw beneath them, straight to the foundation of me. He is one of the few people who knew me with Riley and now without her.

One of my old professors said that when two people have chemistry, it's the result of magic. It's the creation of a "spirit child," when two souls are tethered together in an inarticulable way. A spirit child is said to be an unbreakable bond, similar to society's definition of a soul mate. But the term soul mate refers to the mating of souls as a monogamous process. My professor argued that we don't have one soul mate, but many people our souls are tethered to.

172

Although we can physically extricate ourselves from others when we break up, we may never be able to terminate a spirit child. Thus, no matter how much time passes in between seeing each other, the chemistry will remain. You pick up where you left off.

I remember I asked that professor what happens to a spirit child that's created, but ignored by two people? What will happen when two people who feel chemistry don't confront this chemistry? My professor told me that ambiguity and fear of instigating a relationship will keep the relationship stagnant—the spirit child will exist, but it will not be nurtured.

So, that's what I will do with Todd and my spirit child. I will ignore it.

Even as the thought flows through me, my legs are swinging over the edge of my bed as if they have a mind of their own. I slowly tiptoe down the stairs, debating with myself the entire way. I find the guest bedroom door ajar and hold my hand on the knob. What am I doing?

My thoughts and heart are waging war, but I know who will win. I open the door and take shy steps to the side of the bed, hesitating the entire way. I lower myself down on the bed and stretch out beside Todd. His breath is a slow, steady melody of inhales and exhales that immediately calms me.

I'm almost back asleep when a whisper brings me back to life. "Ruth, what are you doing here?" The voice is not accusatory, but strains with…something. Hope? Still, I freeze as if I have been found out. I stay facing away from him, calculating my next move. Should I tell him I didn't want to be alone? Or that his presence puts me at ease? Or that there is an invisible ribbon connecting us that we do not dare speak of?

When I don't respond, he lightly grabs my shoulder and rolls me toward him. I'm glad it is dark, or else I would have no shield for how this one motion renders me into rubble. I look in the general direction of his eyes and hold my breath. He doesn't say a word, but begins to lift the covers I'm lying on top of and motions for me to get under.

I am suddenly nervous of what he expects of me, but then I remember it's Todd. He's the most respectful man I knew.

Once I am under the sheets, my feet find his out of a misplaced instinct. I want to be near him. I can't. I want to. I can't.

He doesn't move his feet. They are warm, comforting.

"I'm sorry. I guess I wasn't ready to tell you to go stuff your face with chocolate-covered gummy bears."

He laughs out loud, brightening the room tenfold and shaking the thick tension. The sound makes me smile too. I let the smile linger, testing the way the action makes me heart feel.

"Good night, Ruth."

"Good night, Todd."

Chapter 34

Todd

I don't know where I am when I wake until I see Ruth's body next to me. I feel nostalgic at first, but then I let myself breathe easy at the sight of her. Of Ruth. Not Riley.

My mind drifts to the string of events of yesterday. Finding her at the cemetery, seeing the ring of grass on her finger and realizing that it was her—it was Ruth who stopped in front of me at Lake Harriet when my stomach was empty and my heart a bag of stones. It was Ruth who reached her small hand out to me and pulled me up, out of a dark pit of loneliness.

Her father made the call that changed the trajectory of my life, but Ruth and that wide, toothy smile softened me to the point where I could fully hear her father. It was the memory of her that continued to dissolve me through the days of meeting Pat, because like Pat, Ruth had been the only one rooting for me.

Ruth stirs slightly next to me, and I am an instant away from closing my eyes to pretend I wasn't just gawking at her. But she doesn't wake.

Her face is quiet, vulnerable.

I already know I'm falling, like feathers floating down.

Down.

Down.

All five fingers curl into a fist as I hold back the temptation to reach out and brush that strand of hair falling down her cheek. The bed sheets barely cover the black tank top she's wearing, and don't cover her cleavage completely. She has a mole on her right breast.

My face flushes knowing that her freckles don't stop on her face but cover the intimate parts of her body, too. With a bit of imagination, I could trace the constellation of Cassiopeia on her collarbone.

I have never seen her this exposed, both in her vulnerability and in appearance.

She is beautiful.

Instantly, I remind myself she's not the same beauty as Riley. I'm not feeling anything for Riley's sister because they were twins.

They are different. This feels different.

I have to move to shake myself out of these thoughts. I gently roll off the bed and out of the room, grabbing my clothes in the process. I dress in the kitchen and begin making coffee. It feels strange being here without Riley, but then again, it doesn't feel strange without her either. Ruth and I are used to this type of closeness, usually because of Riley's absence.

I've sipped half my cup of coffee when I hear Ruth shuffle into the kitchen.

"Hi," she starts. She's put some other, less revealing, clothes on.

"Good morning," I say.

She crosses the kitchen to get herself a cup of coffee. I watch her concentrate on pouring her cream in.

One.

Two.

Two seconds it takes for the cream to reach her cup.

She clears her throat. "Look, Todd—"

"No," I interrupt her. "I already know what you're going to say. And you don't have to."

Her mouth twists before she smiles, reassured. "Okay."

She leans on the island across from me, cupping her coffee in her hands.

"Did he call?" I ask.

"Did you wake up and stare at me?" she counters, deflecting.

I could lie. I should lie. "No. That is mildly disturbing. I woke up and made coffee."

She glares at me playfully. "Good, because I slobber when I sleep."

"You weren't slobbering."

She points her finger at me. "So you did look at me!"

I close my eyes—found out. And then we laugh. I bring my coffee to my lips and shake my head. "Only for a minute."

She rolls her eyes. I'm thankful for her indifference. And I realize I've never felt awkward with her. She's never made our circumstances uncomfortable.

"And no," she finally answers my question. "He didn't call. He texted me to tell me he was sorry that he didn't call earlier."

"That's big of him."

"Oh, don't be mean. I'm sure he was busy." She waves her hand in the air. I want to ask why she is sticking up for him, but I take another sip of coffee instead and let the warmth wash away my words.

"Plus, it's not like he is the only one who makes mistakes," Ruth's eyes are downcast. Shame and guilt creep up her neck in red. Somehow, I know she is referring to the time we shared yesterday.

"I see no mistakes here."

"Would you like it if Riley had slept in another man's bed?" Her eyebrow quirks.

Good point. "But we are different. You are practically my sister." Even as I say it, I know it isn't true. By the look in her eye, I could see she doesn't believe it either. I can see the words she wants to say tumbling around inside of her. Say it. Get it out.

"It's only a big deal if we make it a big deal." She shrugs. "Right?"

"Right," I say, to calm her guilt.

The silence settles between us. I finish my coffee and put the mug in the dishwasher. "When are your parents coming home?" I ask, simply out of curiosity. I walk closer to Ruth so we are on the same side of the island.

"This morning sometime. You know Mom—she likes to get out of Dodge as soon as she can."

"That she does." I think of Mrs. Schneider and any event she has ever attended. She usually leaves early and normally says goodbye to no one. It had been running joke amongst their family friends.

"I'll have a couple hours alone, and yes, I will be fine."

"Good. That was my next question." I hesitate, not quite ready to say goodbye.

"When did we start to know each other like this?" She tilts her head in question.

Like this…like we truly see each other for what we are, straight to the bones of us.

"Since the beginning," I say. But that doesn't resonate with her. And it wouldn't, because she doesn't know how far back we go. I sneak a glance at her pinky finger where the blade of grass was yesterday.

I kiss her on the forehead, a moment longer than I should, and then make my way to the front door.

Chapter 35

Ruth

I am sitting in my car outside of the little Mexican restaurant near Trip's apartment where he and his friends drink tequila like water once a month. Out of all the Mexican restaurants in Minneapolis, this is their favorite, because after they drink, they can walk to Trip's place to drink more and eventually pass out.

Every month, Savannah and Ali insist I go to these gatherings, claiming that Trip's drinking is insufferable without me being there to monitor. And every month I sit in my car for at least twenty minutes prior to entering the restaurant, preparing myself for the night.

I look at the clock. My head finds the headrest. I still have ten more minutes before I will get out of this car.

My mind wanders to Todd, as it usually has these past few days.

The mere mutter of his name in my head make my heart fissure, just a bit, in a good way. Todd and I simply laid next to each other. No touching, hardly any talking. It was completely innocent, and thus I have nothing to be ashamed of. I am not promiscuous, and he did not cross any boundaries and yet…I feel as if we did.

I tried to see traces of guilt on Todd's face the next morning, but I only saw contentment. Unless…he did feel that that night was a bad idea and was masking his feelings? The thought is ridiculous. No. He wasn't a masquerader. He has a way of speaking out loud the exact words hovering in his mind—no barriers, no waffling. It's one of the most freeing things about his presence.

Todd's personality is steady, patient. He has walls built from past hurt or misunderstandings, but still leaves his heart open for interpretation. He doesn't fear what others think of him and stands tall with a grounding confidence. He gets respect from men who aren't the competitive kind and swooned over by females of any and every type.

A direct contrast to Trip.

Trip has an avid look in his eyes at all times, and I'm never sure what side of him I would encounter from one day to the next. He was the first to wrap his arms around my broken heart. I can't say he has mended it, but I'm not sure I wanted him to. In the beginning, he wanted to be there for me in my grief. Lately, he's become my deflector. My distractor. Not because I want him to be, but because he can't hold my grief anymore. Not alongside his own, which is still there, in his heart. I can see it simmering like the thunder before a grand storm.

Trip has challenged me. He made me discern and fight for us. I thought the process of me fighting for us implied that there was an "us" worth fighting for. But he hadn't been there for me when I needed him most. And isn't that love? To show up?

When I finally gather the courage to leave my car and go inside, I locate Trip's friends easily. They are the loudest bunch in the restaurant. I look from Terrance to Vince and then the two girls, but see no Trip. I slowly back away, slithering against the wall toward the front door.

Outside, I lean against the brick building, inhaling the smell of tacos. My stomach rumbles. I wait another ten minutes, but still I don't see Trip's Toyota pull into the parking lot. I text him and wait ten more minutes. Nothing.

It's only a few blocks to his house, so I decide to walk there. Maybe I would meet him halfway. At least then we could enter the restaurant together.

I take the stairs in his apartment building two at a time. When I reach the fifth floor, I am out of breath. I round two hall corners before I am standing in front of his door. It's ajar. That's odd. My instincts tell me to proceed with caution, because Todd's paranoia doesn't call for such carelessness. There are red flags in my vision, warning signs. Something is array.

The stench of his apartment reaches me first. Old pizza boxes, dirty dishes, and past spills on the carpet make the small space rancid. Now this catastrophe is normal. It's been a while since I had been in his apartment. Usually he comes to me. Now I can see why.

I step with vigilance past the dirty clothes and trash like I'm tiptoeing around landmines, like any minute there will be an explosion, a surprise, something I don't want to find. My instincts flinch the closer I get to his bedroom. The silence of the place is louder than I could have imagined, igniting my nerves. I want to hear something—anything.

I push his bedroom door open. At first, I only see piles of clothes. Heaps of dirty clothes on the bed, on the floor, on his dresser. Then I see a limb. I think it's a foot, jutting out in front of the bed. My shoes are filled with concrete. I'm stuck. My gasp is the only thing that moves forward, out of me, and closer to him.

Fear, a wrangling, terrifying fear consumes me. I think of Riley on the road. Dead. I am not sure I am brave enough to walk around the corner to see more than his foot.

"Trip?" I whimper, hoping he will hear me. Wake up. Move. Do anything so that I don't have to take those last steps toward him.

He doesn't budge. Nothing.

"Trip!" I yell. I wait.

Nothing.

I close my eyes. I'm breathing out, but can't breathe in. It makes me dizzy. I know I should go to him. Life or death. Life or death. Life or death. It would be life if I move now. I inhale and take a step forward.

One.

Two.

Three steps.

I am to his body.

He is white. His mouth is slightly parted. He looks dead, but then—but then I see his chest rise and fall. It's a microscopic movement.

My eyes are frantic, moving in a thousand different directions at once, trying to find something stable and steady and okay to land on. Then they stop. My eyes stop. They sharpen in on what is next to Trip's arm, almost tucked under the bed. Almost hidden.

A needle.

A spoon.

I fall to the ground next to him. Slapping his cheeks and yelling his name. It takes days, hours, minutes, I don't know maybe seconds for him to flutter his god damn eyes open. And when he does, I back away from him. I back far away. I hit the wall and bring my knees to my chest, breathing heavily.

It takes a minute for him to wake up to this reality, to being found on the ground, with a breathing rate that is almost undetectable. I see his head spin around until he finds me. We lock eyes. I am backing far away into what feels like my own tomb, because this feels a lot like death.

"Ruth." He plays coy, confused, like he fell asleep on the floor. "What are you doing here?"

I know better than to fall for his act, but I can't tell him anything. I can't say a word, because my heart is sundered as if it was Riley I'd found. Like she is lying in front of me dead. Except Trip is there and he wakes up.

The syllables to all the words I want to tell him are lost, and I'm reaching

reaching,

reaching, trying to find them to hurl them at him because he deserves that. He deserves my fury.

He cocks his head at me. "What's going on?"

Like he doesn't know. Like he doesn't think I see him crawl his fingers closer to the needle and the spoon, pushing them and urging them to hide under the bed. His eyes shift then, briefly. Maybe I even imagined it. He knows that I know.

I curl my fingers into fists, digging bloody moons in my palms. "What is that?" I ask, even though I know. Even though he knows I know. Still, part of me is hoping it's not real, that that isn't his spoon. They're not his needles. That he hasn't decided to fade into the darkness. He hasn't made the choice to.

He stares at me, a dark glare that sends a shudder to the end of my toes. He is debating.

"It's heroin." There is no remorse. No sadness. No shame.

No. I grab my stomach as if he has punched me, a hundred times over. I ache. His eye contact does not waver.

I pull in a shaky breath. "How long?"

"A long time." Still, he does not look away from me. And I hate it. I want him to look away, to break this trance I am in because it feels like I'm wilting, and he is making me, and he is enjoying it enough to not let it stop.

Get up, Ruth.

I thought I heard Trip say it, but his mouth isn't moving. If he didn't say it, then I must have imagined it and then there is the fear again, rumbling through me.

Stop it. Get up, Ruth. Now.

No. I didn't imagine that. It's an old voice. A familiar one, as close to me as my own heartbeat, except it's not my heart speaking. It's my brain, and it's telling me to leave. To get away.

It's Riley.

Get.

I grab on to the windowsill.

Up.

I push myself up to standing.

Ruth.

I walk past Trip, out of his room, and toward the front door.

I am almost here, almost gone, when Trip comes up behind me and grabs my arm. I back away from him like he's on fire.

"Ruth—" he starts.

I yank my arm away. "Don't. Touch. Me."

The words are foreign, unlike me, but then I know the source of the words—the courage behind the words—it's Riley. Again. It's like we are little again and she is screaming for me to cross the cattle guard. To go fast and be brave and get through this difficult part of the journey so that we can play in the wild fields of Montana.

But I'm not little anymore. I don't hesitate.

This time I run.

Chapter 36

Todd

I stand on the banks of Lake Harriet, waiting for the sun to go down. Out of the 10,000 lakes in Minnesota, Lake Harriet is by far my favorite. It's a perfect circle. Happy families roam around the circumference of it, taking advantage of the long summer days and humid heat.

I feel a short pang of sadness, thinking of the family I would never return to, the family that long ago put me second. Then I think of Pat and know that God works in mysterious ways. She became my family, and if I wanted to, I could return to her home tonight. I could be within the confines of coziness too.

"Talking to trees, are we?" Ruth asks as she timidly walks toward me. I give her an easy smile, trying to convince her that she didn't just startle me. The skyscrapers behind her twinkle in the descending sun, creating a halo above her head. A serendipitous sensation washes over me, in complete awe of her. I didn't think she would come, considering I had just texted her an hour ago.

She is wearing black linen overalls with a white crop top that's really fulfilling its mission to reveal her midsection. I try with all my might to avoid staring at the small amount of skin showing. Her hair is in a high messy bun and dark-rimmed glasses rest on her nose. She is sad. I sense it instantly.

She sits next to me on my bench, nestled between two large aspen trees.

"They are good listeners." I motion to the trees. She doesn't respond. No witty comeback or snide jab.

Her energy is quiet, tense. Her eyes move absently from one pedestrian to the next, so unlike her normal intentional stare. She isn't analyzing. She is lost in her thoughts, and I am surprised how badly I want to know those thoughts, word for word.

She grinds her teeth.

"You're angry," I observe.

She strains her head further away from me. Her tiny fists are clenching and stretching. When she opens her palms, I see pink half-circles. This isn't the first time she's squeezed an imaginary stress ball.

"Yes," she says simply. She leans over and plucks a blade of grass from the ground. I watch her twist the blade around, making knots.

"Your left foot is tapping a million miles a minute," I point out.

She sighs and stills her foot. "Yes," she repeats.

"Look at me." I grab her chin gently and swivel her head to me. "What happened?"

Her face is still, but her eyes are restless. They ask and answer and get lost in mine.

Her lashes flutter. "Everything. Everything happened," she says vaguely.

My hand is still gripping her chin and it feels intimate—too intimate perhaps. I let go and rest my arm on the bench behind her, creating distance between us. I nod and look at the lake in front of us. I'd let her think in silence if that's what she needed right now.

We sit like that, in comfortable silence, until the day's light has faded a bit. The pedestrian traffic has slowed. The crowds have dispersed. I hear crickets begin their night song. In the distance, I see two younger girls rollerblading. They are hand in hand and coming toward our bench. I wait for Ruth to notice, because the image will to do something to her.

They are twins.

I hold my breath.

When the girls have rolled past our bench, Ruth breaks the silence. "Can I ask you something?"

"Anything," I say, and I mean it.

"Your parents were addicts. You were headed in that direction in high school, but you stopped. You don't drink anymore. Why?"

Of anything she could have asked, I don't expect this. One strand of her dark hair falls in her face, her wide eyes patiently anticipating my answer. I follow the path of freckles from her left cheekbone, across the bridge of her delicate nose, to her right cheekbone.

It's the easiest answer of my life. "If I didn't break the cycle, I wouldn't be any better than them."

A nod. Understanding. Sadness and realization cross her face. "Sometimes you're the only one I talk to these days who seems to understand how I feel." Her voice drops low.

I don't know whether I should pull her to my chest or destroy whoever made her feel this way.

"I am not used to this anger I feel," she confides, a voice barely above a whisper.

"Tell me about it. Sometimes I get angry for no reason. It scares me." My jaw tenses slightly at the sudden vulnerability.

Ruth takes my truth in stride. "Anger can be really loud you know. It's almost like anger has to be loud so that we will listen to it. Maybe..." she tapers off. "Maybe anger tries to tell us something, like a messenger of sorts."

"And what do you think your anger is telling you?" I counteract.

She hesitates, her voice faint. "That I am afraid." I wait, sensing she has more to say.

"I'm angry that I am so afraid of life without Riley. I don't know how to do life without her. She was my compass. I knew who I was because I knew who I was not. She was my other half. And now that she is gone, I don't trust myself to make the right choices about me, people around me. Trip..."

She stops as if she is trying to find the right words. She has a hard time speaking about Trip, and I don't blame her. I have a hard time hearing about that asshole.

"Ruth, you are becoming who you are supposed to be," I console.

"Oh yeah? Who is that?"

"Whole," I say. "You're not a half. Your identity is not based on what you are not; it's based on what you choose to be. Fear and anger are messengers; everything after that is a choice."

Suddenly, the sun goes behind a small cloud and a child begins to cry in the playground in the distance. My training tells me to turn toward that cry—to check for danger—but I cannot drag my eyes from Ruth.

"The only time I feel like I am truly healing is when I am with you." Her voice breaks.

I inhale sharply, taking in the naked truth of her words. She's right. And I'm the same way. The only time I feel like I'm remotely moving forward in my grief is when I was with her. This is the first time either of us has called attention to the unspoken exchanges and feelings between us. She did it—not me. Whatever this is between us, she feels it too.

Relief floods me. I gather my thoughts and step into the door she's opened.

"Me too. A little piece of my soul is lost each day I know Riley isn't here with me." I pause and steady myself. "On the flip side, a little piece of my soul is put back together each day."

"How so?"

The sun breaks free from the clouds and shines on Ruth's freckled face. I've never had to answer this question before, much like her other frank questions. I say the first and only thing on my mind.

"We love."

"We love?" Her face scrunches in confusion.

"Well, what if grief is just a mirror of love? Grieving Riley has shown me how much I have loved her. It has shown me the capacity I have to love, and to be loved in return. There is hope in that. It feels nonexistent some days, but it's still there. Hope is still there. The size of my grief is the epitome of my love for Riley and its sheer massiveness will eventually have to overflow out of me and into the world."

"A love forged from grief," she adds. Her words push the dark out of the crater in my stomach. My chest releases.

"Something like that."

"So what you are really saying is that you give your grief to others?" Her eyebrows lift with her playful tone. I take her joke as an invitation and smile a real, unapologetic smile.

"It seems selfish to keep it in." We both laugh out loud. I finally see her face revert to the Ruth I know, gentle and genuine.

"What did you love about my sister?" she asks. We've never spoken about my love for Riley. Not specifically.

I can't look at her as I mull this question over. It's one I have laid with into the early hours of the morning. The love was real, but did it come from my own natural inclinations, or because I thought she was Ruth?

"I loved that she was my light in a dark time, whether she came at the same time my life was taking a turn for the better or she was the reason I took a turn for the better, I'm not sure. I guess it doesn't matter either way, now that I think of it. I loved her regardless."

"But what did you love?"

I clear my throat, diving deep into the past. "I loved the way she didn't hide how she was feeling. What you saw is what you got. She was unapologetic for who she was." I continue to envision Riley, trying to push away the grief I thought had been old grief, gone away. But this grief feels new, because the more I talk about Riley, the more I realize I am falling for Ruth now. And in a way, this love for Ruth—old, but new—is pulling me further away from Riley.

"I loved that Riley was strong, really mentally strong. I never doubted that she wouldn't succeed. I loved that she brought a random bicyclist home for Christmas despite all our reservations, because she had a big heart. I love that she taught me about love."

"How so?"

"Well, I am not sure love is enough, honestly. It takes communication, commitment, having the same values and beliefs, the same stance on finances. I mean, the list goes on. But Riley taught me more than that. She taught me that love is a choice, and sometimes we have to let people go in order to see if they come back."

"And did you let her go?"

"Never," I say and finally look at Ruth straight on. "I didn't let her go, and that was problem. I'm not sure I gave her the chance to go, and hence didn't give her the chance to love me for me—for real."

Ruth seems to be soaking in my words, and I can't help by wonder if she is applying this conversation to her own relationship. What's going on with you and Trip, Ruth?

When she doesn't speak again, I stand up and offer her my hand.

"Come on. Follow me."

"I don't like surprises," she responds, echoing what I had told her on her birthday. I squeeze her hand, letting her know I was fully aware of how she was making fun of me. When we start strolling, I loosened my grip, thinking she will let go. But she doesn't. If anything, she holds me tighter, like if she doesn't anchor onto something she will float away.

Chapter 37

Todd

    I lead Ruth down the paved path that contours the entire lake until we reach the marina. I see her eyes brighten when we step onto the wooden pier lined with an array of sailboats. Her face lights up in a half smile. Loose strands of hair fly across her face, and I have to force myself to not reach out and tuck it behind her ear.

    We stop in front of a catboat called Swift Sammy. Ruth's whole body seems to relax in delight at the mere sight of it. I have to force myself to break my gaze from her innocent giddiness to check lines and tie a figure-eight knot on the bitter end.

    "What are we doing?" she asks with trace of disbelief.

    "What does it look like, Sherlock?" I tease.

    "You're taking me sailing?" She can hardly contain herself. I love seeing her this way, thrilled with the simplest of adventures. Does Trip ever do anything for her? Does he care about the sparkles in her eyes the moment she realizes she's about to jump into spontaneity?

    I shake my head, trying to get a grip, and finish untying the boat.

    "Are you okay?" Ruth asks.

    I keep my hands busy preparing the boat, annoyed that my thoughts are spelled out so clearly on my face. Or that she can read me like I read her. "Yeah, I am okay," I assure her with a smile.

    "It's like the children's book you chose at the bookstore," she says. "A boat to take you far away from here."

    "So I can sail away and be happy." I look up. We share a small smile.

    "Can I help you with that?" She gestures towards the knot I had failed to tie. Without waiting for my answer, she reaches down and ties a cleat hitch like it's nothing.

    I rub my chin. "Hmm. That looks better than mine." She scoffs and moves to sit near the tiller, checking to see if it's secure.

    I bend on the sails. She watches me attach the jib halyard shackle to the corner and then helps to attach the grommet in the tack to the fitting at the bottom of the forestay. We continue to move in harmony, her hanking the jib on the forestay and me running the jibsheets. Her smile grows into something contagious when the mainsail is raised and cleated.

Ruth takes us away from the dock and into the middle of the lake with the grace of a veteran sailor. She is all concentration and seriousness—simply adorable.

"Where did you learn to sail?" I ask, even though I already knew the answer. And Ruth doesn't know I know, because she doesn't know I saw them sailing before we met that day long ago.

"My dad. He used to take me when I was younger. We had a boat parked here until I left for college. Because I was the only one who enjoyed it as much as he did, and I wasn't around to do this with him, he got rid of it. I forgot how much I loved it, though." Ruth shakes her hair loose from the bun and lets the lake's breeze hit her face like she did when she was eight years old. "Where did you learn to sail?" she asks me.

"Pat sent me to a sailing and rowing summer camp one year. I kind of just fell in love with it." I smile at the memory of steering the boat for the first time. Absolute freedom.

In fact, this is the exact lake I learned on—Minneapolis' skyscrapers peeking up behind the lush, green trees surround the lake, just as they are now. I remember thinking how strange the stark commercial buildings looked in juxtaposition to the natural habitat of the lake. The air still carries a trace of fusty moss with contradicting hints of fresh, floral scents from nearby gardens. It may have been a mix of sensations then, but now when I look across the bow I feel a great sense of balance.

"Riley never liked to sail," Ruth reminisces, following my gaze across the bow. That's probably why you never knew that Dad and I used to do it."

At the mention of Riley's name, my mind tries to shift to memories of her and the deal Ruth and I made to share one memory every time we saw each other. But for the first time in a long time, I want to stay in the present moment.

"I know," I say, pointing out yet another difference between the two. "You didn't have much in common."

"No," she agreed.

We let the boat come to a standstill, the only noise when a small wave meets the hull. Ruth sits crosses her ankles under her and faces me. The sun is just beginning to set, and I can feel the temperature drop. The skyscrapers in the distance look bland without the sun's rays.

"A penny for your thoughts?" I prod.

"This is hard," she starts. I wait, hoping she will let me in. "I just can't help but wonder what Riley would say, or what she would feel, if she saw you and me—" She pauses. "Together."

I hold my breath.

"And what about Trip?" She stands up and paces the small walkway in the boat. She is on the verge of something, almost ready to share her thoughts about Trip to me. "I mean, we are still together, I think. I don't know. I still love him despite some horrible things he has done. I still love how he used to be."

I feel a pang of jealousy, quick and fleeting.

Ruth's hand flies to her forehead and she frowns. "Love isn't enough, though." Her hand falls limp at her side and she sighs, but only briefly. Then she begins pacing the small boat again, the strides matching what must be her racing thoughts.

"And," she continues. "And then there's you." She waves a hand in my general direction. I remain seated, slightly amused by her erratic demeanor, completely the opposite of what it was on land moments before. She talks as if she cannot hold it in any longer, like she has found the key to unleash the pent-up thoughts she's been carrying.

The boat moves in a teeter-totter motion, creating small ripples that extend from the hull to the distant shores.

"I get so excited when I see you, and it freaks me out. Am I betraying Riley?" She points to herself with both hands. "Am I betraying Trip? Although I feel as if he is the one who as betrayed me. I'm such a fool."

I want to stop her here, to ask what she means, but she saves no room for interruption. I cross my arms and let her continue.

"There are so many things you don't know about me, that if you did, you might not look at me the same. And…" She stops pacing to look at me. "You're Todd, for fuck's sake. You're nice to everyone, so of course you're going to be nice to me. You get what I am going through, because you are going through it too. Whatever I feel with you means nothing." She covers her face with her hands, the perfect image of confused, lost, and torn.

I can't see her like that any longer.

Before I know what I am doing, I tug at her arm, bringing her down to the bench with me, her hands still shielding her eyes, hiding her gaze from me. I take a deep breath and let the words rush from my heart into the open air between us.

"Ruth, do you want it to mean nothing?"

She spreads her fingers just enough for her green eyes to shine through with stern intensity, as though a mix of emotions are ping-ponging back and forth within her. It's like I can feel her resisting when I am leaning in, and I swear she leans in closer, longing for me, when I try my best to resist. We seem suspended in this moment until she drops her hands and bombards me with one little one-syllable word.

"No."

Something untamed flashes through her eyes. Her hair is a wild, careless. I clench my jaw in attempt to control the blush I know is blooming on my neck and cheeks.

"Do you trust me?" I mumble, grabbing her hands and rubbing her knuckles.

"Yes," she says, more quickly than I anticipate. I am glad she does, because right now I don't even trust myself.

I stand and step onto the seat, pulling her up with me.

"What are you doing?" Her voice hitches.

I take one more step closer to the fringe of the boat's hull, which sends me into a balancing act. There is more weight on this side of the boat. Ruth gasps in delight and looks at me with wonder. A huge smile spreads across her face with the realization of what we are about to do. Even still she questions me, "What are you doing?"

I tilt my head as if to say, you know what, but instead say what we always seem to say when we are together. "Follow me."

She throws her glasses onto the boat's deck with her right hand and holds my hand tightly with her left. I help her onto the ledge of the boat, both of us trying not to tip it before we are ready.

The water below is murky, and I check to see if Ruth is game for what we were about to do. My eyes are squinting with the width of my grin. Her face is full of desire. Desire to jump. Desire to feel free. And because I can see myself reflected in her eyes; I know she feels this desire to let go completely.

A small breeze brushes passed us, sending the loose strands of her dark chocolate hair flying. There is nothing in this moment I want to change. I try to keep my feelings in check, to hide my reactions to her beauty and to cut away the invisible strings pulling me towards her. I try, but this version of her, utterly content in this moment, unravels me.

"One," I count, looking away from her towards the dark water.

"Two," she follows.

"Three!" We yell in unison before we jump off the side of Swift Sammy into the water below.

I let the chill consume me, awaken me, and cleanse me. I stay underneath the surface a few moments longer, allowing the spirit of spontaneity to do its job and make me feel truly alive.

When my face breaks through the water, I gulp down a breath of fresh air. My clothes are soaked, making my body feel heavy. I work a little harder to stay afloat and twirl around two times before I see Ruth's head emerge.

I swim until I am close to her and her infectious laughter. She is moving her arms in slow circles, staying afloat despite the water's pull.

I am struck then by a new thought, so transforming and monumental.

I don't see Riley. I don't see Riley's twin. I don't see another man's girl. I don't see a girl with a broken heart, overcome by grief.

I see Ruth.

I see her in her entirety.

Chapter 38

Ruth

When Todd and I finally make it to his apartment in the city, I am shivering in my wet clothes. We were a slippery mess crawling back onto the sailboat after we had jumped into the water, both chortling after our third failed attempt to lift ourselves onto the stern. Eventually Todd swung himself over the boat's ledge and then proceeded to haul me up by my armpits. Just that slight touch awoke every sleeping cell in my body.

I'm becoming familiar with his hands, hands so unlike Trip's. Every movement Todd makes is with careful intention and a certain protectiveness. His gaze, his touch, and his words are a subtle reminder that good men exist. He's proof that there are men out there comfortable in the space of vulnerability, men who can express their feelings.

No wonder Riley fell in love with him.

And the way he looked at me...

Trip has never looked at me the way Todd did in the moments after we had jumped into the water. Like he didn't want to change a thing about me.

The thought of Trip puts a damper on me, sending my insides into chaos.

My thoughts are interrupted by the sound of Todd unlocking his apartment door.

For a bachelor, he is surprisingly tidy. I am impressed by the order and simple yet tasteful style. The apartment is small enough that when I stand at the front door, I can almost see every room. The kitchen is in front of us, with basic necessities sprawled out on his countertop. The living room is to the left, and his bedroom to the right. I glance at his bed, sheets pulled tight and tucked to perfection. What other military habits has he held on to?

Todd watches me take inventory of his apartment. "I know it's not much, but it works for now. There is a bathroom right over there." He signals to a door to my right. "I can get you some clothes to wear while we dry yours."

I slip out of my sandals and wait by the front door. He walks to the room with the perfectly made bed and comes back holding sweatpants and a shirt. He hands them to me, eyes never leaving my face, but I avoid his gaze by focusing on the clothes in front of me.

All the words I unleashed before we jumped into the water come back to me. There is no hiding from him now, not after what I shared. Whatever lines were drawn between us are now faded.

I take the clothes he offered and turn in the direction of the bathroom.

After I shut the door, I strip my heavily drenched clothes and start the shower. I let the hot water cascade down my body, trying to wash away the doubt. I shouldn't be here. I should go confront Trip about his drug use. I should force him to tell me what happened. Why he would do that to himself and to me? I want Trip to break down, to be vulnerable. I want to know if doing that will be enough to make me stay.

When I step out of the shower, my wet clothes are no longer in a pile on the floor. My skin flutters at the mere thought of Todd's proximity to my nakedness. I dry and dress quickly. I roll Todd's enormous pants by the elastic waist two times until I can see my red toenails peek out of the fabric. The shirt is plain and reaches my knees. I look ridiculous. My hair is another hopeless mess. I let it fall down my back, a tangled mop that dampens the back of the shirt.

I come out of the bathroom to silence. Todd is nowhere in sight. The laundry room must be a shared facility in the building. I notice a tea kettle on the stove, which seems peculiar for a bachelor.

I open drawers, looking for something warm to drink. I find tea tucked behind other random kitchen staples: peanut butter, jelly, rice, cans of beans, and so on. Once the stove is turned on, I scavenge for two clean mugs and some honey.

When I close the refrigerator door, Todd is standing in front of me. He leans against the kitchen counter, an amused twinkle in his eyes. He too has changed into sweatpants and a hoodie. There is something about men in sweatpants that make me suck in air. He puts a hand through his damp golden bronze hair and sweeps it to the side.

"Finding everything okay?" He grins at me, a grin I've seen him give Riley once upon a time, except this grin is slightly different. This one is mature, defined. And it for me.

I stop gawking and shut my gaping mouth, not sure if he is teasing me or being sincere. "Sorry," I finally pipe up. I didn't realize the way I moved about his kitchen without permission. "I thought maybe we could drink some tea?"

"You found tea in here?" he asks, sounding surprised.

194

My smile turns into panic. Did someone else—another woman—bring over tea? Did he have one-night stands? Is that how he coped with losing Riley? The thought makes my stomach lurch.

"It must have been Pat," Todd assures me, as if reading my mind. "She is a tea fanatic. What kind is it?"

I look down at the tea bags sitting in the mugs. "Peppermint."

"Yep. That's Pat."

I turn my back to Todd, not wanting him to see me as my heart expands with relief.

The tea kettle whistles.

"Honey?" I ask.

"Sure," he says, before walking into the living room.

"Cream?" I call after him.

"Nah." He returns to the kitchen with an afghan. I sit down at the table, and he wraps the blanket around my shoulders. His hands linger just moments longer than necessary. I don't even deny it. I wanted to feel him hold me—to put his arms around me.

"Thank you," I mumble.

"You're a natural in here." His eyes scan the kitchen before landing on me. "I haven't had anyone in here like this."

I raise an eyebrow. "You haven't had a girl make you tea?"

He laughs and clarifies. "Someone in my space, making me tea, who seems so comfortable in my home."

I look around. I am comfortable here, more comfortable and safer that I have ever felt in my life.

Before I can respond, Todd asks: "So how do you know where everything is? Have you been stalking me?"

I give him a sharp look, peering up at him. "Says the man who showed up at my clinic for a massage the day after he saw me for the first time in a year."

He laughs, a loud and wholesome sound. "Point taken."

"I don't know why I know where everything is in this kitchen. My gut tells me that the silverware is here." I point to a drawer near the sink. "Knowing you, you want to plan the path of least resistance, so you'd put the cups right beside the coffee pot. Military men don't indulge in delicacies like honey, so I knew that wouldn't be in a main cupboard if you had any at all."

"Wow. You're good."

"It's a science, really."

"How do you know what military men are like?"

Because I read Riley's journal and know more about you than you'd want me to.

"Like I said. Gut feeling." I try my best to put an authentic smile on my face.

"You're wrong about one thing, though," Todd teases, taking another sip of his tea. "Not all military men are the same. I happen to like honey, in case you hadn't noticed."

"Oh, I noticed," I say, meeting his stare. I noticed that and so much more.

Who is this version of Todd? This person who doesn't appear like the boy in Riley's journal or the grieving man who lost his girlfriend. No, he is different. Funny. Lighthearted. Embodying the kind of safety you feel with an army behind you. Like you can face anything.

I press my back into the chair, keeping my distance and reining in the desire pulsing through me.

He leans forward on his elbows. His face turns somber. "Ruth, I—"

"No," I interrupt, not sure if I'm ready for him to ask about whatever this is between us. "Don't. Not yet. I just want…" I hesitate. What do I want?

I think of Trip's lies, his pain, the heroin, the broken promises, my inability to let fully him in, the hole in my heart where my sister should be.

What I want was a night without grief, without lies, without surface-level choices.

"I just want to be in this moment, drinking tea with you, for a couple more minutes before I have to go."

He doesn't seem to like that answer, but he doesn't press me. And I think I love him for that, but then the silence settles between us and it's heavy with all the words I should say but am not ready to.

I focus on my breathing and examine the mug in front of me. My face has to be flushed, because my insides feel like they are boiling.

He is your twin's boyfriend.

Was…

Todd tilts his head, as though attempting to read me. I cover half my face with my mug of tea, hiding. He brings his cup to his mouth, mimicking me. His golden eyes peek over the mug. We both take a drink.

"Are you happy?" Todd asks. I watch the steam from my tea.

"I think I will be," I say.

"Are you happy with Trip?" Todd clenches his jaw, a nervous habit I've noticed.

"Sometimes," I say honestly. I almost tell Todd everything, because the layers upon layers of anguish that have built since I found Trip passed out in his apartment are ruining me. I can't taste my food. I can't sleep. I can't focus. I want to rid myself of those tiers of anger and sadness over Trip, over Riley, and I think telling Todd would be the antidote to begin the process of ridding these layers over my heart. Still, indecisiveness sews my mouth shut.

Soon. Soon, I will tell him everything.

I look at the stove and my heart leaps when I see the time. I know I could stay here tonight. Todd would let me. But I can't. Not until I know what's happening with Trip and me.

I scoot the chair back and walk over to the sink. "I better go." I dump the remainder of my tea and start walking, then I stop. "Laundry room?"

"Just past the bathroom," Todd says, and runs a hand through his blonde hair.

"Thanks."

I move out of the kitchen and toward the laundry room, nudging the door closed behind me with my foot. My linen overalls are still slightly damp when I pull them from the dryer, but better than drenched. It would have to suffice.

As soon as I slide my underwear on, I hear a sound behind me. Shit. Instinctively, I cup my boobs with my hands before twisting toward the origin of the noise.

Todd.

And his eyes. And his body. And everything about him.

His eyes try to stay on my face, but he fails. I see his head and his heart spar. When his eyes travel down my body, soaking me in, I know his heart has won.

I see his chest rising and falling. I don't know what I will do if we stay in this moment. If he keeps looking at me like he is. I don't trust myself, not even to move. My toes curl, trying to grip the earth. Anything to keep me grounded, because right now I am floating up and further away. I am being torn in two. My body in the air, my heart gone to the floor, in pieces. And I might shatter even more underneath his longing gaze.

I want him.

I can't.

We are dangerously close to the beginning of what could be.

I turn around, shaking, and try to put my bra on. I can't clip it together. Then I do. The straps hang loosely down my shoulders and I know I should pull them up, conceal myself, but I…

"Todd—"

"No, I'm sorry. I'll go. I should go." His words match my feeble resistance to him.

I turn back towards him, still exposed. Still not caring. "Wait—" I start with no idea where to take that sentence. The cracks in me pulse with eagerness. My willpower screams in protest, but my heart inches closer to him.

That is all he needs. Me to give an inch.

He takes two strides across the laundry room, reaching for me.

I meet him halfway. Every particle of my body wanting him, needing him close to me.

He is right in front of me. I am staring at his chest, watching him breathe. Heavily. My eyes move to his throat. He swallows. I lean into him, because I need him to hold me up, to be my strength because I am spinning. My bones are weakening. I am spiraling, spiraling, spiraling.

He brings his hand to my face, rubbing circles. My breath is hitching over and over again. His fingers curl around my neck, his thumb traces a gentle line on the apple of my cheek. He has me.

He draws my crumbling body to his. I arch into his embrace, wanting to savor this feeling but unable to grasp it. My feelings and my thoughts are fleeting, rushing through me as if I am a ghost.

He leans down as if he is going to kiss me, but stops.

Our eyes met. He looks at me as if he isn't' sure I am real. Like this isn't happening.

"I don't know what I am doing," he whispers, inches from my face. I'm worried I will vanish completely if he doesn't come closer because what I need is him near me to hold me together. He still looks at me, questioning, curious, frightened. He wants me to decide what's next.

"Me neither," I utter.

My body inches forward. I slowly stand on my tiptoes. My lips meet his. We both stay still, lips touching.

This is it. This moment. We've crossed the line of then and now. His heart beats wildly. I can hear mine pounding in my ears although I am not sure how it's still beating because I feel dead. A goner.

If he is surprised by my boldness, the surprise is short lived. He nudges my lips apart and sweeps his across my own. I dig my fingers into his back, pulling him closer to me so I can taste him—pine and wind and cinnamon. We don't think. We don't talk. We don't do anything but feel. And what I feel is like Christmas morning, straight A's, the moment before you drop on a rollercoaster. It's wild and free.

A small moan escapes me and it's like kindling, making our kisses desperate and urgent. Like we need each other to keep standing. To be okay. I stumble backwards. My back runs into the dryer. Todd grabs my hips and lifts me up in one swift motion. His mouth never leaves mine. He opens his eyes. He is looking at me and searching me like he still isn't sure this is real. Like he is waking up for the first time. And I want him to keep going, so I can drown in him. So I wrap my legs around his sturdy frame and tug him to me. My entire focus narrowing to the muscles of his back. I'm clinging to him, wanting him to be closer to me than he is.

He moves quickly. His hands. His kisses. He kisses my collarbone. My shoulder, my cheek. And then my mouth. Again. For a long time. He seems to be making up for lost time, for a year without touch. Then, an image comes to my mind.

I see Riley. She is staring through the rearview mirror of Todd's truck. She is watching me watch Todd. I am back to reality. It's cold and dark and I am back in my body.

"Wait," I urge.

I painfully pull my head away from Todd's. Our breathing is heavy. I untangle my legs from his midsection. His hands rest on the dryer near my thighs. His head hangs low. I can feel his hair brush my stomach. Impulsively, I run my hands through it and place a kiss on the crown of his head. "We can't do this."

"I know." He brings up head up, slowly, and now we are eye level. "You're right." He steps away from the dryer, and I hop down. I am wobbling in front of him, trying to regain my composure. We stand staring at each other and my heart pulls me toward him, untrammeled. He can feel the invisible tug on his own heart. I know he can. He steps toward me and pulls me against him. Again. His lips are soft but determined, like this will be our last kiss. Ever. I kiss him back feeling every ounce of regret, passion and longing. My eyes squeeze shut tightly. My insides ping and pong.

Don't stop. Ping.

We have to stop. Pong.

He releases abruptly me and walks out of the room, shutting the door behind him. I am left reeling. My body swirls in circles and my mind follows. My hand flies to my chest in attempt to calm my fluttering heart.

What did you do?

My stomach is sick.

Oh Trip...what did I do?

I dress quickly and go to the front door of his apartment. He is waiting for me there, head hung low and hands on his hips. His jaw clenches, one, two, and three times before his tortured, golden eyes look at me.

"Ruth," he says in a strangled voice, like my name is both an apology and a craving.

"It's not your fault," I say to both of us, in hopes that this guilt will subside.

"I shouldn't have. I know it's wrong. But dammit, Ruth"—he grabs my hands in his own—"I..." He is on the verge of saying something but thinks better of it. His gaze searches me. His hair's disheveled.

"I should go."

He only nods, fighting whatever compulsions he has left. He opens the door for me, and I step through. Normally, I wouldn't look back. But today, I want to. I peer over my shoulder at Todd's figure leaning against his door. A mix of emotions on his face. I can't read them all, but still I let myself look.

200

Chapter 39

Todd

I am destroyed. Ruined. Utterly wrecked. Any ounce of willpower I had in resisting Ruth has been demolished. I can't go back, not after knowing what she feels like against me. Not after feeling her soul in that kiss. We gave in, and that decision created a crack in both of us. And I felt her soul, like a living creature, came forward from the depths of her to peek out of the crack. Whatever lived in her came out to greet whatever lived in me. When our bodies pulled apart, and I felt the hollowness in my chest, I knew. I knew she was my lacuna—my missing part.

I felt her...

Her body pressed against mine, those perfect breasts matching the curvature of her body. Her tender and all-encompassing warmth. Those green eyes fighting so hard not to feel what she really felt. She was a mess. Such a beautiful mess that tasted like honey and peppermint tea. I wanted more of it.

I roar in frustration. I messed up. How can she trust me now that I've given in—pushed the boundaries when she was clearly with someone else? It's disrespectful. I know it. Who's to say I won't do that with another girl if I were to be with Ruth?

No.

Fat chance.

There is no other girl.

I can only see Ruth, and my God, I can't go back to whatever person I was before that kiss.

I almost went to her at least five times last night, but what was I going to say? What if Trip was there? Hey Trip, your girlfriend and I just made out. It was the best kiss I've ever had in my life, even compared to her sister, which is all disturbing in itself, okay. But I can't live without your girlfriend so could you just...get out of the picture?

I bang my head against my bed frame and try to ignore the fact that Ruth's presence is still lingering in my apartment. I can practically feel her.

I will fight for her when the time comes, if the time comes, but until then, she has to be the one who made the first move. Even if that means she doesn't make a move at all. Even if that means she hates me and doesn't ever want to talk to me again.

I know I will follow her lead. I have to.
I owe her that much.

Chapter 40

Ruth

My hands start shaking the moment I get into my car and keep shaking as I clutch the doorknob to my apartment. They're still trembling when I unlock it and walk in. I take my shoes off and head for the bedroom. I don't need the lights on to maneuver my way through the living room. My body remembers where every piece of furniture sits. I know how many steps it will take to reach the comfort of my bed.

The darkness is interrupted. A lamp in the living room flickers on.

I yelp in surprise and my hand flies to my chest.

Trip.

Bloodshot eyes, solemn stare. Drunk Trip. On instinct, my eyes shoot to his arm resting on the side of my couch. Flashes of him lying beside his bed hit me. I remember the inside of his elbow. Trip crosses his arms on his chest as if he was just tracing the flow of my thoughts.

I take in his demeanor in attempt to gauge what type of drunk he is, how drunk he is. A tall glass of tequila and the tequila bottle sit on the side table next to him. His eyes are fiery red, either from drinking or crying. Perhaps he's angry. I know it's best to wait for him to speak first.

"It's late," he says, his voice accusatory. I keep my distance, waiting, hoping he'll let me by him so I can go to bed.

"Yes. I know it is." I keep eye contact, praying he won't smell my deceit or my sudden fear.

He reaches his hand in the crack of the couch and pulls out what appears to be a book. It takes me a moment to register what's in his hands.

Riley's journal.

I had left it on the couch earlier today.

I look between him and the journal, trying to predict where he was going to take this conversation. Unease writhes in my stomach as I think of Trip handling my sister's journal. I don't want him to know her private and sacred self. I don't want him to know Todd, because they needed to be separate. I want and am trying to keep them separate.

"When were you going to tell me about Todd?" he spits.

Not separate. The unease of Trip and the safety of Todd can never be separate.

My lips seal into a tight line. I don't know what he wants me to say. Does he know what just happened between Todd and me? Is it spelled on my face?

"Answer me!"

I jump slightly but then square my shoulders and ground my feet into the wood floor. He will not see me afraid.

"What do you mean?" I ask. He can't know what just happened...unless he was following me? He must read the confusion on my face, but he doesn't acknowledge it.

"Don't lie to me, Ruth." The fire in his eyes never banks. "I know about Todd. I read about him in your little journal."

Oh my God. The fear in me builds at the insanity of Trip's words. My mind scrambles through all Riley's passages, wondering how he could possible mistaken Riley's journal for my own. There is only one explanation, and it's terrifying. He is too far gone to register that I didn't go to medical school or that I didn't go to Guatemala. If Trip was sober, sane, here in this dimension with me and not so fucked up, he would see that these facts are as plain as day.

But he can't.

I gulp down my horror.

"Real cute how you two met. It's right out of a fucking storybook." I can see his fingers turning white from his hold on the glass cup. He throws the journal on the couch beside him.

"Not only did you fuck Todd, but you also decided to fuck Zeph. That's a lot of fucking. I'm curious though"—he brings a finger to his lips—"did Todd know about Zeph? Or would he be just as confused as I am right now to know you're a sneaky slut?"

"You have no idea what you're talking about," I mutter.

"Don't look so goddamn dazed, Ruth. You've been with someone this whole time—" His face goes blank. He's just realized something. After he chugs the rest of the tequila in his glass, he starts laughing. It's a manic, villainous laugh. "You're unbelievable. I met Todd outside O'Reilly's. You were in the alley with him. What were you doing then?" He cocks his head. "Screwing me over behind my back?" I watch his eyebrows rise toward his hairline. He is taunting me.

"Stop." I attempt to sound assertive. I've handled many versions of drunk Trip, but this is one I have yet to experience. I can see the hatred in his eyes and the tendrils of a familiar dread creep up my spine. "That is not my journal, Trip. That's my sister's. If you weren't so drunk, you'd be able to see parts in there that point to that."

He considers this for a brief moment, but I can tell he doesn't believe me. He doesn't want to. I back up towards the door. He sees my feet shuffle and stands up from the couch, drink still in hand. He sways and tries to maintain balance. He closes his eyes and rests his palm on his stomach, like he is about to be sick.

"I'm so sick of this, Ruth."

"Of what?"

"You! Your lies!"

"I told you, Trip. That journal is not mine."

"All you do is mope around. You're depressed and you're not doing shit about it. I'm sick of you being like a zombie!"

I'm flabbergasted. Where is this coming from?

He walks back to the bottle of tequila to pour himself more. "You walk around like a ghost. I'm making love to a ghost." He starts laughing hysterically and slams down the bottle. "Wait—is it making love? I mean—do you even consider it making love, or do you use me at your convenience?"

No more. I won't take this.

"You want to talk about sorry-ass behavior? Tell me about the heroin, Trip. Tell me why you keep drinking when you told me you'd quit over a year ago." I can't stop. Everything that's piled up comes spilling out of my mouth. It's terrifying. It's invigorating. "Let's talk about why you do it, shall we? Tell me how you blame yourself for your father's death and you find it necessary to owe yourself spoonful of regret with each stiff drink you suck down. Tell me why you cover up your own insecurities with drugs."

My hands are shaking again. My body is trembling. My face has surely gone crimson, heated by uncomfortable anger. I feel like I might faint.

Trip stares at me with wide eyes, as if his own father had slapped him. I stare back.

"You of all people should know what it's like to lose someone," I go on. "How dare you point fingers at me and say I'm moping around. So what if I am?" I throw my hands up. "My twin sister died!"

"A year ago!" Trip fumes. His arms spread away from each other, as if he has to get bigger. Louder. I watch tequila spring out of his cup and onto the floor, almost in slow motion.

"And that..." I pause. "Is precisely what you don't get." He doesn't understand. Even if I open my heart to him, he won't understand. He won't understand that there is no timeline for grief.

And then it hits me.

He's been running his whole life. Not once did he face the hard truth of what happened to his father. He stores the memories in the deep crevasses of himself and does all he can to forget. Trip doesn't want me to remember Riley. He expects me to tuck my pain away, just as he did.

But I won't.

I let that conviction ripple through me like thunder, letting the spark ignite a part of me long forgotten. I feel my shoulders relax down my back. He can't hurt me.

Trip eyes me with a serpentine glare.

"Tell me why," I cry out. "Why are you doing this to yourself?"

He takes a drink of what's left in his glass. "Because the alcohol isn't enough."

My eyes jam shut. I swallow the lump in my throat. How did we get to this point? My brain says to turn around and leave this place, this space Trip and I are in. And yet, despite the heartache, I can't bring myself to leave. Not yet.

I try one last time.

"You don't have to do this to yourself. We can get you help," I say.

"Me?" He gestures at himself. "You really think I am the one who needs help?" He paces back and forth in front of the couch. I keep my distance near the door; I've barely moved an inch since this all began. "When you get help for your depression and stop fucking Todd or Zeph, or both, then I'll consider getting help."

"This isn't about me."

"Oh really?" he chides. "I think it is."

"Fine. If I go see a therapist, then you will go to treatment?"

"You forgot one piece."

"I'm not doing anything with Todd." Just kissing him...

"So it's Zeph, then?"

"No."

"You're unbelievable," he says before storming past me towards the front door. He zigzags the entire way. And even though I can't stand to be near him, I can't let him drive, either.

"I told you," I go on. "That journal is my sister's. Not mine. You have to understand that at least."

Trip looks at me with empty, cold eyes. And I know then that I have lost him. Anything rational won't reach him. It won't matter. He's already made up his mind.

"Trip. No," I say. "Please. I will leave. Just go to bed."

"Oh yeah? Leave to go where? To snuggle up close to Todd? I'd rather I'd leave and spare myself the mental image." He violently shoves his feet into his shoes and reaches for his keys. I step in between him and the door.

"Please. You shouldn't be driving. You know how I feel about you driving like this."

"It's not your choice to make."

I push my back into the door behind me, fusing myself to it, anything to create a barrier between Trip and his own destruction.

"No."

"Move," he says through gritted teeth. I can smell the stench of tequila.

"No."

"Ruth. Now."

I recoil at his intensity. We are at a standoff, vehemently staring at each other.

"Damnit, Ruth," Trip says. Then he takes me by the shoulders and shoves me aside.

I hit the corner of a table before I fall to the ground. All of it happening too fast for me to comprehend. Pain, like lightning, shoots down the side of my body.

I catch a glimpse of Trip rounding the corner of the hallway. His stomps echo as he runs past the elevator and down three sets of stairs. Moments later, I can hear the door of my apartment building being slammed shut.

I inspect my throbbing arm and bruised leg, in too much shock to move.

I keep waiting, hoping, for Riley's voice to come to me like it did the night I found Trip out cold in his apartment. I want her to tell me to stand up. To move on. To get myself together. But I hear only the dull thud of my heart.

Chapter 41

Ruth

My phone's vibration brings me out of a trance. I've been reading and rereading each line of Riley's journal, trying to pinpoint the exact part that set Trip off. But now, I close the book and look at my ringing phone.

Monica, it reads. Trip's Mom. And God, it's two o'clock in the morning. Worry floods me. Something isn't right.

My heart accelerates and a zap of adrenaline hits my stomach. "Hello?"

"Ruth," Monica says, her voice breaking. "It's Trip. Something happened."

Time is frozen. I've been here before. I've had this call this before. The last time I had heard those words were from my own Dad when he told me Riley had gotten hurt, and the prognosis wasn't good. I don't realize I haven't responded until I hear Monica repeat my name over and over.

"What?" I manage. "Tell me."

"He's in the hospital. I just got here."

I make my way to the door, replace my socks with slip-on shoes and grab a jacket.

"Which one?"

"Regions. Fourth floor."

I hang up and tear down the stairs, deciding to bypass the painfully slow wait of the elevator.

Don't be dead.

Don't be dead.

Don't...

~

I break into a jog as soon as I park my car. I reach the front desk of the hospital in two minutes, steadying my breath.

"Trip—" I don't have time to finish before Monica comes out of nowhere and grabs my arm.

"This way."

I give her a sidelong glance as we rush down the hall, almost afraid of what I will see. She stands tall for a woman with a son in the hospital, which makes me think his condition may not be that bad. Her eyes are slightly red from crying, but that is the only sign of her worry.

"What happened?" My words are rushed. I know I should have stopped him from leaving the apartment. She looks back at me, weighing how much information she can divulge, but I can tell she will not hold back. Not with me.

"Police officers found him in his car...off the side of the road. No real damage to him, or the car for that matter, so he didn't hit anything." I wince at the word. Monica's face scrunches in pity and she swears. She squeezes my shoulder, an apologetic gesture.

"He was highly intoxicated. The doctors said that alone was worrisome, but then they told me he had heroin in his system. They found pills, God knows what kind, in his car..." She stops in the middle of the hall way and looks away, distraught. Her lips quiver before she puts her hands on her hips. Her chin reaches her chest. "How did I miss this?"

How did I miss this? I think. How did I miss it for so long until now?

"He is good at hiding—even from me." I bring her into a hug, suddenly exhausted from the emotions surging through me. Disappointment, anger, and above all sadness for Trip. To go to such great lengths to escape...to avoid feeling. Was his reality that bad? Should I have done more? Been more? I push the thought aside while simultaneously pushing Monica away. A nurse passes us in the hall and eyes us with pity.

"I want to see him," I say and continue walking the direction we were headed.

She follows me, but I see her shake her head. "I don't think he is in any condition to see anyone."

We reach a fork in the hallway. "Where is he?" I press.

Monica gestures to the left, either too tired to fight me or knowing that eventually I'll get my way. I pivot left and start down the hallway as she mumbles out a room number.

When I get to Trip's door, I pause. I'm terrified of what I will find. The only reassurance I have is that he is not dead, that Monica is still upright, and thus hasn't been broken by what he's done. She did not have the face of a mother who had just lost a son. The fact consoles me as I inhale. Exhale. Inhale once more and open the door.

At first, all I can hear is the beeping of machines—a welcoming reprieve from the hospital silence, proof that he is alive.

Beep.

Beep.

I count the beeps in my head, still afraid to hear that one lone, flat line of dread. The sign of death.

Beep.

Beep.

The room is dimly lit and eerily quiet. I walk to the side of his bed and stare down at his frail body. Purple fingers protrude out of a cast on his right arm. A gauze bandage wraps around his head. He looks like he barely survived the biggest fight of his life. Like he was wrestling with a demon, and the demon won. I can't take my eyes off his skin, pearly white except for the black and purple bruises under his eyes. I look at the IV drip near his bed and the slow rise and fall of his chest under the thin hospital gown. I glance down at his hands and remember how they used to wrap around me. How can those same hands be the bridge to his destruction, or the hands that pushed me to the ground hours ago?

Oh Trip, what have you done?

I don't know how long I stare at him—it could have been minutes or hours—before a soft touch brushes my shoulder. Monica looks kindly at me, offering a sterilized hospital blanket.

"The doctors say he has a lot of recovering to do— internally," she says. "He has to detox, which is never a cakewalk. I remember." Her eyes go to another place, and I feel like an intruder sharing this moment with her, so I force my eyes to look at Trip.

"Being here under these circumstances is not ideal, but…" I start, treading lightly. "But I'm glad he is here. We can't go up until we hit rock bottom."

I don't exactly know what I am saying, but regardless the words slip out, rounding and forming a phrase resembling hope. Monica's eyes meet mine and we are clearly in silent agreement: how much worse this could have been. How fortunate Trip is to be alive.

Beep.

Beep.

Beep.

"Why don't you go home and rest?" Monica suggests. "I'll call you if anything changes."

A nod. I don't move. She tries again. "You will be the first I call when he wakes up." At this small assurance, I stand up and walk to the door, looking back one last time before I leave.

Chapter 42

Ruth

I'm groggy when I wake, and the dregs of a deep, exhausted sleep try to convince me to go back to bed, to put the pillow over my head and disappear, but then I wouldn't be any better than Trip using whatever he could to escape.

I will be strong. I will not run from this tidal wave of emotion. The events of last night flash before me, one short scene, then another.

I scream into my pillow.

I look at the clock. Noon. Shit. How did I sleep that long? I instantly feel guilty. I should be in the hospital. I should have stayed with him all night.

Should. Should. Should.

The shoulds are suffocating. The opposite of what my heart wants.

There are four messages on my phone, all of them from my mom. Monica must have taken the liberty of calling my parents to check in on me. I count to ten before dialing my mother, knowing I would have to pacify her and convince her of my sanity.

Two rings. "Ruth, thank God. Are you all right, honey? Monica called. She told us. I just can't believe it. Heroin?" She says it like a question. I maintain deep, even breaths in and out waiting for her to take a breath of her own. "He must be going through some dark stuff, really—"

"Mom," I interrupt, "He will be okay. I am fine."

"Please!" She dismisses me. "Come home right now. You need to be with your family." In the past, I've learned that refusing her would bring us to an impasse, but today I hold my ground.

"Mom, I am okay. I'm going back to the hospital in a few and then I will call you later."

She continues like I didn't say a word. "I just worry about you, honey…I'm not saying Trip is a bad man, but this…this is not like you to be with someone with so much…" She grasps for the correct word. "…baggage."

I close my eyes. Leave it to my mom to say the truth out loud, no matter how sour it may sound. It's ten minutes before I tell my mom I am really leaving now and hang up the phone.

I think of the baggage my mom mentioned. My mind wonders to Trip as a young boy, standing over the body of his dead father, and then as an adult feeding this seed of guilt with alcohol. I ache for that young boy who lost his father. Would Trip's life have been different if his father were here? Would he still use drugs to cover up his pain, even if that pain wasn't death?

I think of my own loss. I think of what Todd's lost.

We can't choose what we lose. But we can choose how we react to it.

The answer, the answer to whether or not we heal at all, seems to be wrapped up in choice.

~

When I get to the hospital, I have to reach into my foggy mind for the vague directions Monica had given me when Trip was admitted. I turn right instead of left on the fourth floor of the hospital, I have to backtrack until I find Trip's room. When I round the corner, I notice he is alone save for that damn, irksome, wonderful beeping from the machines. The blinds have been lifted, allowing rays of light to pour in and rest on his gaunt face. Despite the shadows under his eyes, he looks serene, so unlike the man bellowing at me last night.

I walk to the windowsill, my eyes never leaving his face. I watch him silently for a few moments, his chest barely rising and falling. I don't want to wake him from this deep sleep, so I sit and wait.

What will happen when he wakes up? Will this accident be the tipping point toward change?

I position myself on the wide windowsill with my legs stretched in front of me. Sirens roar in the distance, the sound making me think of heartache and of tragedy. I block the noise out and rest my head on the wall behind me, focusing on the sun's heat kissing my skin. I watch Trip, waiting for any movement.

Four painfully long hours pass. The ticking of the clock and the beeping of the machines nearly drowns me. I am hypnotized by the way his chest rises and falls, slowly. They are short breaths. I fumble for words, rearrange the syntax in my head so that when he wakes, I will know exactly what to say. A speech prepared. But my mind is blank.

214

"Ruth," a voice croaks at last. My eyes must have shut, because I feel them snap open quickly. I jolt to sit up and feel the blood rush out of me. Trip is awake and too weak to sit up himself, but he is trying. I watch him for a minute, wondering if I should go help him, but I don't. He eventually lies back down, defeated.

I hop off the windowsill and force my shaky legs to carry me to the chair next to him. I keep my distance, hesitant. His dark, hollow eyes stay on me, waiting. Filled with sorrow and longing.

"I'm so sorry," he starts. His voice is soft, questioning. He closes his eyes for a split second, and when he opens them, a single tear falls down his face. I want to reach out and catch it, save that proof that he feels something and is still alive, that reminder that pain won't kill him. He can do this. He can face his pain.

"I don't remember everything, but I know I must have been terrible if I deserve that look you're giving me now."

I try to rearrange my face, but nothing happens. My features stay stone cold.

Blacking out isn't something unfamiliar for us; this isn't the first time Trip had lost consciousness and left me to fill in the pieces for him the next day. I've done my best to minimize his behavior, but not this time. I want him to know how his actions impact me, how they stab a thousand little needles into me.

I hardly hear my own voice when I tell him, "You were an ass."

I sit down in the chair next to him. He scrunches his eyebrows together and mutters, "What happened?" I lean forward, resting my elbows on my knees, my fingers in prayer formation, temporarily sealing my lips shut. Because even though I know what I need to say, I need the right words to say it. To say it in a way he will understand. Because if I do this, then I need him to change.

"Trip, so many things happened. I don't know where to begin."

"Anywhere," he pleads. He seems desperately afraid of seeing me in this state. "Begin anywhere." His eyes beg me to speak.

"First, I need you to tell me more about your dad."

I wait for him to respond, and watch him shift around, clearly uncomfortable with the truth pushing its way up his throat.

We hear a knock on the door and a nurse barges into the room. She looks back and forth at us, a welcoming smile on her face. "Just here to check Trip's vitals." When we don't respond to her, she averts her eyes and quickens her movements. She leaves without so much of a word. Trip's gaze never leave mine the whole time. I didn't think he would open himself up to me, but then he begins.

"I've lived my whole adult life without a father. I know other kids who lost a parent, sure, I know that it happens. Most of those kids have parents who die in a car wreck, or drown, or cancer, or God forbid in a fire as they were trying to save a helpless child, something like that. Don't get me wrong; any kid who loses a parent, no matter how that parent dies...that's catastrophic for that kid. It's a tragedy, but the real tragedy..." A second tear fell down his cheek, "The real tragedy is when your parent dies by choice."

I stay mute and neutral in hopes that he will continue on.

"He didn't leave a note. He didn't leave us anything, but the messy pieces to pick up in his wake. I found him—" Trip doesn't even try to wipe his tears away now. I stay still, despite already knowing bits of this story.

"I found him dead in his room. I was so excited to come home that day because it was my birthday. I knew he and I would go to the airport that night, watch those planes. But as soon as I saw him lying there so lifeless, I knew we wouldn't make it. How silly is that? That my father is lying dead in front of me and all I can think about is how we won't make it to the airport to watch the planes take off. How selfish."

"Typical," I murmur. His head swivels fast. I prepare myself for a fight, but one side of his lips twitches upward in a small, affirming grin.

"You're right. I am selfish."

I reach for his hand, that familiar, yet strange, hand. His eyes fall to our entwined hands, and then they meet my stare. There's hope in his eyes. An image of us lying on the hood of his car at the airport sends a ripple of nostalgia down my spine.

"I don't deserve you." His eyes are fixed on me with so much intensity that I have to look away. We both know I don't deserve this.

"You need help," I insist.

"I know."

216

"The doctors said you could have died, Trip. Do you understand that?"

He takes a moment to think about the question, the pause saying more than any words ever could. "I thought for a long time I could deal with my dad's death on my own, if you call ignoring it dealing with it. But then I felt this darkness blanketing every inch of me—my heart, soul, skin, thoughts...I was dark. You know when you're little—" He pauses, as if pondering how to best articulate his thoughts. "You're scared of the dark because of the unknown, but then your parents come into your room and reassure you that you're not alone? They are only ten feet away if you really need them.

"This darkness isn't like that. This feels like a never-ending eclipse, and I am alone, and I can't see where I am going. When I drink, I feel...I don't feel great, but I feel something. That feeling gets me out of the darkness and into the present moment where I can see." His eyes widen, like he is witnessing something for the first time.

"When I drink, I can see you, and God, you're so beautiful." His body sags. "I can see Vince, Gus, and the others right in front of me. I can feel the music. I can...feel. And when I wake up, and I am sober, then the darkness tiptoes in again. Sometimes, the only way I can see what is in front of me and feel anything is if I am drunk."

His mouth makes a tight line, but his body relaxes, relieved to be telling me the pieces of this internal world he's kept hidden for so long. We both let the dust of those words settle around us. I remove my hand from his and brace myself for what I'm about to say.

"Trip," I begin gently. "One day, you will kill yourself. It may not be pills. It may not be a gun. All the same, you will hurt yourself to the point of no return, and I don't think I can stand by and watch you do it.

"Your mom didn't know about your dad's depression or his opiate use, but you bet your ass she would have done something to help him if she knew. I know. I see you. You're crumbling in front of me."

His face contorts like a wounded animal's. He stretches his hand out, wanting me to take it again. But I keep my distance. I have to.

"This version of you, the one I was so graced with last night, is one I cannot live with. You hit me, Trip." He cowers. "You accused me of cheating. You were determined to believe I wrote that journal that actually belonged to my sister. You would have known better if you read closely or if you asked me. You got in the car drunk. Do you even remember how my sister died? Do you not even care?" My lips start to quiver, and tears threaten to come down. And then everything that was building up—the emotions, the thoughts, the resentment—comes tumbling out of me in one final blow.

"I'm sorry you lost your father, I really am. No one should have to go through the death of a parent, let alone to find them. You might destroy yourself and call it healing from a pain you never thought to explore, but I refuse. I will not go down with you, as much as I love you."

"I am going to change. I swear. I love you, Ruth. I'm sorry. You're right. Please—" He stops when I get up to put on my coat.

Out of everything my heart has just spilled onto the table, all Trip heard was love. But if he loved me, he'd know that love alone is never enough. It never is.

"Ruth. Don't leave. I...I can fix this," he stammers and sits up in bed. "I'm going to get help. We can get through this."

I look at him, really look at him in this moment. All the times I saw him and felt love seemed like a distant memory and I can't grasp a single one. All I have left is pity, and even though there is a scar across my heart, I don't feel any hostility towards him.

He suffered a great deal. He needs help, and I know in this moment that I'm not meant to be a savior.

Only he can be that.

I kiss his forehead and turn to leave, but not before I see him bend in half, head in hands, tears falling freely, and a phrase that I can barely make out, but sounds like "I love you..."

Chapter 43

Ruth

After I leave Trip, I drive. I don't know where I am going, but I keep my foot on the gas, making random turns,
Right.
Left.
Left.
I keep going, just to propel myself forward. It's a strange feeling, a welcoming one, to feel lost and relieved at the same time. I thought relief would come after Trip and I had been broken up for a while, months maybe. It didn't come to me when I walked out of the hospital; it came before then, right as the words I told him flew out of my mouth. Free—the words were finally free to leave me. I felt empty in a good way. I had purged myself of the doubts. The fears. The staying with someone just because.

The day is hot, but still people are bustling around the city with the kind of energy that only summer can bring. I turn the radio on and roll down all my windows.

I could be driving in circles for all I know. It could have been minutes or hours since I left the hospital, I don't know. The sun setting is the only sign that I have been lost in my mind for quite some time.

My phone buzzes. It's Beth. I curse, frustrated with myself. I forgot to text her back after she asked how the massage went with Todd. I also forgot to reply to the other texts she sent me after seeing Todd again, all of them alluding to his godlike physique.

Beth: Come to the W? Party going on there tonight.

The W is an upscale hotel in the city, and parties there are not unusual and almost always involve dancing. Should I tell her what happened? Tell her it's a terrible time to go to a party, or that I just can't in this emotional state? Then I think of myself siting alone at home, or worse, in front of my parents. Maybe, just maybe being distracted will be good for me? Just for this one night. I'm too far from home at this point, so going back to change was out of the question. I let the thoughts ruminate and magnify. I ponder both possibilities.

I pull into a quiet, older neighborhood. The streets are clean—clean and well-off, judging by the Tesla in one home's driveway. I park my car under mature trees. I take a deep breath before I look at my face in the rearview mirror. I do my best to rub off the mascara that has smudged under my eyes.

I twist my body to glance in my back seat at the box of random clothes that had been stashed at my parents' house and that I had yet to unpack into my own apartment. I rummage through the mess of clothes, trying to find something resembling decent. After some digging, I find a simple dress and throw it onto the passenger seat. It's slick but not slutty.

Perfect.

I'd go for one hour. That's all.

I make a U-turn in the small street and drive in the direction of the W.

~

I park in a nearby parking garage and climb into the backseat to change into my slightly wrinkly dress. I quickly text Beth back that I'm here and will meet her at the top.

The W is about as posh a hotel as they come: velvet furniture, white marble floors, chic light fixtures, men in suits, women wearing swanky name brands, high ceilings, fresh flowers delivered on a daily, and a small replica of the Trevi Fountain in the center of the lobby.

I step into the elevator and instantly feel like I am in a fun house. Each wall is a mirror. I pinch my cheeks, giving myself some color. I comb through my hair the best I can and pull down my dress that shrinks up my thighs when I move. The elevator climbs higher and higher. I watch the numbers change in front of me, counting every one until I reach the 57th floor.

It's noisy as soon as I leave the elevator. People are everywhere, dancing, mingling and lingering near the bar. There are tables tucked away in different corners on the rooftop, offering privacy for those who seek it. Tall trees grow out of gold planters, wrapped in white Christmas lights. I walk around the roof twice, peering in different booths and eyeing the dance floor, but still don't see Beth, so I decide to sit on a stool at the end of the bar that has a full view of the restaurant in case I spot her.

The bartender asks me what I will be having, and I stutter for a moment. My rational mind knows drinking is not the greatest idea in my emotional state, but I don't feel like being responsible tonight. Just once, I don't want to overthink. I order a glass of wine, the healthiest pour they have.

"You look lonely." I hear a voice say. I ignore it. It can't possibly be directed toward me. But then he repeats the phrase. I almost laugh out loud. Not because I am being hit on, but because I had no idea I was. I am naïve. The man is wearing a business suit, charcoal and polished, like he just came from work.

"I'm not," I respond with a small smile, hoping he'll leave me alone.

"Do you mind if I sit?"

"Sure," I answer, despite my internal waffling. Maybe a distraction wasn't so bad, at least until Beth showed up. There was no harm in talking.

"What's a pretty lady like you doing here alone?" His voice saunters as he speaks. Suddenly, I want to vomit.

"Waiting for a friend." I keep it short.

"Me too," he responds. "What's your name?"

"Ruth."

"I'm Jax."

Or that's what I think he says—I miss the name. Right over my head. But I raise my glass anyway in a mock toast and take a sip.

The more Jax-Jack-Whatever talks, the more I feel myself leaning into the superficial encounter. In this moment, there's nothing serious or outlandish going on. It's me talking to a stranger on a roof. The simple idea of it makes what happened with Trip and me seem further away. And tonight, I want what was happening with us to be as far away as possible.

Jax-Jack-Whatever has ordered me another drink by the time Beth arrives.

"There you are!" Beth squeals. "I've been looking for you."

"I have literally not moved from this seat," I say, slightly annoyed, but also playful with her. I should have known she'd be late. She's wearing a gold, tight, shimmery dress that doesn't leave much to the imagination.

Beth's face turns serious. "What's wrong?" she asks. I see Jax-Jack look at me quickly, confused.

"Nothing," I say, hating how old friends can see right through your masks. I grab her hand and pull her away from the bar. I tell her everything about Trip. When I finish, she grabs my shoulders tightly.

"You did the right thing," she assures me. "Trip was a jealous asshole and he didn't deserve you." I laugh despite myself. She would say that, even if Trip wasn't an asshole. Beth would defend me until the end.

"Now that Trip is good and done," she says and I wince. "Who is that guy at the bar you were talking to?"

"I have no idea. Jack, I think?" I'm surprised that I can't remember his name. I'm usually good with details.

"Well, he is hot and he is coming over here. Play it cool." She straightens her shoulders and puts on her best smile. I roll my eyes and turn around.

"Here is your drink." Jax-Jack-Whatever hands me another glass of white wine. "Want to dance?" he asks.

I hesitate.

"Yes, she definitely does," Beth answers for me. I want to strangle her. Jax-Jack-Whatever looks confused, but still puts his arm out for me to take. As he is pulling me away, I stick out my tongue at Beth.

The dance floor is filled with bodies; no matter where you are on the floor, someone's inches from your front and your back. Everyone's dancing, or more like grinding, in one large group. I can feel the wine in my system, making me a little lighter and lot looser. Here's to a night of not caring, I repeat in my head, trying to let go.

I sip my drink, doing my best not to spill it. Jax-Jack-Whatever turns me around so my back is against his chest. His hands are on my stomach, pulling me tighter against him. One hand inches lower and the other comes just below my breast. I shift in his arms so we are facing each other. He gives me a sly smile, like he knows exactly what I was trying to avoid. He grabs my waist, pulling me to him. I watch as he looks down—to my cleavage. I'm annoyed, but I let it go. He is a terrible dancer, which satisfies me. You can't be good looking and a good dancer, Jaxy boy.

Someone bumps into my shoulder and quickly apologizes. It takes me a millisecond to remember who he is. Todd's friend. I can't put my finger on his name, because Todd had only mentioned him a couple times, but I know him. The way his face lights up, I can tell he recognizes me too. He keeps his eyes on me but shuffles off. I follow his body weaving through the dance floor, through the crowd of people meandering around, and then to the outskirts of the bar. He stops in front of a group of men. Three stand tall and one leans relaxed against the wall. He looks at his friend, confused, and then over his friend's head to the dance floor. To me.

Our eyes lock.

Todd.

Suddenly, I'm embarrassed to be this close to Jax-Jack-Whatever and even more ashamed to be slightly tipsy. Todd doesn't reveal any disapproval or judgement, he only smiles at me as if to say: We meet again.

My body responds instantly, my heart shooting against my ribs as if I'd been dead and then shocked back to life with an AED.

I see two girls come up to Todd and his friend, and I know they are asking them to dance. Todd is nervous, judging by how he fidgets and looks to me. Eventually, his friend walks toward the dance floor—toward me—and Todd follows with a blonde girl who is wearing far too much makeup.

I don't say a thing yet, not until they've pushed their way through the crowd and are right next to me. Todd is dancing practically at my elbow with too-much-makeup blonde and I know he is looking at me. My body can feel him this close, and it's so intimate, it's as if he's within me, knowing me, filling all the emptiness from today with something warm.

When the song changes, I watch Todd glide stealthily away from the blonde. He cocks his head, wanting me to follow.

Jax-Jack-Whatever has turned his attention to his backside where a girl in a scandalous dress is rubbing herself on him. I take the opportunity to step backward, until I am face to face with Todd.

All the indifference I've built around me tonight shatters when those golden eyes lock on me.

I am not all right, I want to tell him.

He inclines his head as if he knows, surveying me in this raw form. A shadow of understanding crosses his eyes and relaxes his features. He gulps and nods, like he is seeing all the pain pooled in my heart.

I know, he conveys and pulls me to him.

I wrap my arms around his waist, and I bury my head in his broad chest. It's comfort. It's safe. It's home. We are in a crowd full of people, but I notice none of them. He leans down and nuzzles his head against my neck. He kisses me behind my ear, and I sag even more deeply into the steadiness of him. I am suddenly so tired. His knee comes between my legs, keeping me upright.

"I've been thinking about you," he whispers in my ear. He begins to sway us to the music.

I turn my head so our faces are inches apart. I can't hear much of anything and my body gets even heavier, but I can feel his heartbeat, strong and wild, and I secretly love that I am the one making it pound so erratically.

I close the distance between us and gently place a kiss on his lips.

He doesn't hesitate. He cradles my head and deepens our kiss. Warm, warm, I am warm all over. I want to stay stuck like this forever.

"Todd," I mutter, feeling faint, and not a good faint. My body feels as if it is losing control and I am on the verge of passing out, fading between twinkling lights and complete darkness. The feeling frightens me. "I don't feel good. Something is happening."

My legs give out.

My fingers clutch his arms. I'm trying to stay upright, but…

I'm plunging into darkness.

"Ruth," he yells. "Hey, stay with me. Ruth." He pats my cheek.

I hear Todd demand that his friend carry me downstairs to the car. I feel someone, I am assuming Todd's friend, pick me up. I feel like a feather, weightless in his arms. My head feels heavy, like I can't fight gravity any longer.

The dance floor wavers in and out of my vision. The last image I see before darkness completely consumes me is Jax-Jack-Whatever falling to his knees in shock, clutching his bloody nose.

Chapter 44

Todd

My blood is boiling.

If there's an emotion greater than livid, I'm feeling it.

I've been in life-threatening situations before, physical hardships that push and define my edge, but none of that compares to seeing someone you care about collapse. Seeing Ruth like that instantly made me think of Riley, helpless, gone, drained of color and life. I can't bear to lose Ruth too.

I could kill him. Whatever his name is. He deserves to put in jail for giving Ruth rohypnol. If he drugged Ruth like this, how many other girls did he try to take advantage of? I see it all the time as a paramedic. Girls passing out in clubs only to wake up and not recall a thing, or worse, waking up naked in another person's apartment. I'm disgusted.

As soon as I catch up with Xavier and Ruth, and catch sight of her again, I almost turn around, right then and there, to finish off the guy who did this to her. She's sprawled out on the backseat, limp. I grit my teeth. She is what I need to focus on now, not him.

"Thanks, Xavier," I say and jump into the driver's seat.

"No problem. What happened to her?"

"Rohypnol."

A few muttered swear words from Xavier. "Asshole. Take care of her. I will call tomorrow."

I'm too busy backing out of the parking lot to respond. My eyes shift to the rearview mirror, watching—waiting, even—for her to disappear in front of me or wake up. I want her to wake up, to give me that reassuring smile she usually does.

I don't know what overcame me when I saw her on that roof. Relief, jitters, jealousy, and hope surged through me. It was as if no one else was there. I went to her like a moth to a flame, craving her warmth. My muscles demanded that I reel her into me, attach her to me, so close that the scent of her skin enveloped me.

It takes me half the time to reach my apartment than it normally would. I don't bother with the parking garage but park my car in the first space I see in the lot. As I gently pick Ruth up in my arms, waves of that cinnamon scent hit me, and I want to stop and smell her and take her all in. But I use my foot to shut the car door and jog-walk up to my apartment.

Once inside, I lay her on my bed and put a damp washcloth on her forehead. I pull the covers up to her chin. At this point, all I can do is wait. I wait and let her ride the wave and when she wakes, I'll fill in all the missing pieces. I will be here.

I stretch out beside her on top of the covers and move her hair from her face. I keep my eyes open as long as I can, watching and making sure her chest is rising and falling.

~

"Todd."

My eyes flutter open at the sound of her voice. I shoot up out of bed, quickly. Then I remember what happened, slowly. The details are crystal clear in my mind, but I don't wish to recall them. So I don't. I let what happened go, away, gone forever from this moment where I am lying in bed with Ruth.

I'm lying in bed with Ruth.

She is wrapped tightly in my sheets. Her head is all I see, and her eyes look foggy and confused, like she is in between asleep and awake. The sun is shining through the window onto her pale face, which means we had slept all through the night and into a better portion of the morning. She squints and stretches her arms long above her head. I see her back arch and that's when I let myself fall back down to lie next to her, because at least then I don't have to stare at her. Because staring at her makes me want to be inside her, and I'm not sure we are ready for that yet.

"How are you feeling?" My voice cracks.

"What happened last night?" Her forehead crinkles in confusion and then her eyes widen. "Wait. You punched someone. Why?"

"Because he did this to you."

"What happened to me?" Her voice is curious, scared.

"He roofied you," I admit, painfully. Her mouth drops open. "Did you leave your drink somewhere last night?"

She stares at the ceiling, as if the answer will be written there. "When Beth arrived, I walked away from my drink and he brought me a new one." She sighs in exasperation and slams a palm to her forehead. "How could I have been so careless?"

"If anyone is to blame, it's that asshole. I could have killed him."

Ruth gently glides her hand down my cheek. I hold my breath. I can see the effort it's taking her to hold back her smile, like she knows what her dainty touch does to me. "Is that a hint of protectiveness I hear?"

"Call it what you want. No one will hurt you while I am around."

Now she doesn't even fight her smile, but lets it go, and it flies directly to my heart. We stare at each other and fire fills my blood with intense speed.

"I better get home," she says meekly, but remains still. Right next to me. Staring at me with those big green eyes.

I lift my arm in an inviting gesture. She smiles shyly and scoots her body closer into me. Her head nestles into my shoulder, a leg draping over one of mine. I drop my chin on her head, amazed at how this tiny gesture can send me falling.

We are quiet for a while. Still. As if moving will disrupt this moment—this moment of utter perfection.

And then she begins with the details of what happened since I saw her last. She tells me about Trip, her guilt about the kiss we shared prior to breaking up with Trip, and the way she longed to be close to me. I listen without interrupting, a hundred emotions coming and going through me. And when she is done, I hold her tighter.

"I feel like a cheater," Ruth admits.

"It takes two to make a relationship work," I say. "If one person fails to meet the other halfway, in every single sense, then it's a lopsided relationship. It will wither and die. When we are unhappy, it's only natural to seek happiness if we have the capacity to do so."

"It doesn't make what we did right, though," Ruth argues.

"No. Maybe not. But what happened was the result of your broken heart fighting to be whole, at whatever cost. Cheating on Trip allowed you to admit—to come to a conclusion—that the path you were headed on was not yours to begin with. Your heart knows what will make you happy, and sometimes it asks you to jump. Jumping is terrifying, but you did it."

"We did it," she says.

"Yes. And I don't regret it. You're the strongest girl I know, Ruth, don't get me wrong. But love shouldn't leave scars on our hearts."

I can feel the moisture of Ruth's tears seeping through my shirt, and I let them be, as much as it pains me to see her cry. I give her time to cry, because I don't know how often she lets herself go like this.

Gradually, her sniffles stop. Still, I wait to say anything. She sits up on her elbow. Quickly. "Oh my God," Ruth says.

"What?"

"How could I have not put two and two together?" She her palm to her forehead.

"Put what together?" I ask, worry creeping in.

She brings both hands to the side of her temples and repeats the same phrase over and over. "Oh my God."

"Ruth, you're scaring me."

She stops and looks at me, her body deflating. "I'm sorry. Nothing is wrong. I just realized something." She kisses me and crawls over my body toward her shoes. I want her to stop and replay that moment. I want her to stay on top of me, to kiss me, to stay.

"I have to go, but everything is fine. I promise." She smiles, that reassuring smile I had been waiting for since last night. My heart releases.

"I trust you. Can I see you later?" Please say yes.

She leans against my bedroom door and nods. She fidgets with her hand, gaze downwards. "Todd. There is something of Riley's I want to give you."

Hearing that name makes my muscles halt and melt all in one, it's a confusing reaction. "What is it?" I ask, nervous for the answer.

She bites her lip. God, I wish she wouldn't do that.

"Come with me," she whispers. She looks back up to me, debating. I can hear her release all the air inside of her before she says, "I want to give you Riley's journal."

228

Chapter 45

Todd

Xavier tried to get me out of the house three times this week. Each time I politely declined, and when the fourth text came from his wife expressing concern for my lack of contact, I hid the phone in the laundry room.

I didn't change my clothes. I barely ate. All I did was read Riley's journal, some passages twice: the first time to see the world from Riley's eyes, the second time to gauge how Ruth would have felt reading the passages. Then, sometimes, a third time in order to reflect and sort out my own feelings about Riley's words.

It was almost too much to take in. The woman I was going to ask to marry me. The woman I thought was my person. But this pain associated with loss was not new to me, and so I pressed on.

Reading Riley's account of her spying on me through the hold in her bedroom floor made me unexpectedly chuckle. My own laughter transported me to the picnic table near the Mississippi River where we would go and talk on those first dates. Sadness overcame me as I read onwards, not because there was a hollowness in my heart, nor for the mere fact that I was reading Riley's journal, but because I could read this and not be completely distraught.

I sit back, leaning into that thought. I can read her journal and not feel as if I wanted to crawl into a hole and disappear. I find myself more focused on Ruth's reactions to Riley's words, and the unease she must have felt reading these entries of Riley and me being intimate and yet…Ruth still came back to me. She hugged me goodbye. She kissed me goodbye. That has to mean she worked through all this in her heart—alone.

A knock at the door interrupts my thoughts, and I snap my head up. I mark my place in the journal and make four brisk strides to the door.

"Did you not hear me knocking?" Pat says, obviously piqued. "I have been out here for at least five minutes pounding on your door."

"I'm sorry Pat. I was"—I look around, suddenly aware of my personal hygiene—"busy."

"I see that. You look like a disaster. What is going on with you?" Her tone is both perturbed and accusatory.

I sit at the small table in the kitchen, watching her put groceries away that I hadn't asked her to bring over. I learned long ago to pick my battles with Pat, and if she wanted to bring me food, how could I complain? Eggs, spinach, cream, and yogurt all go in the vacant fridge.

I make music with my fingers, drumming them on the table.

"Why are you fidgeting like that?" she asks. When I don't answer she demands, "Spill it."

My fingers stop. I sigh. Pat will find out eventually, so I settle on telling her the truth. "I am reading a journal that Ruth gave me. It's Riley's journal."

I wait to fill Pat in on the context of Ruth and me, as I am still not even sure what we are. Only my therapist really knows about Ruth and me. I had to tell someone with an objective perspective, or I would have gone insane. And since Pat's only prerogative is to have me be happy, no matter who I choose to be with, she's not entirely an objective sounding board.

My quasi-mother finally takes a seat, as if the gravity of my statement is physically pulling her downwards. "You've been reading this journal." More of a statement than a question, really. I nod. "Why did Ruth give it to you?"

"I think I haven't read that far yet?" I lift my shoulders, uncertain. "My guess is that she wants me to have some sort of closure and thinks that my reading this will help in that process."

"It's also very invasive."

"I know." My eyes cast downwards.

"Is the invasiveness worth it? Have you found your closure?" As if there's ever closure in death. Pat and I both know that healing from loss is not a linear process.

"I think we both know closure is not the same as accepting what my life is now without her."

A nod and a wave of her hand. "You know what I meant."

Am I ready to admit that Ruth is the main reason I have survived the loss of Riley? I proceed, conscientious of how I form my words.

"It's strange. When I lost Riley, I understood my life would go on, but I was convinced the shape and depth of my happiness would change drastically. I would feel numb. I would not feel the happiness I felt with her again, with anyone. That's what I thought." I look at Pat to see if she's following. Her eyes are steady, waiting.

230

"Reading this journal reminds me of why I love—loved—her, and I know it was real, but…" I hesitate.

"But what?" Pat says patiently.

"Do you believe that we can love again after so much heartache?" I hold my breath. I need to hear this answer before I tell her about Ruth.

"Good heavens, yes," Pat says. "Of course I do. We can love many people. We are compatible with hundreds of people!" She must see the relief on my face, because she eyes me suspiciously. "Why do you ask?"

My eyes flutter around the kitchen, trying to find a calm place to land.

"As I'm reading this journal, I can't stop thinking about Ruth, who also read the journal. She…had to do this alone. But that's beside the point." My legs are dancing underneath the table as I anxiously try to find the right words. "I can read this journal and not feel myself going back to square one about Riley, because of Ruth and her choice to give this to me."

Pat tilts her head in confusion, like she hasn't fully registered what I said. I don't even know what I am saying.

"I am in love with Ruth," I blurt out. Then my forehead hits the table. I wait for the reprimand or the gasp of disbelief. I hear neither.

"Oh child, I know."

I peel my head up. "What?"

"I know you love Ruth. In fact, I think you've loved her a long time."

I gulp and sit up straight, regaining my composure. How much does she know?

"What are you saying?" I ask.

She gives me a look as if to say, come on.

When I don't budge, she begins. "You see, I met Ruth first. It was she who came to dinner the first time we met. I know it was, because when I met Riley, you were not the same." She shakes her head and gazes into the distance. "It was almost like"—she rests her chin in her hand—"almost like you fell into step with Ruth. She made you seem…well, she made you seem at ease. Like you could feel at ease with her."

My mouth hangs open. All these years, Pat knew. And she never said a thing. "What was I like with Riley, then?"

"Like a puppy trying to please its owner but being disappointed time and time again." Her words are quick, clipped, with undertones of sadness.

"And why didn't you tell me?"

"Oh child," she repeats. "What good would that have done? You were destined to make your own choices. I knew you would figure it out."

I am speechless.

"Besides," Pat goes on, "It was Ruth who told me that you ran into your parents outside of that dance club in high school. It was Ruth who was worried about you that night. She's kept me in the loop, for years."

"I didn't know," I say, still in utter shock.

"She told me what they said to you," Pat declares.

I think back to that night. Ruth and I were waiting outside the dance club, letting Riley expel her energy until she was too tired to dance anymore. We were getting air when two people walked by pushing a grocery cart. They were homeless. I stepped out of the way, but not fast enough. The man saw me and called me by name.

He was strikingly familiar in all the wrong ways. I shrank back to a boy that was both terrified and waiting to be loved. Even after all those years a part, my dad still had a hold on me. I remember that feeling as it was distinctly how I felt for the first eight years of my life. Afraid. Lonely. Waiting for him to approve of me.

Ruth had stepped in front of me. Somehow, she knew those two strangers were my parents. She must had seen the resemblance or perhaps she felt the dramatic shift in my body language. She asked me what I wanted, like I had a choice. She told me I could pretend they were just meaningless strangers, or I could face them. Either way, she was with me.

She has always been there.

I decided to pretend I didn't know them just as they had done to me for years. I turned away, but not before my haggard mother said "Don't think you're better than us. You are a part of us." She pointed between herself and my father, who was nodding vigorously.

I was speechless at the time, but Ruth said something. I didn't hear what she said, because my worry shifted to Riley, who had tumbled out of the club and vomited on the ground between us.

I look at Pat, who's patiently eyeing me. "I guess in a way, I have always loved Ruth."

232

She sighs. "You are in between a rock and a hard spot aren't you? Who else knows?"

"No one," I say. Pat squints at me and I sigh. "Fine. Ruth probably knows too. How could she not? I'm not good at shielding the truth, especially not with her. I don't know what to do, Pat. How could this have happened?" Pat surveys me with both pity and understanding—all, of course, from a place of love.

"Todd, Riley is gone. No matter how you sugarcoat it and no matter how painful that fact is, she isn't coming back to us." Her voice cracks.

"Riley wouldn't have wanted you to wallow in your sorrow and pity yourself. She would want you to move on, and to find your portion of happiness. Whatever you find out there, and it sounds like you found it with Ruth. Whatever is going on with you two is not supposed to be like the love you had with Riley. You were a different person when you fell for Riley than you are today. How could the love possibly be the same?"

We stare long and hard at each other. We have always been able to communicate about words; that was, after all, the start of our relationship.

"You never really stopped being my counselor, did you?"

She smiles coyly. "I won't ever stop either. That's what mothers do."

A moment of silence grows between us, the word mother reverberating through the room. I am filled with gratitude for her relentless drive to give me a better life without the substances that threatened to destroy my future.

Pat clears her throat. "So, have you finished this journal?"

"No. Almost."

"Then you haven't yet found the reason Ruth gave it to you." I hadn't considered that the ending would be any deciding factor. "I suggest you finish it," Pat says before standing up and grabbing her purse. "And then take it to therapy with you. It's always helpful to have someone near when important information is presented to you." I think of Ruth finishing the journal alone and a pointed pain stabs my heart.

Pat stands at the door and says, as if she is just now arriving, "I brought you groceries. Take a shower. Eat. You look terrible." She blows me a kiss.

When the door is closed behind her, I stand in between the living room where the journal lies and the laundry room where I had hidden my phone. I argue with myself about where to go. Do I finish this journal, or do I leave the house, get some fresh air, be human?

I walk to the living room and read the last pages of Riley's journal.

Chapter 46

Todd

The concrete steps outside my therapist's office are numbing my behind, but I welcome the pain. Bystanders are marching past me on the city streets, some teenagers are smacking each other around, cigarettes dangling from their lips. Others are professionals wearing business suits trudging home after a long Monday.

I watch their faces as they pass, trying to detect their feelings and wondering briefly where they're headed. Do they make a long commute and return home to the suburbs? Are they in love? Do they want to be married? Will one of those teens grow up to cheat on their significant other?

The outline of the skyscrapers grows more defined, darker, as the sun sinks below the horizon. The traffic comes to a lull and the honking of rush hour subsides.

Heidi, my therapist, opens the heavy glass door behind me, and it's only then that I can't recall how long I had been sitting on the steps watching the city transform before me, preparing itself for night.

"Todd?" She treads lightly. "Is that you?" She takes one step down and peers around until she can see my face.

"I'm sorry I missed our appointment," I say. "This is as far as I got." Heidi stays silent but takes a seat next to me on the stairs. Her knees fall towards me and her feet jut out to the right, trying to sit as modestly as she can in a skirt. I know she is waiting for me to say something. I hand her Riley's journal instead. I give her no explanation. She takes the hint and begins reading a passage here and there.

I don't know what I want her to say. I don't know what I want to say, but I do know how I feel, and that alone is taking me more time to process than usual. As soon as I turned the last page of Riley's journal, I felt relief. In some sick way, I felt that her decision to cheat on me gave me the permission to love Ruth in the way that I have always wanted to love her.

There is no doubt that I loved Riley. Her love set me back on track during a chaotic phase of my life; it fundamentally changed me. But I wasn't her person if what held us together was so easily cut.

It was love, but it wasn't the kind of love I wanted in my forever. I want a love where the idea of her and the real her were one in the same, and no amount of distance changed that.

When Heidi finishes the entry she's reading, she closes the book lightly and lets out a small sigh. She doesn't look at me. I don't look at her.

"Would you have fallen in love with Ruth today if Riley were still alive?"

I mull over this question until the silence unnerves me.

"Yes," is all I can muster. I swallow back my emotion.

Three images flash before me. The first is of Ruth kneeling in front of me under the tree at a lake when we were little. The second is of Ruth jumping off the sailboat into the frigid water; and the third is her pained face when she pushed away from me after we had been kissing, like she didn't want to let go, but she had to.

"I know what people will think. They will think that I didn't fall in love with Ruth as Ruth, but Ruth because she is the twin of my deceased girlfriend. They will think I settled with Ruth because I long for Riley. They'll think…" I can't finish.

"And they can think whatever they want. What do you know for sure—not what you think, but what you know?"

I look at her then. Are thinking and knowing not one and the same? I try to separate my thoughts from what I knew to be true in my gut.

"I love Ruth. I loved Riley. Our loves are different, just as the two of them are unequivocally different as people."

"I have no doubt that they are different people, and thus of course the love you have shared with them will be different," she says. "It sounds as if Riley loved you, but she concluded that love alone was not enough for her to be fulfilled."

There's the truth, all in one succinct and precise statement.

"That doesn't mean that you were not enough as a person, but that perhaps she grew in a different trajectory than you did. If a person chooses not to communicate those changes, that is of no fault to the other individual in the relationship."

I remain silent, biting the inside of my cheek and tasting blood.

"Distance does funny things to people in love," Heidi continues. "No matter how determined you are to beat distance and stay in love, the miles between remain and impede on any act of love you could have between each other.

"I wonder…did you hold tight to the idea of the Riley you met at eighteen or to the Riley who was right in front of you?"

Neither. I'm about to tell my therapist the truth about the start of my infatuation, but I realized I don't have to. I don't need her help with this because I already understand.

I made a beautiful mistake that had somehow came full circle.

"I guess I lost sight of what was right in front of me."

"All I can say is that the Riley at the beginning of this"—Heidi holds up the journal—"does not sound like the same one at the end of it."

"You're right. She was happy toward the end." I feel a smile start to form on my face. "And that makes me happy, too." My shoulders drop in resolution. I have no anger toward Riley. Not even toward Zeph.

Heidi looks across the street at people waiting in line to enter a restaurant for dinner. "They're more than love," she says absentmindedly.

"What is?" I asked.

"Relationships. They take more than love to make it work. It's possible that she loved you and Zeph, just as you have loved her and Ruth. You could make it work with both women, just as she could with both you and Zeph. Who, though, will touch your soul and make you the best version of yourself?"

Ruth. A quick and short response. No hesitation.

Heidi glances at her phone and stands up, handing me the journal. "I need to go. Next time you decide to sit on the steps outside, why don't you give me a call? I'll meet you down here."

I make a weak attempt at a laugh. "You got it."

"And Todd, I'd suggest you go talk to whoever just came to mind a few moments ago. I think you and I both know life is too short not to."

As she descends the stairs I yell, "Hey, Doc!" She turns to me. "Thank you."

She resumes her steps down the stairs. "I'm not a doctor!"

When she is no longer in sight, I stand, looking both directions before crossing the road to my car.

I click my seatbelt on and drive the familiar roads to Ruth's house. I don't know if she will be there, but I do know life is too short not to try to see her tonight.

Chapter 47

Ruth

I'm going to visit my sister's killer, and I need to do it alone.

I need to see the man who killed Riley, because he also was the one who loved her.

The truth didn't hit me until I was lying in Todd's arms, recounting the incidents that led to Trip's wreck. The fight. How Trip thought I slept with Zeph.

Zeph. My sister's lover.

Zeph. The man who's awaiting trial. A trial I didn't want to partake in, but now…now I want to know him. To see for myself who Riley fell in love with and to know the truth of that night.

My hands shook when I called Zeph's lawyer to explain the motive behind my meeting and ask to be put on the visitors list. They shook when I called information to determine the jail's visiting hours. They shook when I typed in the address in Google Maps for the two-hour drive there, and they shook when the jail's gates creaked open.

I immediately find a bathroom and locked myself in a stall. I spin small circles in the tight space, trying to envision this meeting and how I want it to go.

I thought of the questions I wanted to ask. I thought about Riley. I thought about Zeph, the mere syllables making his name a catalyst to the sob stuck in my throat.

As much as I should be angry, livid, and seeking vengeance, I can't do it. I can't hate a man who loved my sister, even if he was ultimately the one to end her. Yes, my anger could coil in me and strike at him today and every day onwards, but I don't want that anger. If he loved my sister as much as I think he did, he will be feeling enough anguish for both of us.

No matter what I do today, my sister isn't coming back.

I open the stall door and look for a mirror, but there are none to be found. I am wearing an ugly, brown sweater over a flowy sundress. My best attempt to appear homely. I tug the sweater down over my knees and mess my hair up, just slightly. I take a deep breath and walk out. The smell of jail is rancid, like a combination of iron and grade school cafeteria. A wave of nausea shoots through me. I pass through a short security line, leaving my belongings in a gray metal locker.

I do my best to avoid the eyes and unctuous faces of the other inmates walking from their cell towards the glass pane separating them from their loved ones.

"Right this way, ma'am." A large man in uniform directs me to a seat furthest from the door. Before I can turn around to ask the officer what will happen next, the door across the room clicks and opens.

When I see a man walk through those doors, everything falls into place. I know it's him, instantly, because he is looking at me as if he may die right then and there. My jitters are gone by the time he sits in front of me, because I have nothing to fear. Riley didn't fear this man. So neither will I. I give him the decency of my undivided attention. My eyes never leave him.

I watch his mouth open in awe. Nothing can prepare you to see your love reincarnated, even the fact that he knew I would be visiting.

His hair is jet black and long. I try to envision him with shorter hair. I try to see him as Riley did. His eyes are blue, strikingly beautiful. His nose is sharp, and large. His face is gaunt, likely from poor nutrition, but what his face lacks, his body makes up for. He is lean and surprising muscular for being in jail. Everything about him is an aberration in this setting besides his orange jumpsuit.

His mouth hangs open. He leans forward. I see teardrops build in the corner of his eyes. Then, and only then, do I drop my gaze, offering him this small moment of privacy. I pick up the phone. So does he.

"Hi," I start, saving him the trouble. "I am Ruth. Riley's twin sister." Like he didn't already gather this from the visitors' log. Or from the way I look. "She may have not mentioned me. We weren't as close as I thought we were..." I falter. "Or as much as I would have liked."

He bows his head slightly in understanding. He still is speechless. He is scared. He thinks I am here as an angry family member accusing the perpetrator. I'll save him from that anxiety as well.

"I didn't come to your hearing, because I didn't care about you then. I wanted nothing with my sister's killer. But I came today because...now I know. I know about you and Riley in Guatemala."

240

A tear falls down his face, as if he is remembering each moment with her on that trip. If he is worried about other inmates judging his public display of emotion, he doesn't show it.

"I read her journal. That's how—that's how I know about you...and her."

Another nod. He speaks at last. "I know it's ridiculous, to love someone after such a short time, but I did. I loved her very much."

It's the first time I've heard him talk. I repeat his words in my head, trying to hear his voice as Riley had. I can hear the traces of a once assured, hopeful man, but just barely. He appears to be breaking right in front of me; his shoulders shake and his lower lip quivers.

"Listen, I don't know what it's like to be on the other side of this wall," I say. "I don't know what happened that night, but I do understand losing someone you love." The words are pure agony coming out of my mouth, but I have to say them. "And I am sorry you have to do it alone, over there."

Gratitude fills his eyes, another nod of appreciation. "What did the journal say?"

I give him only what I can, and I hope it's enough to lift the torture in his eyes. "She talked about you towards the end. She was prepared to give up her life for you, maybe not medical school, but I have a feeling you wouldn't have wanted her to do that anyways." I leave out Todd on purpose. What point would that piece of information serve now?

"The journal must have been detailed if you know this about me."

I nod and throw him a bone. "She loved you. That's all I know." And because this somehow seems to make him feel worse, I add, "If she were here today, if she heard about this story, this story of you and her... she'd say that everything happens for a reason and that whoever was behind bars didn't deserve to live the remainder of their days without hope and in perpetual guilt."

"Why are you being so nice to me?" Zeph asks, voice breaking. I look at him long and hard.

"Because we all deserve second chances."

Moments pass between us.

"She was supposed to be with me that night," Zeph says unexpectedly. "We hadn't landed but a few days before that night. I was so excited to see her again. I couldn't believe my luck in having her on that trip. She was bright, stubborn, independent, intelligent, and so…" He tries to find the right words. "Driven."

You can say that again.

"I'll never forget that month. People think I am crazy when I say I found my future wife in a month." His smile is a little crooked. "It's true, though. I found her. She was it."

I force my mouth shut and bite my lip, hoping this will keep the sadness at bay. I think of Todd—my solid ground—and this small image makes me sit up straighter.

Zeph takes my posture as a sign that I want to know more. And I do. I want to hear his story. To have her come alive in this moment with two people who loved her dearly.

"She was supposed to come meet my friends at a gala in the city but decided to stay back and study. She acted different once we landed in the United States, kind of aloof. At times, she was withdrawn from me. She told me she had unfinished business that was on her mind. Other times she seemed to melt into me. We were great together. That night…I was on my way to visit her at the library at the college, where I assumed she would be studying. The library was, as you know, her second home. I guess she had decided to take a break from studying and go on a night run."

Each word appears to be pure agony, but he continues. "I drank too much that night. I should have never gotten in the car. I should have never gone to visit her at the library."

He gasps, trying to catch his breath. "I did this to her. I didn't see her…I was going too fast." He puts his head in his hands. He begins to rock back and forth, moaning slightly. His knuckles are turning white. The inmate next to him gapes between Zeph and me, and behind Zeph, the guard's forehead creases in concern.

"Zeph," I say, attempting to get his attention. "I need to tell you something." At first, I think he doesn't hear me, or he is ignoring me, but then he slowly moves his hands from his head so that he is cupping his face. He looks at me with anticipation—or dread; I can't tell. His eyes are pools of despair.

I take off the gold ring that's tightly wrapped around my index finger and hold it up to the glass for him to see. I wish I could give him this one small symbol of hope, this part of Riley. His icicle-blue eyes follow my every movement. His brows come together in confusion.

"What is that?"

I hesitate, because I'm about to lie to him and I have never been good at lying.

"This is Riley's ring. Someday, when you're back out in the world, I will give it to you. You're not crazy. She thought she met her future husband in one short month too."

A small smile creeps onto his face, and my heart aches for this man who made one horrible choice after a million wonderful ones. I hurt knowing his guilt is not like my own. His guilt and grief are intertwined in such a way that he may never be able to tell the difference between the two. And I hope that guilt won't be the weight that stifles the next million right choices he could still make.

Chapter 48

Todd

I go to Ruth's apartment first, but she doesn't answer. Then I go to her parents' home. They tell me she went to visit Zeph at the jail. They are not pleased with her choice to visit the man who killed Riley, but that has to be because they didn't read the journal.

What happened to Riley was in no way excusable, but the fact that Zeph loved Riley shifted something. It turned his poor choice into a grave mistake, a freak accident. It made him human. If Ruth and Riley's parents knew about the journal, they'd see that Ruth had no option but to go. It's in her nature to offer condolence, to offer a grace that transcends hardship.

After I left Ruth's parents' home, I went back to her apartment to wait. I needed to talk to her, especially now, more than ever. She couldn't be alone after she met Zeph.

It's dark by the time her car pulls up. I push off the steps of her apartment and approach her, intuitively taking in her body, her face, looking for anything out of the ordinary.

"Todd." She smiles apprehensively as she steps out of her car. She seems fully intact, stable, and this relaxes me. "What are you doing here?"

"I..." I don't have any words for this moment, and words to tell her, because they are all inside of me. Screaming. She waits for me to answer, but I can't. I'm afraid to move, because when I do, that will be it. The end of control. She looks behind me toward the front door of her apartment building, and then back to me. She bites the edge of her lip.

It drives me insane.

I take one step toward her. She takes another. I close the distance, grab her hand, and walk with her the rest of the way up to her apartment. She unlocks the door and steps inside, turning to me quickly.

She doesn't hesitate to pull me close. Her small arms wrap around my waist and her cheek presses against my heart. I rest my chin on her head. I want to kiss her, to tell her I love her, but I don't know where she is mentally and the last thing I want is to scare her.

She slides her hands into the back pockets of my jeans, pulling me even closer, and tilts her head back so she can see me, her wide green eyes scanning my face. "Did you read it?"

"All of it."

"Oh." Her mouth rounds. The expression makes me excruciatingly still. She is surprised, almost cautious.

"And it didn't change how I feel about you right now." I kiss her forehead. My pulse quickens.

I move to hover over her lips, waiting for her to go the last ten percent. This has to be her choice, not mine. I mentally snap a picture of this image—her presence consuming me, her innocent, pure gaze lighting me up.

Her soft lips brush mine. I do my best to go slow, letting her lead, when what I really want is to unleash this fire I have within me, building and building and building. When her hands move with more urgency, I know it is safe to take the lead.

This kiss is unlike the kiss we shared in the laundry room, because now there are no barriers. No Trip. No Riley. No lies. No what-ifs. Nothing is hiding from us in this moment.

She tugs at my shirt and urges me to lift my hands. I let her pull my shirt off, watching her as she does it. There is no regret in her face, just pure love. It ignites me. It sends fireworks through each cell in my body.

She removes her sweater, revealing a dainty yellow sundress that has buttons down the middle. I make my way button by button from bottom to top until my fingers linger near her breasts. I shake a little staring at the perfection of her. My breath catches in my throat when she loosens the straps from her shoulders and shrugs off the dress. Her bra is lace, revealing. I can see her completely and it's doing wild, dangerous things to my mind. I want to pull her backwards, so I don't have to take my eyes off of her, but my lips are unwilling and find hers. I gently press into her, both of us walking backward toward her bedroom.

A nervous and happy giggle escapes her mouth in between kisses, and I feel it shiver through me. I grab ahold of her waist and hoist her up. She wraps her legs around me. Her arms cling to my neck. We are so close, so close. I stop when the back of my knees hit the bed.

I feel her lips hitch into a smile, and I match it with my own. She untangles herself from my embrace.

She is so beautiful, and I'm about to tell her as much, but she covers my mouth with her own and unclips her bra. I want to look at her—all of her—but there will be plenty of time for that later.

Chapter 49

Ruth

As I drove home, emotions and thoughts outnumbered the mile markers from the prison to my apartment. The further I drove away from the prison, the clearer the difference between my guilt and grief became. The guilt of leaving Trip at his worst, of having feelings for Todd…it was slowly subsiding, softening into something malleable. And in a strange way my grief was too, as if I could finally see that the true remedy for healing from a relationship destroyed was to lean on the relationships that were not.

One simple truth consumed me for the last hour of the drive: there was no one I'd rather lean on in these moments than Todd.

When I saw him sitting on the steps, everything drifted away. My thoughts. My feelings. The past. He was all I could see.

He was still all I could see.

He is standing in front of me with his shirt off. The warmth of his nearness turns my breath shallow. I wanted to spend time examining the tattoos covering his chest, learning the stories behind them, but there will be time for that later.

He loops his fingers around my underwear, drawing me closer to him. There is no reluctance. His hands slide behind me, into my underwear, so he is touching my bare skin.

His hands caress my bottom and then he squeezes it to lift me. My legs know what to do. They wrap around his midsection, straddling him. His hands push into my back. There is nothing between us now. There is no room for anything but us. Me and him.

He turns us around and slowly lays me down on the bed like I am treasure. Gold. Something he has been waiting for a long time. He lengthens his long body on top of mine, and I run my fingers everywhere. Memorizing each curve. Every freckle and shiver of him. I want to know all his thoughts and everything else he traps inside of him. I want nothing to be off-limits.

I reach between us, unbuckling his pants. His eyes search my face in awe. I keep eye contact with him, not wanting to miss a thing. I remove his pants with his help. I can feel him hard against me, and he inhales sharply, surprised, thrilled. I see a sheen of gloss cross his eyes that match his hungry hands.

He is on his elbows, one on each side of my face. He looks to his hands on either side of my head and then back to me. He is in disbelief. "Do you even know what you do to me?" His voice strains in a shaky whisper.

I kiss him in response—my entire world centered on the focal point of his lips. A moan escapes me when his hands move from beside head to my breast to the space in between my legs.

He draws circles and stops every once in a while to fill the hole within me. I groan and bite my lips enough to draw blood. His eyes lock with mine while he touches me, and for a split second I become self-conscious. He senses this slight insecurity. "Look at me, Ruth."

I look. I'd do anything he asked me to. I'm floating again, just like I was in the laundry room. I'm gone. Out of this moment.

"You are what I want. And I don't mean just in this moment."

The words are lava, pouring into me, grounding me from the weightless feeling of being in the clouds. I lift my head until my mouth is close to his ear and playfully bite his ear lobe. His muscles tense, making me feel more confident than I was moments before.

His fingers slip inside me one last time and I cry out. A shock reverberates through my entire body and each muscle shudders. My toes curl and I bury my head into Todd's shoulder, breathing his name. I turned my head until our lips meet again, this kiss more intense than the last.

I wanted to feel him inside me. It's a need so overwhelming it's threatening to overtaking me.

He leads a trail of kisses from my neck down my collarbone and chest, and then to my nipple. I separate my legs to make room for him. He inches closer. I hold onto his masculinity with my hand, guiding him into the deepest parts of me. We both became still.

He's reached the end of who I am, and suddenly, the end of me is just the beginning of us. His elbows are on either side of my face. His hands brushed my hair aside. His eyes devour me.

We are finally one.

I am overcome. I feel like everything is okay in this moment. I am safe. A tear falls down my face. My hand flies to my mouth and I squeeze my eyes shut, because I know the tears will come full force if I don't stop them now.

Todd scoops me into his arm and rolls so that I am on top of him. He has managed to stay inside of me. He doesn't say a word, but he doesn't have to. He can feel this too—this overwhelming feeling of love. His hands move up and down my back, consoling me, fingers dancing from my hair down and past my shoulder blades. When the tears subside, I bring my chin around and rest it on his chest. He peers down at me through his long eyelashes. My heart thrashes against my ribcage. A shadow crosses his features, like he had just been digging for a memory from long ago.

"I have loved you a very long time." My head is heavy and light all at once.

"I love you too," I said. There are no red lights. No warning signs. This is green lights all the way. I arch my hips into him, hoping to distract him from whatever caused the sliver of sadness on his face. He takes this as in invitation and rounds his hips into mine. I tug his shoulder, wanting him on top. He flips us over again.

I move my hips to match his cadence and it doesn't take long until we are lost in the raw, vulnerable moments that be two minutes or two hours. I don't know. Small noises escape with each thrust inside of me and when he pulls out ever so slightly, my body screams with protest. I grab hold of him and bring him back into me.

It is almost painful to keep my eyes open when I only want to feel, but he keeps looking at me and that makes me feel more than his touch could. I feel the tether between our souls. I feel the beat of my heart matching the tempo of his body. There are no other thoughts—just him. Just me and him in that moment. My person.

We come together, both sweating and shaking against one another. My fingers dig into his back before we both collapse.

Afterwards our breathing is sporadic, echoing off the walls of the room. Emotion dominates me again, and I feel compelled to either cry or laugh. Todd rolls to his side, his breathing slowing to an even tempo. His lips brush my forehead for a long moment.

When he pulls away, his eyes shine with an effervescence I know is in my eyes, too.

He traces a long line from my shoulder down my back and past my behind. My face flushes. I am speechless in this moment.

The hint of a grin sweeps his face before he repeats what he had said before. "Do you know what you do to me?"

Chapter 50

Ruth

My parents wanted to visit Riley's grave tonight after I was done with work, and I reluctantly agreed. I haven't gone back since my birthday. I don't need a gravesite to talk to her. She's not a marble stone. She's not dirt and grass. She was made of stardust, and so I'd rather look up at the night sky and imagine her dancing through the tails of other stars.

She'd be up there. I would be rooted here. We'd maintain our polar opposites, but sometimes, just sometimes when I peered up and thought of her, a shooting star would streak across the sky, fulfilling the final line between the constellation of us—destined, connected, and complete.

My one task today is to pick up the flowers for our visit to her grave.

I smell the scent of flowers before I even cross the street—lilies, roses, and lilacs all overpowering, hints of lime, peppermint, pinecone and orange peel not far behind. When I nudged open the doors to Monica Makes Potpourri, I hear the familiar chimes announcing my entrance and almost stumble as the aromas crest over me like a gust of wind. No matter how many times I enter this shop, I still can't prepare myself for that overtaking gust.

I spot Monica right away, holding up two flower bouquets for a customer who appears distraught in her indecisiveness. I take my time walking around and viewing the new merchandise, as well as the numerous bouquets laying around the shop, each one color coordinated and theme-based. Purple china-asters are mixed in with yellow sunflowers to represent Minneapolis' football team in one bouquet. Another bundle has a dozen black roses circling one yellow rose and the note: "Will you still be my friend?" taped onto the vase.

To each their own, I thought.

The only other customer in the shop, the one with Monica, finally decides to pick the bouquet with the wildflowers. Monica sighs with relief and walks to the front desk, stopping when she spots me.

"Ruth, honey. Hello!" At the sound of my name, Trip comes from around back to greet me, his eyes alive with consternation. His apron is on, just as it was the first day I properly met him, and his hair is no longer in the neat style he normally wore. He's also shaved his beard, leaving him completely transformed. And perhaps he has transformed. Near death experiences can do that to a person.

"Coming to pick up your mom's order? Aunt's? Or both?" He gives me a crooked grin, and I politely smile back.

"Just my mom's order today. I wouldn't want to spare you the opportunity to spend some time with my aunt. I know how much you're looking forward to seeing her."

"Funny," he says dryly, knowing perfectly well that older women do indeed love him and almost always look twice when they spot him across the room. He leaves the front to go pick up my mom's flowers in the back, and when he returns, I see him holding a small pouch filled with minty green leaves. That was not a part of my mom's order, but I didn't ask.

"How are you, Ruth?" he asks with what seems to be genuine curiosity.

"I have been well. Things were a little shaky at first, but I am on a good road right now." My walls are up. I can feel it. I won't be able to divulge any more even if I want to.

"That's good to hear. I think about you...a lot." He shifts awkwardly, and glances around the store nervously before adding, "I still miss you."

There it is. Right in the open. After all this time, here he is, sober, and from the looks of it maintaining his health. According to Monica, Trip went into treatment shortly after the car accident.

He stands, waiting for me to respond, and I think of how easy it would be to tell him "I miss you too." How easy it would be to walk to him and hug him, telling him I want to start over. But I know where that would lead us.

"What are you doing working here? I thought you were still with your consulting firm?" I decide to keep it casual. He nods slowly and then averts his eyes, but I know him better than that. He avoids looking at me for two long moments, not because of what I said, but what I failed to say.

"I am. I work here on the weekends, and most Friday evenings to help her close the shop up. I worry about her leaving the city at night."

250

A nod, and then a delicate silence. How was there ever a time when we couldn't stop talking?

"Well, it was good to see you, Trip. Thank you for these flowers. She will love them." I smile, a courtesy. The customer walks back to examine another bouquet, and Monica makes a subtle blah blah blah gesture, indicating this customer talks too much, and rolls her eyes. I laugh under my breath and give her a small wave goodbye.

Before I am out on the street, I hear the ding of the front door and turn to see Trip jogging up to me. His longer hair bounces along the way.

"Ruth, wait! This is for you." One final gesture. He throws me the small pouch he was holding. It is sage. My favorite. He waits for me to respond, and I know he's hoping this will ease the tension in our story, hoping we can go back in time to where we—almost—began.

I bring the pouch to my nose and inhale. Memories from a world away fill me. His idling eyes are longing. He doesn't realize that the girl he knew then, who fell in love so easily, doesn't exist anymore.

Time changes us. That is what time and distance do to love—it gives two people the space to change, to bend, to break, and to form or destroy ties. If two people are lucky, then the ties between their souls will remain intact despite distance and despite time. Change will have been made, yes, as it is inevitable. But this change will have been for the better and enhance the pair.

I looked at Trip closely, and know I'm a better person now than I ever could have been with him. I know he's not my person, but right now, in this moment, it's a cemented fact that brings me great joy. Closure.

I give him one last cordial grin before I step outside. Our spirit child lessening its hold on me.

And it was only when the aromas of the shop were far behind me that I finally understood what my professor had said all those years ago: the only difference between a spirit child meaning everything or meaning nothing is choice.

Chapter 51

Ruth

I gently rest the vase of my Mom's flowers on Greta's old but reliable backseat and then enter the building where I now do massages—my own private practice of sorts. I sneak a glimpse of the sign hammered down in front of my parking space and feel a rush of pride. Reserved for Ruth Schneider.

The parking lot is empty, which isn't too ominous considering it's a Friday evening. No one wants to work now, but I found Friday evenings to be the most productive part of my week. The office is be quiet, and thus no one would bother me. No noises would disrupt the massage.

Last week, I decided to take one new client, as that was all my schedule allocated for. Laura filled it instantly. She had moved with me to the new building in order to work the front desk. I should have known asking her to come work with me at this new space would have only caused me more grief in the long run. She hardly cleans, misses half the calls people made, and almost always forgets to put the name of my clients into my schedule. She's the worst assistant I've ever seen, but I don't have the heart to let her go.

After the bed is prepared, I text my mother to tell her I'm working late with a new client and would be there at some point tonight to deliver her flowers. My phone vibrates with an emoji from her at the same time the bell rings for the front door. I shut my phone off and take one last look at the room to make sure it was presentable before walking the short corridor to greet my last patient.

When I reached the glass door, I see a man, instantly familiar. I began to assess his body posture. His back is facing the door, but even from behind I could see this man is confident. His broad shoulders are squared. He's wearing well-fitted jeans, comfortable looking shoes, a plain V-neck and a black hat, backwards, with a colorful logo on the front of it. His hands are in his pockets, and he looks...relaxed.

I adjust my own posture and open the door. The man hears the jolt of noise behind him and quickly turns to face me. My heart flutters and sinks to the floor. Will I ever get used to this feeling?

"Hey stranger." Todd smiles at me, lopsided and goofy. "What's a guy have to do around here to get a massage by Ruth Schneider?"

"What are you doing here?" I practically yell, thrilled to see him, even though we saw each other two nights ago.

He raises his arms, resting his elbows on the door frame, and leans his face closer to me. "Taking you out," he says matter-of-factly.

I step forward and put my arms around him. He drops his hands and interlaces them behind my back. "I can't. I have an appointment at five." Now I feel like I could kill whoever made an appointment for a massage at 5:00 p.m. on a Friday.

Todd kisses my nose. "I scheduled that appointment, under my alias." His grin is mischievous.

"You are Sammy Swift?" I bark out a laugh. "I should have known." I go back to the office to get my purse and turn off the lights, relieved at this sudden deviation from my expected plans this Friday afternoon.

I lock the front door and turn to Todd. "So, what now?" I ask.

He loops his hand in mine and pulls me down the street. "Follow me."

Epilogue

Ruth
Then

I loved these days most. The days when dad took me sailing, alone. There were no complaints from Riley's mouth to cut the excursion short. This was one-on-one, uninterrupted time with Dad. Because it was summer and almost dusk, we would have at least another hour of daylight for sailing. It wasn't much, but I would take it.

I let my hand create waves out the window as we drove to Lake Harriet—our favorite spot to sail. The air was still humid, warm and sticky against my skin. My hair drifted past my face, clouding my vision, but I let it.

"You and Riley will be nine soon," my dad said, stating the obvious. "It's time you learn how to tie all the knots associated with sailing."

"But when can I actually steer the boat?" I whined.

"Perhaps this time." My dad winked at me before his face turned serious. "If you can manage to tie all the knots I teach you today."

I sighed. Always a lesson with my dad.

After we parked, I grabbed my small leather backpack that my mom insisted we bring and waited by the car. I didn't have to look inside to know that there were sandwiches, a sweet of some kind, and without fail—water.

"I'm going to get everything set up, but when it's time for knots, I am going to need you, Ruthie. Got it?" Dad asked.

"Yes, Dad," I responded, relieved to not have to get the boat set up for sailing. That was a task I would undoubtedly learn eventually, but not today. He locked the car and headed for the dock. I could see people leaving the lake, probably wanting to get home before night set. That was fine by me, because that meant more open water for us to sail on. That, and we didn't have to compete with other boats for the view of the entire Minneapolis skyline. The city's lights were beautiful at night, shining brightly against the stars that would be waking up soon.

I was looking up to the sky, hoping to spot a star, when a harsh voice brought me back to earth.

"Goddammit, Todd. Get your ass over here now and bring me the soap." A man was standing in the lake up to his knees, wearing thin shorts that were much too short for his grown body. "You no good piece of—" the man said under his breath, although I could hear him loud and clear.

A woman was slowly inching her way into the water, her ankles submerged, but she said nothing of this man's demeaning remarks.

The boy, who I assumed was Todd, had been sitting on grocery bags before he stood up and handed the soap to this father. The first thing I noticed about the boy was his arms and legs. He was skinny, unnaturally skinny. Even from this distance I could see the dark circles under his eyes.

"You need to get in here, Todd," the woman said. "You smell."

Why did they smell, I wondered? Why were they washing in a lake?

The woman finally walked far enough into the lake where she could dive in. I waited for her to come up, and when she did, she was yards in front of the man. The man followed suit. He plugged his nose and sunk down. When he broke the surface, he too was yards away from the bank. I could barely make out their heads bobbing around, as the light was melting into dark by the minute.

I watched the boy carefully. I felt bad for him. I wouldn't have, except for the shame on his face. He was embarrassed. His shoulders were hunched as if he was carrying something too heavy to bear. He hung his head low between his knees before he decided to stand. It was a slow and painful process to watch. He took his shirt off, and I gasped at the shape of his torso. I'd never seen ribs stick out that clearly.

Unlike his parents, he walked into the water without any hesitation. I thought he'd swim toward his family, but he went a different direction, the furthest he could be from them. He floated on his back, looking up to the changing sky.

I rummaged through my backpack, and sure enough, my mom had packed sandwiches, water and chocolate-covered gummy bears. I looked back at the family. There were swimming a safe distance away from me and from the shore. They would never see me walk to their belongings. Even so, I crept slowly to their pile of clothes and torn garbage bags. The sight of it made my heart sink, because I knew these people didn't have much. If they did, they'd have nice towels and wouldn't be washing in lake water the first place.

I found where the boy had been sitting and tucked the gummy bears underneath his worn clothes. It wasn't much, but it was something.

"Ruth! It's ready. Let's do this." I heard my dad in the distance. I looked toward the water. The family didn't hear a thing. Still, I walked slowly away from their belongings to the dock where my dad was waiting.

Once I got to my dad, he put his arm around my shoulder and led me to the sailboat. I felt the urge to look back, one more time, to see if the sad boy with skinny arms and legs had found the gummy bears. I wanted to see his face change from sadness, at least once, before I never saw him again, but my dad was pulling me onwards, away from the boy.

I looked up. Stars were twinkling, forming constellations I was learning by name. A smile came to me, because even though I couldn't see the boy's face change, I could imagine we were looking at the same stars tonight. In a way, he wouldn't be alone.

And today, that was enough.

Acknowledgements

As a social worker, the stories you hear transform you, sometimes they jade you. Reading and writing became my escape— a channel to leave the horrors of the world. There is power in creating. It can heal the parts of you that you don't necessarily clap for. Don't let anyone tell you differently.

Rebecca Mahoney, thank you for your compassionate guidance and patience. Your edits gave this story clear direction and made me realize the difference between showing and telling, because there IS a difference.

Blair Thornburgh, editor extraordinaire. Thank you for diving into the nitty gritty pieces of this story. You helped me find the exact words I was looking for and called me out when some things just didn't quite make sense.

Thank you Tessa Jessop, Hannah Croteau, Kimberlee Bray, Colleen Martin, Emi Strickland, Jessica Curdy and Ally Williamette. Your insight was the exact type of light I needed to bring me back from any shade of dark. You jumped at the chance to read this novel, and for that I will forever be grateful. I couldn't have done it without you.

Nana, you're the real Pat. Thank you for giving me my type of heart. You're my best friend.

My family—Your presence and support run true. Thank you. Ali, Nose. You know what it means.

Garrett, from start to finish you have been my biggest cheerleader. You're my best friend. My partner. My Todd. Our spirit child is the strongest and I choose you, every single day.

Made in the USA
Monee, IL
13 May 2020